ORANGE
ANGEL
DUCK

Patrick The Magnificent

Patrickthemagnificent.com

I dedicate this book to someone very special, who has inspired me. However, I am not the sort of person who could ever make someone feel uncomfortable, so I will not recognize you in print. I will tell you personally about this dedication, and you will be the only person to whom I will tell this because, like the book, this dedication is completely honest in its honesty and truthful in its trueness. Which is true.

Truthfully,
Patrick The Magnificent!

PREFACE

The story you are about to read is true. Actually, it is truer than true in its trueness. No story has ever been written that is truer, except of course when the sequel to this book comes out, which will be as true, if not truer than the original. Which is true.

For legal purposes and to protect the innocent, the names have been changed. However, the names were changed truthfully, which makes the story even truer. Which would be hard because it is already completely true.

Because it is so true, it is important to know the exceedingly, exceptionally, extraordinarily, extremely, exponentially, and especially educating facts pertaining to its authenticate anecdotal accuracy. Therefore, at the end of each long chapter, there is an assessment in the form of a crossword puzzle. The margins are also spacious to facilitate note-taking. This is to help reinforce the completely correct facts in this amazingly true story.

If any reader cannot complete the chapter ending puzzles, it is allowable to continue reading the next chapter, but it would be better to reread the chapter and retake the test or do some sort of penance such as slapping oneself silly and sending the video to Patrickthemagnificent@outlook.com to be posted on Patrickthemagnificent.com. Anyway, enjoy an island of truth in an ocean of lies or an asteroid of accuracy in the multiverse of, dare we say it, misinformation.

Yours truthfully,

Patrick The Magnificent

CONTENTS

Chapter One

FLORENCE

Great cities aren't just born. They're reborn. We've all been told that being born is traumatic, even though there is no reliable first-person anecdotal evidence to support that finding. No one ever remembers their actual birth. Some online psychics may have made this claim, but if they were really gifted psychics, they would know the winning lottery numbers in advance or would have bought Nvidia stock when it was twelve dollars a share and wouldn't have to charge for advice. Being reborn has its traumas too, and they are far easier to recall. Such is the case with the beautiful city of Florence, Italy.

In real estate, the three most important factors are location, location, and location and, believe it or not, Florence has all three. It is situated perfectly on the main road, exactly halfway between Here and There. It is also at the junction of This Way or That Way and is also a place. Florence is also rich in resources. It has air. Throughout the history of humankind, people have overwhelmingly settled in places that have air. Hence, the saying "to air is human," and humans, notably Romans, stopped roaming and built the city of Florence a long time ago.

Just as Rome was born from two brothers, Romulus and Remus, Florence was reborn from the two Medici brothers, Mario and Luigi. The Medici came from the union of two well-connected Florentine families, the Movers and the Shakers. Those two families did not want to repeat the mistake of the Montagues and Capulets from the nearby city of Verona who did not want to have their names associated with each other and, with tragic results told their children Romeo and Juliet to just go to their rooms and listen to Blue Oyster Cult until they forgot about each other. Therefore, the Movers agreed to let their son, and the Shakers agreed to let their daughter marry each other as long as they came up with a new last name. Those children, Siri and Alexa, decided on Medici because it meant doctor in Latin and they wanted to play doctor together. After playing doctor, they were blessed with fraternal twins, Mario and Luigi.

The Medici could use their connections with the Movers and Shakers to improve their stature in the community. Except for the plague when young Mario and Luigi were forced to live in the countryside and write stories for a man who believed he was a painter, they were able to climb to the top of society and enjoy the finer things in life. Things were going well in Florence. Too well, in fact, and Florence would soon be a victim of its own success when Mohron, the man who would usurp their power, showed up.

Mohron had come from Genoa with an infectious smile and lots of promises. Florence had become a victim of its own success. After the plague subsided, the city bounced back quickly. Already known for its high-quality wool, it was also producing its own silk. That meant more prosperity for more of the people. But not all the people shared in that prosperity, and those people were jealous. So jealous that when Mohron promised them free everything, they took to the streets. They burned and looted for equity until the merchants and guilds were ousted, and the people helped Mohron, their champion, seize power. He demanded that the wealthy hand over their wealth and the means of production, which, of course, the wealthy did not. They hid their wealth and most of their means of production and hoped to wait things out.

The means of production that Mohron could seize soon became useless. Tending enormous flocks of sheep for their wool and mulberry orchards for silkworms was hard work, and weaving them into expensive fabric was even harder. Lamb chops with mulberry sauce provided much quicker gratification to the unwashed masses. It was especially gratifying when consumed next to a roaring fire of mulberry logs. The peasants did not need chickens and ducks as food when they ate the lamb, which made things even easier. Back in those ancient times, chickens, ducks and other fowl reproduced by splitting in two. When a bird grew to maturity, it would begin a quick process of separation where it would divide itself into two identical birds. The problem with this was that during the hot summer months, which was usually when they reproduced, they would overheat while reproducing and blow up. This made raising fowl for food a messy and dangerous business, so the peasants were more than happy to feast on lamb and mutton. The problem was that feasting on the free lamb and mulberries Mohron promised meant there was no wool or silk to sell to pay for all the freebies. Shortages replaced the freebies. That is for everyone except for Mohron and his cronies. They always had plenty. When the people complained about the food shortages, Mohron suggested they could eat their pets. Some peasants got so desperate they began following the flocks of chickens and ducks that were no longer being farmed and were now feral nuisances in hopes one would overheat and blow up and they could make a meal of the pieces they could collect. They were relegated to this because Mohron had convinced them to turn over any weapons they had in exchange for free stuff, so they could not hunt the foul feral fowl. As the peasants got hungrier and hungrier, they became more restless, but Mohron wasn't concerned. He was so sure of his control, he even began reducing the number of mercenaries he employed to keep order. Though it meant he could keep more gold florins for himself, it turned out to be a mistake as the peasants became more and more emboldened in their restlessness. On one particular day, the restlessness was so intense it got the attention of Mario and Luigi, who, like the other merchants and guild members, had been lying low and waiting for their moment to take back the reins of power.

"What is that loud noise and commotion I keep hearing from the Plaza?" Luigi Medici cried out to his brother. "It just can't be chickens exploding? It's too loud for that."

"The ducks are blowing up too," his brother Mario replied.

"I hate it when it gets this hot," said Luigi. "The chickens and all the other birds burst into flames when they split into two."

"I know," lamented Mario. "Wouldn't it be great if there were a better way that fowl could reproduce?"

"Sometimes I almost wish they wouldn't reproduce at all," said Luigi.

"But then there would be only sheep to eat, and the wool trade would never come back," said Mario.

"Then I just want the ruckus to stop," sighed Luigi.

"It isn't chickens causing the ruckus this time, and it looks like a good ruckus," Mario said to his brother Luigi as he peered out the window of one of their family tower houses toward the commotion that was going on outside the Palazzo Popolo. "It looks like something we've all been hoping and waiting for."

From where the brothers stood on the house's third floor they looked out over the center of 14th century Florence with its grand public buildings, soaring gothic cathedrals, warm, colorful tower homes, merchant row houses, and rent-controlled igloos for the formerly working poor. Outside the massive stone fortress that was now the seat of power of Mohron, the poor unwashed masses had finally turned against their champion for equity. Mohron had seized power from the guilds and merchants by enticing the city's poor into rebellion with promises of golden free stuff. Now that the free stuff had run out, they stood as a mob against him in the Piazza della Signoria, where they had torched the houses of the ruling classes just a couple of years before and propelled Mohron to his position of power.

Inside the Palazzo, Mohron hunkered down with his loyalists, determined to weather the storm and remain in power. The sturdy walls of the Palazzo and the dozen or so mercenaries he still employed could keep the mob at bay for a few more hours, but eventually the mob would breach their stronghold and bring his reign and perhaps his life to an end. Mohron realized that he needed more mercenaries, and he needed them quickly to put down any dissent once and for all. Suddenly, he came up with a plan.

"We must put down this insurrection immediately," Mohron shouted to those around him.

"What is your order?" asked Azhull, the leader of the guards.

"We need more mercenaries," explained Mohron, "You and your top lieutenant must make your way through this filthy mob and bring back an army of mercenaries to cut them down. Let each mercenary know I will pay for their red blood in gold florins."

"But how will we get through the mob?" asked Azhull

"Remove your armor," said Mohron. "I will find you some rags for you to wear. You should fit in well."

Mohron dispatched two other guards to bring some prisoners from the prison cells in the Palazzo. He stripped them of their ragged clothes and used them to dress the two guards so they would blend in with the mob during their escape to bring more mercenaries. Then, he instructed the remaining guards to march the stripped prisoners to the Palazzo tower that soared above the city and to dangle them over the edge.

"Hang them over the side, but do not drop them," he yelled to his guards. "We do not want them to double their efforts to take over the palace."

All he wanted was a distraction. Something to hold the mob's attention while his messengers could slip out of the Palazzo, evade detection by the mob, and come back with enough mercenaries to quell the riot and keep his seat of power. From the townhouse, Luigi and Mario continued to watch in amazement. Then they saw something happen on the tower that even shocked them.

"They're dangling prisoners from the tower," said Luigi. "The tyrant Mohron has been a black spot on the city, but even this is a low point for him. He's gonna drop those poor people to their deaths."

"No, he isn't," answered Mario pointing to a door opening on the opposite end of the Palazzo from the tower and two figures in peasant clothing making a dash for the cover of the shops, row houses, and tiny igloos that surrounded the Palazzo, "It's a diversion to send out messengers. Mohron must be desperate and vulnerable. Now is our chance."

"What do you mean?" asked Luigi.

"I mean, we strike now," said Mario. "We must send out all the loyal servants immediately to bring the heads of all the patrician families to an emergency meeting at the Basilica. We must waste no time. Also, intercept Mohron's messengers and take them to the Basilica. It has been a while since the crypt and catacombs of the Basilica have been of use. I'll have the

Bishop Dividend open it up for us. He probably misses being paid by us much more than he'll miss paying Mohron. I have an idea, an awful idea. I have a wonderful awful idea. This is our chance not only to rid Florence of Mohron the Dictator and the unwashed hoi polloi that supported him, but to recreate Florence as the center of glamour that leads the world out of these dark ages."

Mario laughed fiendishly. Luigi laughed fiendishly. They continued laughing together until a loud bang interrupted them.

"Was that a chicken or a duck?" Luigi asked.

At the Palazzo, Mohron had just given the order for the nearly naked prisoners to be pulled back inside the tower after being dangled over the walls. The guards dragged the three grimy and terrified peasant plebeians — an emaciated man, woman and child — down the spiral steps of the tower back to the dungeon. Mohron stood on top of the keep and addressed the rabble that stood in the square below him. "Dear people of Florence, am I not a wonderful man? Are you not impressed with my act of mercy? I would be within my rights as Grand Protector of Florence to throw them from the tower. For they were all guilty of breaking the unwritten law. Now, I cannot tell you what law they broke, for it is unwritten. But they surely broke it. I have shown them great kindness in sparing their miserable lives. At least for the moment. And this merciful act will not be the extent of my kindness today. For my beloved proletariat, I have a splendid gift for all of you. As I speak, I have my finest men coming to give you the sum you so richly deserve. Soon none of you will live—that is, in poverty," Mohron sheepishly continued. "Yes, you will no longer be living in poverty. Just remain calm and please don't storm the Palazzo. Just wait or go back to your rent-subsidized igloos, and before nightfall my special friends will bring you your reward."

In the square below, the plebeians began talking among themselves. "What does he mean?" Asked an old crow of a woman in a dusty burlap cloak.

"Don't give him a chance!" screamed an old man with wild gray hair wearing a rumpled brown tunic. "He's a tyrant!"

"But he might give us free stuff," came a cry from deep inside the mob.

"Free stuff?"

"Free stuff."

"Free stuff." Soon the murmur of free stuff began bouncing around the mob's conversation.

"Well, if there's free stuff to be had, maybe we can give it a few hours before storming the Palazzo," said the old man in the brown tunic. "Free stuff, you know."

Meanwhile, the heads of the patrician families and major guilds, who had controlled the politics and commerce of Florence before it was usurped by Mohron, began filtering into the Basilica. They each took a few moments to gather themselves after their journey. They had been told to dress as plebeians and to take evasive action while traveling to the Basilica. This meant moving in a zigzag pattern through the cobblestone streets and pathways of Florence, which caused them to constantly bump into each other and further dishevel the fabric of their coarse brown tunics. After collecting themselves, they jostled for position for the seats in the chancel nearest to the podium where Mario Medici and the local bishop would speak. Vito Lucchese, the round, balding patriarch of the Lucchese Family and head of the shearing guild, was about to sit closest to the pulpit when Guido Gambino, whose family controlled the Weaving Guild, challenged him.

"The Gambino Family deserves the closest seat," he announced.

"What good are looms without sheep?" Asked Cleetus Columbo, whose family literally owned the Sheepherder Guild. "The Colombo family should have the favored spot."

"If there is a favored spot, it belongs to the Genovese family!" bellowed Skeeter Genovese.

"There is no guild in North Italy that the Genovese family does not influence. The Genovese will take the most prominent spot!" exclaimed Genovese, throwing the dark straw hat he had worn to conceal his identity as he followed Colombo into the Basilica.

"Just sit anywhere," called Mario Medici, who had unbeknownst to the arguing elites, taken up a position behind the podium. Half a dozen of the most prominent patrician men stood behind him, wearing peasant clothes instead of the finery that the city leaders usually wore before Mohron's peasant rebellion drove the city's power brokers into the shadows. This mirrored the other elites who had recently filed into the Basilica and also dressed to blend in with the plebeians and not arouse suspicion.

"None of you has any special status anymore," Mario continued. "That ended when Mohron usurped the power of the Grand Protector and made himself lord and dictator. If we act together in the next few hours and you do exactly as I say, you can have your little empires back."

"Why should we listen to you?" Skeeter Genovese asked.

"Look at how you are dressed," answered Mario Medici. "Would you have been sneaking through the streets in plebeian clothes before Mohron took away all of your power and made you bend your knee to him? And, would you have humiliated yourself to even come to this meeting if you did not think this was the only chance you and the rest of the guild-leading families had to regain your power?"

"Then what is your proposition?" Cleetus Columbo asked.

"We use this peasant revolt to oust Mohron once and for all." Mario replied.

"How do we do that?" Guido Gambino chimed in, "What's keeping the rabble from trying to take over everything for themselves?"

"The Movers, the Shakers, my plan, and of course, your complete cooperation," declared Mario. "In one fell swoop we will deal with the tyrant Mohron, retake complete control, rid ourselves of the rabble-rousers, and most importantly make beautiful Florence the envy of the world."

"What is this plan, and what do you mean by complete cooperation?" Cleetus Columbo asked nervously.

"Come with me to the crypt and all will be revealed," Mario replied.

His brother Luigi walked further behind the pulpit, past the shining white altar and into the lady chapel. There behind a small golden altar decorated with red candles, he opened the door that led down to the Basilica Crypt.

"How do we know we're not walking into a trap?" Skeeter Genovese asked.

"You don't," said Mario, "but the first one in gets the best seat."

"Festival seating?" Genovese asked.

"Like Day on the Green," Mario replied.

In a rush, the family heads raced to the crypt. After they entered the crypt, the family members jostled for position among the dozen chairs around a rectangular, ornately carved, dark wooden table that was set up for the meeting. The crypt below the Basilica was a cavernous space with a bumpy gray stone floor and smooth stone walls with tall archways that divided it into several chambers, some visible through the archways and others sealed behind large wooden doors. Positioned in rows along the floor were coffins, some plain and some ornate, most distinguished with a plaque or marker bearing the title and birth and death years of the interred.

There were also markers on the stone walls for ashes interred inside the walls and chests and crates containing church records, keepsakes, relics and dust. A thick layer of dust covered nearly everything in the crypt. Beneath the dust, there were more layers of dust.

"Let's all be seated quickly," Mario said. "Our very success depends on quick action." The established patrician men took their seats at the side of the table farther inside the crypt, with Mario in the center and Luigi and Bishop Dividend on his right and left-hand side, respectively. Colombo and Genovese quickly took the seats directly opposite Mario and Luigi, and the rest of the patricians hesitated for a moment and then filled in the remaining seats. Mario briefly made eye contact with each person seated at the table and then described his plan.

"In case you haven't noticed, the mob of rabble-rousers that Mohron used to gain power has now turned against him. He's holed up in the Palazzo waiting for the messengers he dispatched to return with enough mercenaries to slaughter the mob leaders and then probably anyone at this table not willing to give him their full allegiance and most of their fortune." Mario said, surveying the room.

"How do you know he has sent messengers for that purpose?" Genovese asked.

"They told me." answered Mario.

"Where are they now?" Colombo asked. Mario put his finger to his lips to silence the room and then pointed to a far corner of the crypt where two heavy gray stone sarcophagi sat among the other stored and largely forgotten relics. Then, he and Luigi put a hand to their ears, encouraging the others around the table to do the same. As the crypt got even more silent than crypts normally get, the group could detect the faint sounds of muffled screams undefined at the table.

"You will not leave them inside there to die, will you?" Columbo asked.
"We're businessmen, not barbarians."

"But we're not particularly nice businessmen," interjected Genovese,
interrupting Columbo's rare moment of compassion. He stared directly
into Mario's eyes. "So what is your plan?" he asked. Mario drew a quick
map in the layers of dust on the table and pointed to a boxlike shape in the
center surrounded by circles and rectangles he had drawn around it.

"Mohron is waiting in the Palazzo for his messengers to arrive with
enough mercenaries to put down the mob that is screaming outside. We
intercepted those messengers, and they are enjoying our hospitality inside
those sarcophagi in the corner. I have taken the liberty of sending my
own agents to the local Mercenaries R Us and Mercenary Depot to hire
our own mercenaries to quell those disgusting rabble-rousers. Once the
mercenaries, who are now loyal to us, show up, Mohron will open the
doors of the fortress to greet what he thinks are his forces. At that point, the
mercenaries we are employing will storm the Palazzo and remove Mohron
once and for all."

"And what is our part in this?" Colombo asked suspiciously.

"I'm going to need to hold on to your money," Mario replied.

"For what reason?" declared Genovese.

"To pay the mercenaries," answered Mario. "They won't get rid of
Mohron for free."

"How do we know you won't keep our money?" Colombo demanded.

"I won't touch your money," Mario answered. "The new Bank of
Medici will receive your florins. All payments, mercenary or otherwise, will
go through the bank. Your money will remain in each of your individual
accounts. The Bank of Medici will hold your money, but you will own it."

"Why should we trust this bank?" Asked Genovese. "You and the rest of your family obviously run it." He said, motioning to the Movers and Shakers seated on the other side of the table from him.

Mario elbowed the Bishop who was sitting next to him, getting his attention.

"The Bank of Medici has the endorsement of the church," he said. "Bishop Dividend can attest to the church's support in the Vatican."

Bishop Dividend recognized his cue from Mario.

"The Bank of Medici has the full blessing of the church," he assured Genovese and the other guild leaders. "Your deposits will be safe."

"As a matter of fact," Luigi chimed in, nudging his brother Mario, "to show you how much the church supports the Bank of Medici, we've teamed up for a new promotion."

"We have?" asked Bishop Dividend.

"Yes," said Luigi, hoping Mario and the Bishop would catch on. "For every deposit today, you get one free indulgence compliments of the Vatican."

"Indulgences?" asked Columbo. "You mean we're getting indulgences?"

"Sign me up!" Lucchese exclaimed.

"Can I make more than one deposit?" asked Gambino.

"Let me get this straight." Genovese said to Mario. "If we deposit our money and gold florins into the Medici Bank, in addition to indulgences, we regain control of Florence and our influence over all of North Italy."

"You all return to your previous positions of power and build a Florence that is not only the world's envy, but leads that world out of these dark ages." Mario replied.

"Build Florence?" Asked Genovese.

"Yes, build Florence." Answered Mario. "Mohron was able to take power by manipulating the lower classes. We cannot let that happen again.

From now on, only the cool people get to live in Florence. We must rid ourselves of the wretched rabble forever."

"We can't kill them; that's bad juju," said Columbo.

"And bad for business," Genovese added.

"We'll banish them," said Mario.

"We can't banish all of them," said Genovese. "Who's gonna tend the sheep and run the looms?"

"And servants, we need servants, we will not do things for ourselves." Lucchese said.

"And who's gonna fill the churches?" Bishop Dividend asked.

"Okay, we'll only banish the worst of the worst." Mario said. "But we can't let the ones who stay feel like they own the place. We can't let the lower class feel at home. We need to make everything frilly and fancy and florid. Artsy-farty feasts and festivals. And no more tunics. Everyone wears tights and bodices and codpieces. We'll feature the most hyped artists and architects. We'll have a Renaissance!"

"What's a Renaissance?" Colombo asked.

"It's a French word, but it's fancy." Mario said.

"I like it; it's time to put the dark ages behind us," said Luigi. "We're having a Renaissance."

"But how do we justify banishing the worst of the riffraff?" Columbo said.

Suddenly, Luigi started fidgeting and murmuring to himself as if he were trying to remember something. He kept chanting to himself, "Book of...book of..." and snapping his fingers as if he was trying to remember something. Those around the table stared at him in silence until Mario spoke up.

"What are you doing?" Mario asked.

"I'm trying to remember something," Luigi explained. "Maybe it's an old wives' tale, but long ago I heard that somewhere in this crypt is an ancient text that contains warnings of bad things in the future."

Suddenly, Bishop Dividend had an epiphany. "You mean The Holy Book of Stupid?"

"Yes, The Holy Book of Stupid," said Luigi. "That's it. Is there such a thing here?"

"Yes," said Bishop Divided. "I know exactly where it is. For ages, people avoided a corner of the crypt, and that is where it is."

"Why is that?" asked Mario.

"In case we or anything we hold dear is in that book," answered Bishop Dividend. "It could prove embarrassing."

"That's perfect," said Luigi. "Any of the rabble-rousers we want to banish, we just say they're in the Holy Book of Stupid and therefore aren't cool enough to be part of the Renaissance."

"Where is this book?" Mario asked Bishop Dividend.

"Do I have to show you?" Bishop Dividend asked. "It scares me."

"The clock is ticking," Mario demanded.

"Then follow me," said Bishop Dividend.

The bishop got up from the table, followed by the rest of the group. He walked toward a dark corner that shared a wall with the corner that held the sarcophagi that entombed Mohron's hapless messengers. He strolled to a booth in the back, in the corner, in the dark. Stopping next to a dusty wooden coffer about the size of a milk crate on the floor inside the booth. Mario and Luigi joined the bishop around the coffer. They knelt down and began blowing off the layers of dust that had accumulated over what must have been centuries. It revealed ornate olive wood carvings on the coffer of a dozen men in robes sitting around a table enjoying a meal.

"I've been told it is in here," said the bishop.

"Help me take off the lid," Mario said to Luigi. When they removed the lid of the coffer, a bright glow emanated from inside the coffer.

"I don't like the looks of this!" warned Bishop Dividend.

"Let's get this box out of the crypt where there's more light," Mario said. "It will be easier to see inside."

Mario and Luigi moved the coffer up the stairs and sat it down on the table in the Basilica where the group had been sitting before descending into the crypt. The rest of the group followed and took their places where they had been sitting before.

"What do we have here?" Mario said, standing up long enough to pull the book from the coffer. He opened it up and handed it to the bishop, who perused it.

"It's in Greek and Latin," said the Bishop. "But most of it is in ancient Yiddish."

"What does the Greek say?" Mario asked.

"I don't know," answered the Bishop. "It's all Greek to me."

"What about the Latin?" Mario asked.

Bishop Dividend quietly began flipping through the book, from front to back, silently reading random pages. It took a minute while those around the tables watched in silent anticipation.

"I've never heard of most of the things in this book," said the Bishop. "What's a French bulldog?"

"Isn't it titled The Book of Stupid?" Luigi asked.

"That's what it says on the cover." replied Bishop Dividend.

"Then that's good enough," Luigi said. "We write the names of any peasant who might impede our Florence Renaissance and use that to banish them."

"Banish them where?" Colombo asked. "I have business all over Italy. I don't want them banished to another city just to start trouble there."

"I agree," said Mario. "Once we have our Renaissance, I want it to spread throughout all of Italy and beyond. It would be great for business. We must banish them to a place where no one would want to go."

"Bishop Dividend?" Luigi asked. "With all your experience, is there such a place? A place where not even the most zealot of missionaries would go even if there were souls to save?"

"I have only heard of one such place in all my travels. It is so poor, so without hope." He answered.

"Where is it?" asked Genovese.

"France."

"Duh!" Luigi said.

"This terrible place is on the coast." Bishop Dividend said. "It's so terrible even the Genoese won't go near it."

"It sounds perfect," said Mario. "Close enough to banish, but far enough where they can't come back. What is the name of this impoverished place?"

"It is called Monaco," the bishop said.

"Then Monaco it is!" Mario declared. "Once we end Mohron's reign, we will have a peasant inspection and ship all the non-renaissance worthy peasants to this Monaco place."

Suddenly two men burst into the Basilica. They were the messengers Mario sent to replace Mohron's imprisoned messengers to get mercenaries in the Basilica's crypt.

"My Lord!" one of them cried. "A horde of mercenaries approaches the city, ready to do the bidding of whoever pays them first. The mercenaries will gather outside the city gates in 3 hours."

The room fell silent. But noisily got up. Mario was the first to speak. He addressed Colombo, Genovese, and the others who sat on the opposite side of the table.

"I will need those deposits in one hour." Mario commanded. "Our plan depends upon it!"

"I'm not sure we can get you the money and gold that quickly," Genovese said.

"Any deposits received within the hour get double the indulgences," Luigi said, thinking quickly. "It is a special offer from the Bank of Medici and backed by the Vatican. Isn't that right, Bishop?"

Mario kicked Bishop Dividend under the table. The bishop did not get the point, so Mario kicked him again. Then Luigi kicked him.

"Okay," the Bishop said pensively.

"Double indulgences?" asked Lucchese.

"Double indulgences," answered Bishop Dividend.

"Double indulgences, I've got to get busy, busy, busy!" Columbo cried, rising from his seat and running out the door followed by Genovese and the other business leaders.

Mario then spoke to the remaining patrician men sitting at the table with him.

"All of you," he called out to them. "I need Medici Bank payment pavilions set up outside the city gates to greet the mercenaries. That way they are already on our payroll before they even enter the city. And keep meticulous records."

"Also," said Luigi, getting another brilliant idea. "Set up each payment as a loan. Not to be forgiven until the job is done. Or better yet, forgive 95% of it. That way they'll have to remain loyal to us."

"And remember to tell them that The Bank of Medici has the best relations with the church," said Mario. "Now get things set up."

With that, the messengers and patrician men exited the Basilica, leaving Mario, Luigi, and a suddenly nervous-looking Bishop Dividend to talk amongst themselves.

"I'm feeling really nervous about this," said the Bishop. "I don't think I can continue to speak for the church on double indulgences, for supporting everything the Bank of Medici might do, and being around that ancient book scares me."

"We need your support for this plan to work," said Mario. "The Medici Bank will give you a generous payment."

"As a matter of fact," said Luigi, "we'll make it a regular payment and in your honor, Bishop, we'll call it a dividend."

"I still don't think I can do this," said the Bishop.

"Either you take our payment and support the Bank of Medici or...," Mario said, pulling a dagger from his waistband and holding it to the bishop's throat.

"I am a man of the church; no one can buy me, and no one can threaten me," said the bishop.

Mario pressed the knife harder against the bishop's throat.

"But if you combine the two, I'm your guy," Bishop Dividend said. "Is it a generous dividend?"

"Quite," Mario replied.

"But I don't want the book here." Bishop Dividend said.

"Fine," said Mario. "Once we've used it to get rid of the Renaissance unworthy peasants, we can burn it for all I care."

"It is still an ancient holy book," the Bishop said. "We can't destroy it. That would still be sacrilege."

"Then let the rabble take it with them to this Monaco place," said Luigi. "There's nothing in it that can be used against us and besides, some of it is in Latin. Latin is down the dumpster. It's so yesterday. All the cool people are writing and speaking like that Dante dude. We have to talk and write like that. There's no room in the Renaissance for Latin."

"Let them have everything in the coffer; it will be a parting gift." Mario said. "What else is in there?"

Luigi reached into the coffer and pulled out a large chalice made of a mysterious golden metal with a dome-shaped base made of chalcedony. Inside the cup was a rolled-up scroll that looked to be well over a thousand years old. Luigi took the scroll out of the chalice and handed it to the bishop.

"What does it say?" He asked the bishop.

"I'm not sure," the Bishop said. "It's all written in Yiddish, so it's probably from Judea. I can make out a date written on it."

"What's the date?" Luigi asked.

"It says April first thirty-three A.D. It looks like some sort of dinner party. I think it's a guest list."

"Are there any names on it?" Luigi asked.

"I can make out Andrew, Bartholomew, Thomas, John, James, Simon, another Simon with Peter in parentheses, Matthew, a couple of others and I see one name crossed out."

"Maybe he left early." Luigi said.

"What else is in the coffer?" Mario asked.

"Just some party favors, some dreidels and what looks like a really old palm buzzer." Luigi answered.

"Let them take it all. Once we write their names in the book, it will remind them not to keep making trouble." Mario said.

Just then, another Medici servant walked into the Basilica. Luigi was instantly struck by the mess on the front of his tunic and the odd design the blood and burnt feathers made.

"What happened to you?" Luigi asked the servant.

"The fowl are reproducing, and I tried to help separate them before they overheated, but it was too late," replied the servant.

"Was it a chicken or a duck?" Mario asked.

"It was a chicken," said the servant. "Actually, two chickens. Well, almost."

"We should have the rabble take the chickens and ducks to Monaco as well." Luigi said. "They make such a mess when they reproduce. I wish there were a better way. Maybe one day..."

"We can't get rid of the chickens; we need the meat," said Luigi. "But we can get rid of the ducks. No one enjoys eating duck. Even that recipe that Marco Polo guy brought back from Peking when he brought them noodles and silk isn't very good. Ducks are not part of the renaissance and neither is Quanjude."

"Once Mohron is deposed, and the mob taken care of, round up all the ducks," Mario told the servant. "In addition to the coffer, all rabble banished get a free duck to take along."

"I will make the arrangements," said the servant as he started toward the door.

"Wait," Luigi told the servant. "Leave your tunic here. The shape of that odd mess on the front of it would make a great logo for the new Medici Bank."

"Then what shall I wear, my Lord?" asked the servant.

"Put on some tights and a ruffled shirt," answered Luigi. "Our Renaissance has no place for tunics."

"And move quickly," added Mario. "We have a renaissance to start!"

Back inside the Palazzo Mohron paced nervously. Outside, the mob was getting raucous again, and chants of "We want the free stuff!" could be heard inside the Palazzo walls.

"Why haven't I heard from my messengers? He asked the handful of loyalists that remained with him.

"Do you suppose the mob got them?" Asked one of Mohron's loyalists.

"Impossible!" Mohron responded. "They couldn't recognize their own butts if they didn't smell."

"Butts smell?" Said another of Mohron's loyalists. "I thought noses did."

"Either way," Mohron said. "Those peasants have their noses so far up their butts there's no way they could smell what's in store for them once my men return with the mercenaries. We just need to keep them at bay for just a little longer."

"How can we do that?" asked one loyalist.

"I've got it!" he exclaimed. "Make an enormous banner that says 'FREE STUFF COMING SOON' and hang it from the bell tower," he told his loyalists. "That should work. Promising free stuff always works with peasants. That's why peasants stay peasants!"

The Medici Bank pavilions, set up just in time outside the city walls of Florence, successfully convinced the mercenaries to open accounts and take out loans exceeding their down payments for services they would soon provide. As a whole, mercenaries weren't a bright bunch. They scratched at their unkempt hair and beards or tugged at their padded quilted garments and chain mail patches as the gold florins were placed in their hands and taken out just as quickly. As Mario and Luigi navigated around the pavilions, they keyed into the conversations that were going on between the mercenaries and the Medici associates at the pavilions.

"If you let us hold the payment in your account, you can choose one of the free gifts on the table," one of the Medici associates told a mercenary.

"What's a blender?" The mercenary asked.

"I think it's for drawing pictures with," said another mercenary.

"I'll take the CorningWare," said a third.

Mario and Luigi smiled at each other. Suddenly there was a loud boom, and they were covered with singed feathers. A reproducing duck had blown up next to them. However, they kept smiling, knowing they would soon banish the ducks to Monaco along with the city's undesirable residents.

Later, Mohron finally received what he thought was good news inside the Palazzo. The mob outside was suddenly silent. Mohron dispatched one of his hunchbacked henchmen to look through the peephole in the massive oak door of the fortress.

"Your Slyness," announced the hunchbacked henchman. "Your messengers have finally arrived with an army of mercenaries behind them. The mob is silent with fear."

"Open the door," Mohron instructed his henchmen. "And set up a pulpit outside. I wish to address the people."

Mohron's minions quickly laid down a wooden platform outside the Palazzo, and Mohron walked out the door of the Palazzo and stepped up onto the hastily assembled pulpit that raised him above the mob to address them.

"Ungrateful peasants," he began. "I promised you free stuff, and now you shall have it. The free blades of my soldiers of fortune upon your ragged necks. Soldiers, cut down this mob!"

The mob recoiled in fear, but nothing happened. The mercenaries just stood there. Mohron just stood there, surprised. He looked at one of his messengers.

"What's going on?" Mohron asked. "Didn't you tell them to attack this degenerate mob?"

"I didn't really get the chance," the messenger said sheepishly.

He pointed behind him to Mario Medici, who was holding a dagger to his back. Mario gave it a turn just for good measure.

"The soldiers work for the Medici family now!" Mario yelled. "Mohron, your time in Florence is over! Get him and all his cronies!" With that, the mercenaries set upon Mohron and his ilk and dragged them away. The crowd of peasants cheered as Mario and Luigi climbed triumphantly onto the platform.

"Good plebeians!" Luigi announced, "Today is your day. Not only have you been saved from certain death by the evil Mohron, you'll also get to march in the parade for Florence's new Renaissance!"

"What's a Renaissance?" a plebeian yelled out.

"It's a new high-end, artsy, frilly, tights and bodices, and talk like Dante sort of thing." Mario answered.

"Go to the Via Camillo Cadaver. The parade is mandatory. The soldiers will escort you there and line you up!" yelled Mario.

"And remember to look your best, "Luigi added. "If our judges select you, you can march in the duck parade immediately after."

The mercenaries suddenly kicked into action, pushing, kicking, and sometimes dragging the plebeians from the square out to the Via Camillo Cadaver, which was the broad cobblestone street that had circled through the heart of Florence since Roman times. When the mercenaries drew their swords, the peasants' arguments were silenced. The mercenaries quickly gathered them in the center of the street, and some of them spread out throughout the town center to find any plebeians that were still in their igloos. Soon the mercenaries had the peasants marching, parading through the center of town along the Via Camillo Cadaver.

A long string of tables was hastily set up at the head of the parade march at the curve in the road directly in front of the Palazzo, and a giant bronze gong, taller than a man, was wheeled out next to it. They moved the pulpit, which had been right outside the Palazzo door, to the left-hand side of the string of tables. To the right of the tables, which were about thirty feet long and about three feet wide, was a large fenced-in area that had been set up that resembled a cattle pen. The workers who were helping the mercenaries at the Medici Bank pavilions outside the city walls were now busy rushing through the city collecting ducks and depositing them inside the pen. The ducks, having grown fat and lazy from city life, had forgotten how to fly and were an easy catch. At the table sat the once again powerful elite of Florence. At the center of the table sat Mario and Luigi, flanked by the wealthy guild leaders such as Lucchese, Colombo, and Genovese. They all wore the finest colorful tights, silk shirts, and velvet coats. The upper crust of Florentine society, dressed in colorful clothing, lined the sides of the streets.

The elite would judge the peasants on their Renaissance worthiness as they came around to the front of the table after being paraded around the Via Camillo Cadaver. They pointed their fingers and laughed at the peasants, and the upper class lining the streets joined in as well. Among the marchers, Mario noticed a dim-looking family of peasants that could barely walk straight.

"They look like wandering cave people," he said, pointing at them.

"There's no place for meanderthals in our Renaissance," Luigi said.

"Gong them!" Mario cried as he pointed them out to a large Asian-looking man in a bright red robe, who struck the gong with a mallet.

Suddenly the mercenaries sprang into action, dragging the entire family, mother, father, sister, and two brothers, out of the street and into the duck pen. An air of excitement overtook the entire Via Camillo Cadaver. Soon, those lining the streets were pointing out any not Renaissance-worthy peasants.

"Gong them," shouted a woman in brand new Lululatin tights, pointing out some Renaissance unworthy peasants.

"To the duck pen!" another well-heeled spectator shouted.

The crowd was now in a frenzy. The gong repeatedly sounded and each time the gong sounded the crowd would break out in a chant of "duck pen, duck pen, duck pen, duck pen!" The frenzy continued until three-hundred of the most pathetic peasants filled the pen which also held a corresponding number of ducks. Mario and Luigi rose from the VIP table and walked to the pulpit, where Bishop Dividend greeted them as the peasants peered through the stockade at those more fortunate outside the pen, like dogs at the pound hoping to be adopted. Mario then hopped up onto the pulpit to address the crowd.

"Those of you still standing on Via Camillo Cadaver, rejoice, for you have been deemed Renaissance worthy," Mario proclaimed. "We have identified the counter-Renaissance, enemies of the people, usual suspects and foulest of the fowls. And they are in the......"

Mario continued to bellow, hoping for a response from the plebeians standing on the Via Camino Cadaver. The crowd, however, remained silent. Mario tried again to get a response from the plebeians on Via Camino Cadaver, this time pointing to the poor pauper peasants and destitute ducks that were penned up.

"And are in the...," he yelled again.

Still, there was no response from the more fortunate on the Via Camino, which caused Luigi to spring into action. He bolted from his place on the pulpit and confronted two mercenaries overseeing the plebeians on the Via Camino Cadaver.

"Get them to say duck pen," he instructed them.

With some prompting from the mercenaries, some in the crowd started shouting "duck pen!" Mario waited until the shouting had permeated sufficiently throughout the crowd before trying to get the call and response started again. Finally, he yelled.

"And they are in..."

"The duck pen," came the response from the crowd.

"And they are in?" Mario called again.

"The duck pen!" The crowd now joined in their response by the cities' privileged citizens.

"And they are in!?!"

"The duck pen!"

"And they are in!?!"

"The duck pen!"

The frenzy continued, but Mario could tell when the enthusiasm was waning, and that was the moment he was waiting for. That moment when his grand plan came together. When he would remove Mohron, his ilk, and the city's riff-raff, reduce fowl explosions, make the Medici family the region's supreme power, and start the rebirth of civilization known as the Renaissance.

"And since the duck pen is unworthy of the Renaissance, I shall banish it!" Mario proclaimed.

The entire crowd, with those on the Via Camino Cadaver receiving extra encouragement from the mercenaries, cheered.

"And the dictator Mohron and his minions shall be banished too!" Mario also proclaimed.

Distressed, Bishop Dividend moved behind Mario and spoke directly into his ear.

"The book in the coffer, make it all go away."

Mario turned and faced the bishop momentarily and nodded before addressing the crowd again.

He also commanded the banishment of any relics from the past that opposed their enlightened future, while the crowd cheered and the bishop sighed in relief.

"Prepare for the second parade!" he announced. "The parade of banishment!"

And with that, so began the Parade of Banishment. The guards matched each ragged peasant in the duck pen with a duck to take. They gave the dirtiest peasants a duck close to reproduction because if the heat from binary fission caused them to combust, it wouldn't look so bad on an already filthy peasant. The citizens of Florence, including the upper, middle, lower, and those who survived the first parade, were told to wear their best Renaissance attire and line the Via Julia Augusta on both sides. They took Mohron and his ilk from their cells in the Palazzo, where they had previously locked up those they perceived to be undesirables. Mercenaries marched them under guard about a mile ahead on the Via Julia Augusta, giving them a head start before those in the duck pen would start their parade to the hellscape of Monaco. Mario figured it would speed up their migration as Mohron and his henchmen would increase their pace to escape the riff-raff's wrath and the peasant paupers would push their pace to punish the perpetrators. Bishop Dividend made sure the coffer containing the Book of Stupid, the ancient chalice, dreidels, and party favors made the journey as well. He selected a failed philosopher and former pauper to the stars named Mediocrities to tend to it during and after the journey and issued a papal directive that Monaco would always have a curator for the relics. As the failed Mohron, the Renaissance-unworthy peasants, and ducks were marched to their dismal banishment in Monaco, those worthy of the Renaissance on both sides of the Via Julia Augusta all sang.

"Yo mama's mama, yo mama's mama, hey, hey, goodbye," they kept singing.

And thus were born the pleasure of the Renaissance and the poverty of Monaco.

Florence review

Across

2. Built Florence originally.

5. Sent to room to listen to Blue Oyster Cult.

9. Got everyone talking real pretty.

10. Ancient Book of.

11. Rewards for bank deposits.

13. Soldiers for hire.

14. Where Mohran came from.

Down

1. Place to buy tights in Florence

2. Replaced the Dark Ages.

3. Brought noodles to China.

4. Source of Florence wealth.

6. Controlled business in Florence.

7. Language of scroll found with chalice.

8. Brothers who invented the Renaissance.

12. Often overheated and exploded during reproduction.

CHAPTER TWO

COLUMBUS

"Christopher Columbus, what do you think of that?" The cabin boy said.

"Think of what, Chips?" Columbus asked.

"My name's Pedro," said the cabin boy.

"Chips is a fine name for a cabin boy," said Columbus. "Tell me about your hat."

"A big fat lady came and sat upon my hat," said the cabin boy, pointing to a crushed tricorn hat on the floor of the captain's quarters.

"So what happened?" Columbus asked.

"My hat, she broke, so what's the joke? My hat, she broke." The cabin boy complained, pointing again to the black flattened hat. "Christopher Columbus, what do you think of that?"

Christopher Columbus thought for a moment before he spoke. The cabin boy was describing the first contact with the native people since the expedition had finally sighted land. The journey had not yet reaped the rewards he was hoping for. Columbus had promised Queen Elizabeth the world, or at least Asia, if she financed his historic voyage, and so far the trip was more bust than boom. It had started off on the wrong foot, or fin since it was an ocean journey. The crew caused delays when they tried to sabotage the Pinta because some felt it was a one-way journey. After that, they went much longer than expected without sighting land. Columbus was so pessimistic about finding land that when one of the crew shouted, "Land ho," Columbus answered back, "Stop calling me a Ho!"

When the expedition finally went ashore, they could not trade for the gold, spices, and silk they had hoped for. The natives, though cooperative and curious about the newcomers, only offered to trade flora and fauna that Columbus saw no market for. His first attempt at commerce on an island he thought was in proximity to India had gained him nothing he felt would have any worth in Europe.

"You're complaining about your hat?" Columbus asked the cabin boy. "What about my lot in this? You just had one native sit on your hat. Look at me. The first haul of my grand voyage and I have nothing of worth to bring back to Europe. Look at these red, sort of fruity things they gave us. What did they say when they gave them to us?"

"Tomato," the cabin boy said.

"I can't imagine bringing these tomato things back to my native Italy," said Columbus. "They won't have any use for these. What are they gonna do? Put it on their noodles? That's preposterous, Chips."

"Surely there's something else," said the cabin boy. "And my name's Pedro."

"Oh, these other things they gave us?" Columbus said, holding up a brownish tuber. "What did they call these, Chips?"

"They called them potatoes." The cabin boy answered. "And my name's still Pedro."

"Who in Europe would ever want these potato things?" whined Columbus. "Even in a far-off backward corner like Ireland, they couldn't possibly find a use for them. I'm ruined. I can see Queen Elizabeth copping one of her attitudes, and it won't be pretty."

"Maybe Luis de Bullchip and Quark de Farrtur will return with something of value that will impress Queen Elizabeth. It's been a couple of days since you dispatched them to the interior. They should be back soon." The cabin boy said hopefully.

"If they come back at all," mused Columbus. "These people on the outskirts of India differ from the Indians I had been told about. Their appearance seems similar, but they speak and act much differently than I have been told."

"I'm sure they will be back," the cabin boy reassured him. "Luis the interpreter knows many languages, and I'm sure he'll communicate with the natives to get their best treasures to bring back to Europe."

"That won't be much help if he doesn't make it back." Columbus said.

"Luis the interpreter is in expert hands," the cabin boy reassured him. "Quark the sailor is not only a skilled navigator, he's well known for his survival skills and mastery of all weapons. They should be back soon."

Columbus went back to pondering the navigation charts he had laid out on a faded old oak chest he had been using as a desk. He leaned back on his rickety stool before he dipped his quill into a tiny inkwell and wrote more of the day's notes in his logbook. The cabin boy, who had no place to sit in Columbus' tiny captain's cabin, crouched on the floor and tried to fix his crushed hat. Suddenly, there was a knock on the cabin door.

"What is it?" Columbus asked through the closed cabin door.

"Luis de Bullchip and Quark de Farrtur have returned." Someone yelled through the door. "Luis de Bullchip has something important to tell you."

"Send him in right away!" Columbus commanded the crewman. He looked at the cabin boy. "Go to Quark the sailor and tend to any needs he may have. After I have spoken to Luis, send Quark to meet with me."

"Will do," said the cabin boy, and he left the tiny quarters. Moments later, there was another knock on the door.

"Come in," Columbus said, facing the door. The door opened, and to Columbus' surprise there stood Luis de Bullchip holding what appeared to Columbus to be a thick smoking stick in his mouth.

"You're burning!" Columbus exclaimed. Luis shook his head, pulled the smoking object out of his mouth and blew a puff of smoke in Columbus' direction.

"Don't be alarmed," he told Columbus. "It's something the natives in a village turned me on to."

"You're not burning up inside?" Columbus asked.

"No, it's something most everyone in the village we discovered does," Luis said to Columbus. "You just inhale the smoke and blow it out. It's some kind of leaf they roll into a cylinder and light one end on fire."

"How does it make you feel when you inhale this smoke?"

"Not very well," admitted Luis. "The first time I tried it, I thought I was going to throw up."

"Then why do you keep doing it?" Columbus asked.

"I can't stop doing it," he said. "Once I finish one, even if I feel bad, I want another one. I'm afraid I'll run out."

"Did Quark do this smoking thing too?" Columbus asked.

"Yes. He can't put it down either." Luis said. "He even marked out a smoking section on the top deck so he could smoke there."

"Do you think there's a market for this stuff in Europe?" Columbus asked.

"Of course," Luis responded. "Once you get people started, they'll probably pay good money for more."

"Then you and Quark go back with the soldiers and get as much of that stuff as you can," said Columbus. "What do they call it?"

"Something like tobago."

"Well then, get all the tobago they have here in...what do they call this place?"

"Tobago," Luis answered. "They say that word a lot."

"What does it mean?" Columbus asked.

"I'm not sure," Luis said. "It's hard to decipher their language, but one thing I am sure of is that they are not the source of this tobago. They did, however, let me know who had it."

"Who?"

"The Fugawi."

"Who the Fugawi?" Columbus asked.

"It's another tribe." Luis answered.

"Where the Fugawi?" Columbus asked.

"The people of the village let Quark know. They even gave him a map."

"Go get Quark. I need to know where the village people told him to go."

Luis left to find Quark, and Columbus sat down at his desk and again poured over his maps and notes. His mind raced with excitement. Had he found something to take back to Europe, that would bring him riches and the gratitude of Queen Elizabeth? What about a passage to Asia? Was he near India? Should he keep searching for a passage or return after finding a supply of this new substance that Luis de Bullchip couldn't get enough of? He was pondering these questions when there was another knock on

the door and an excited Luis and Quark let themselves into Columbus'
quarters.

The campiness of Columbus' small room at the rear of the Santa Maria
was even more pronounced by the smoke that both Luis and Quark both
deeply inhaled and exhaled. His mind raced with thoughts of all of Europe
partaking in this habit and what his share of the profits would entail. He
knew he had to get more of this tobago.

"Did the village people tell you where the Fugawi?" Columbus said to
Quark and Luis as they continued blowing smoke.

"Yay," said Quark.

"What did the village people say?" Columbus asked.

"Go west," said Quark.

"What did they look like? Did they look Indian?" Columbus asked.

"One was an Indian," said Luis. "Another was dressed in leather and one
had a hard hat."

"But the one they called Cop did most of the talking, at least I think it
was talking, said Quark. "The rest just sort of danced gaily."

"Luis said they gave you a map," Columbus said to Quark. "Do you have
it?"

"No," responded Quark sheepishly.

"Where is it?" Columbus asked loudly.

"I rolled some of the tobago in it and lit it." Quark admitted.

"You burned the map?" Luis shouted.

"I needed a smoke." Quark admitted.

Columbus was even more beside himself. The map was destroyed, but
the fact that Quark had sacrificed it because of his compulsion for this new
commodity made him want to find its source even more.

"Do you remember any of it?" Columbus asked Quark.

"I think so," answered Quark.

Columbus turned over one of the many maps that littered his small desk, dipped his quill in the well and handed it to Quark. Quark drew some shapes that appeared to be islands and then drew a straight line down about two inches from the left edge of the paper. In the middle of the paper, he drew two crossed palm trees and then pointed to that spot.

"The Fugawi live here," said Quark.

"On that piece of paper?" Columbus asked.

"No," said Quark. "On a mainland behind two crossed palm trees due west from here."

"How long will it take to sail there?" Columbus asked Quark.

"I'm not sure," said Quark. "We had trouble with their language."

"And the village people seem to want to sing more than talk," added Luis.

"What did you give them for this tobago?" Columbus asked.

"Just a chicken," Luis answered. "They had never seen one before."

"They were amazed," added Quark. "For a few chickens, you'll probably get all the tobago these ships can carry as long as the chickens don't blow up first."

Just then, there was knocking on Columbus' door that sounded like hurried pounding.

"What is it?" Columbus shouted through the door.

"Captain," a voice answered. "The men want more of those smoking leaves."

Columbus looked at both Luis and Quark. "Set sail for the Fugawi Village. I don't care how far it is."

"Aye," said Luis, coughing.

"Aye, aye," said Quark, coughing as well.

Soon the call went out for all hands on deck, especially the irritable hands on the Santa Maria looking for their next nicotine fix. Someone yelled,

"Anchors aweigh," and the Pinta, Nina, and Santa Maria headed due west, each ship with a bone in her teeth. The crew constantly manned the crow's nests to look out for the two crossed palms that marked the location of the Fugawi and more tobago.

A day passed and then another. The lookouts in the crow's nests saw only open ocean. Columbus became impatient. He accused Quark of lying about the whereabouts of the Fugawi and of not remembering what was on the map he destroyed. He kept asking Quark where the Fugawi were. Quark insisted he wasn't lying and said he wanted to find them as much as Columbus did because he was dying for a smoke. He told Columbus that since he had stopped puffing the tobago he was miserable, and the only bright spot was that he had stopped coughing. Still, Columbus gave him no peace and kept constantly yelling, "Where the Fugawi?"

Finally, they sighted land. It was a large landmass that extended to each end of the horizon. Columbus was excited, thinking it could be a continent. He thought it might even be Asia. However, his euphoria decreased when the ships approached the shore, and they did not see the two crossed palm trees that marked the Fugawi village.

Columbus decided the most efficient way to find the crossed palm marker was to split up his ships. He sent the Pinta 20 leagues north, the Nina 20 leagues south, and the Santa Maria would search for the crossed palms between them. After completing their searches, the three ships would meet again at their present location and share their findings. Since time was of the essence and the crew of the Santa Maria was getting antsy to find more of this tobago, each ship set upon its course immediately.

The Santa Maria got as close to the shore as possible and set a course north. It would search 20 leagues north, then turn around and search south until it reached the search area of the Nina and then return to the agreed upon meeting place with the other two vessels. That is unless they sighted a pair of crossed palm trees along the beaches they were searching, which is exactly what happened.

"Crossed palms ho!" cried the lookout from the Santa Maria.

"Get my spyglass," Columbus commanded his crew. "And tell them to stop calling me a HO!"

Columbus made his way to the ship's front deck and looked through the spyglass. There it was. Two palm trees that almost criss-crossed at the top. When Luis and Quark joined him at his vantage point, it was visible to the naked eye.

"Are these the crossed palm trees the village people told you about?" Columbus asked Quark.

"I'm sure of it," Quark answered. "What do you want to do?"

"Seeing the crossed palm trees, I want to get in and out as soon as possible," Columbus answered.

"In and out sounds good right now," Luis added. "Since we ran out of that tobago, I'm always hungry."

"We don't have time to wait for Pinta and Nina to return," Columbus instructed Luis and Quark. "Prepare the boats and form a landing party. In case we meet the Fugawi, we'll need things to trade immediately. Quark, you said the village people liked the chicken. Bring as many as possible and have one prepared so they can sample what a cooked one tastes like. As a matter of fact, fry it in oil; it will cook faster that way."

"Would you like me to select chickens that don't look like they are about to reproduce in case they overheat and blow up while splitting?" Quark asked.

"No, if this tobago sells in Europe like I think it will, we'll be trading a lot of chickens. They'll just have to deal with it like we do."

"Should we bring soldiers?" Quark asked.

"Yes, but not too many," Columbus answered. "We want to approach them peacefully. They should not follow us too closely, but not be too far away. Behind those crossed palms, it could be a mad, mad, mad, mad world."

Within an hour, they took three boats from the cradle of the main hatch. Two of the boats held caged chickens, assorted trading trinkets, and three soldiers each. The soldiers wore conquistador helmets but no armor in case they had to swim. Each soldier carried a short, curved falchion sword to appear less conspicuous and menacing to the natives. One soldier in each boat also carried a matchlock musket for the psychological effect the booming weapon could have if the natives turned hostile. In the third boat were Columbus, Luis, Quark, the cabin boy, and Friar Juan from the monastery.

The boats made landfall about one hundred yards in front of the crossed palm trees. Behind the crossed palms started the thick tropical jungle. Between the palm trees was an undergrowth of bushes and vines that effectively hid the contents of the interior. It was determined that three soldiers would remain on the beach and guard half of the chickens and trinkets. Columbus, Quark, and Luis would forge ahead through the jungle searching for the Fugawi with the cabin boy, Friar Juan, and the other three soldiers keeping a safe distance behind. Since there was very little visibility inside the undergrowth, they would project their locations verbally. At various intervals one party would loudly shout "Marco!" and the other parties would respond "Polo!" Columbus, Luis, and Quark carried with them the fried chicken, a couple live chickens in small cages, and the few tobago leaves they still had left.

"Marco!" Columbus cried out as he and his party stumbled through the thick growth. "Polo!" came a reply from the party trailing them and a very faint "Polo" that could barely be heard from the beach. Columbus, Luis and Quark ventured deeper into the jungle until their cries of "Marco!" were no longer answered. They were no longer in contact with the rest of their landing party and had ventured further into the jungle than any of them had ever gone before. Their minds raced with what dangers could be lurking.

"Maybe we should turn back," said Luis. "There could be lions."

"And tigers," added Quark.

"And bears," said Columbus. "Oh, my!"

They were just about to turn back when Columbus noticed a clearing behind a last stand of extremely thick foliage.

"I think there's a clearing on the other side, if we can just get through this last layer of brush." Columbus told his two companions. Since they had not brought their machetes so as not to look too menacing to the natives, they had to cut away at the dense but thin hedgerow that separated them from the clearing with tiny pocket knives Columbus had gotten from the Swiss army in Genoa. Each of them started carving an oval shape about their size, which they were hoping to push through and fall onto the other side. Progress was slow, but at about the same time they each felt the hedgerow give.

"Let's all push through together," said Quark, pressing a chicken cage into the foliage.

"Heave ho!" Luis yelled, following suit with what he was holding.

"Don't call me ho," said Columbus as he finally pushed through the hedgerow and fell through onto a grassy meadow that lay on the other side. Columbus's fingers felt the short, fragrant, bright green meadow grass and tiny orange and yellow flowers, and he was transfixed until he saw what appeared to be human feet covered in a thin, crude, black coating, which startled him. He looked up to see two natives standing over him and his companions. Columbus, Luis, and Quark slowly rose to their feet, each feigning a smile and trying to look as friendly as possible.

The natives were men of about the same size as Columbus and his party and appeared to be in their twenties. They wore white, what appeared to be cotton, wrap-around skirts that went almost to the knee and sleeveless shirts. Bright red and yellow flower designs embroidered the shirts. They also wore multicolored feathered headdresses and shell necklaces. Both parties stared intently at each other until Luis began trying to speak with the natives. He tried saying hello in Arabic, Hebrew, and Klingon. The two natives glanced at each other and then looked back at Columbus. Luis then tried a couple of phrases he knew from Middle Chinese. The natives looked at Luis, puzzled, and then at each other.

"No entiendo a estos gringos locos," one native said to the other.

Columbus and Luis looked at each other in amazement.

"¿Habla español?" Columbus asked nervously.

"Si," the two natives responded in unison.

"How can you speak Spanish?" Columbus asked the natives.

"You're in Latin America, Homes," replied the shorter of the two natives. "Everyone speaks Spanish here."

"Except in Brazil," added the taller native. "They speak German."

"I am Christopher Columbus," said Columbus, introducing himself. "My crew and I have sailed from far away to make friends and trade with you."

"I am Teepee," said the shorter of the two natives. "What are those weird-looking bird things you have in those cages? I've never seen birds like that."

"And I am Peepee," said the taller of the two natives. "What smells so good? It's making me hungry."

Columbus signaled to Quark to uncover the fried chicken and held one of the caged chickens up for Teepee and Peepee to inspect.

"These animals are called chickens," he said. "And when cooked, they are delicious."

Quark presented the uncovered platter of fried chicken to Teepee and Peepee and offered it to the natives after taking and eating a piece to allay any fear from the natives that the fowl might be foul. Teepee and Peepee each took a piece. Peepee ate his first, followed by Teepee, who appeared to be the more suspicious of the two.

"It's good!" Peepee declared, taking a couple more pieces of the chicken and devouring them quickly.

"Finger lickin' good," added Teepee, taking another piece himself.

Columbus set the cage containing one chicken down on the grass of the meadow and placed what tobago leaves the crew of the Santa Maria hadn't smoked on top of the cage.

"We have come from Hispania to trade," Columbus said.

"You're Hispanic?" Teepee asked. "No wonder you speak Spanish."

"Hispania means Spain," said Luis. "It's from the Roman era."

"How long have you been roamin'?" Peepee asked.

"Like two months," said Quark.

Columbus pointed to the chicken cage and the tobago leaves on top of it.

"We have more of these tasty chickens and will trade them with the Fugawi for as much of this as we can get," Columbus said, picking up the greenish-brown leaves on top of the chicken cage.

"Who the Fugawi?" Peepee asked.

"Aren't you the Fugawi?" Columbus asked him.

"No," said Peepee.

"We're the Guardians."

"Guardians?" asked Columbus.

"Yes," said Peepee. "We used to be called the Indians, but some woke Karens thought it was offensive, so we changed it to Guardians because we guard sacred things in the village."

"We came to trade with the Fugawi for what they call tobago," Columbus said. "Can you help us?"

"Now that I think about it, I recall a tribe with a name like that settled around here a while ago, but they moved on," Peepee said. "If it's those leaves you want, we have plenty. We used to smoke them but gave it up."

"Why?" asked Columbus.

"The smoke turned our teeth brown and made them fall out." Peepee answered.

"In Europe we have people called the British," said Columbus. "They're perfectly fine with rotten teeth. We'll take all the leaves you have."

"We would like more of those tasty things," said Peepee pointing to the caged chicken. "Bring all you have to trade with back here and I will take you to our leader."

"Deal," said Columbus. "We will bring all we have."

Both parties set off to return to their respective groups and get ready to start what would become, for better and for worse, the Columbian Exchange. Once back on the shoreline, Columbus made immediate preparations to meet the leader of Teepee and Peepee's tribe. He wasted no time in returning to his ship and ordered the landing boats to transport trade goods to shore. He figured he could use the soldiers he already had on land to carry the load inland and for protection if he told the Guardians they were only wearing their armor and weapons to bring them for gifts and trade. Columbus refused to trade the matchlock muskets, but he would trade some swords and armor if it got him what he wanted.

Besides bringing ashore all the chickens held on the Santa Maria, he ordered some to be butchered and fried so he could arrive with food at the gathering so the natives would covet the new creatures even more. He just hoped that if any chickens reproduced during the meetings, it was without complications and none overheated and burst into flame while splitting into two.

As the landing party made its way toward the agreed-upon meeting spot, Columbus looked up at the sky. They had made good time loading up, and there were still several hours of sunlight left. It would be advantageous if he could conclude his business with the Guardians before the Pinta and Nina returned. They did not like the thought of traveling back through the dense undergrowth at night as they made their way to the holes that they had cut in the jungle hedgerows. As with all exploration, success can rest on acting expeditiously but without falling into the trap known as haste.

Because journeys are normally quicker the second time around, Columbus' party, along with their chickens, and other wares, moved rapidly. Soon they were at the spot where they had cut through the thin, yet dense, jungle hedge to get through to the grassy meadow where they had earlier in the day met Teepee and Peepee. Quark was about to push his way through the center hole when, several feet from the hole to his left, an opening in the hedge appeared as if a door had swung open and Teepee and Peepee appeared in the doorway.

"What's happening, Homey?" said Teepee.

"You brought some people with you," said Peepee, noticing the rest of Columbus' party, including the soldiers.

"They're here to carry the things we brought to trade with you," Columbus said.

"Those knives look pretty long," Peepee said warily.

"We'd be happy to trade some of them for those leaves, and we have those tasty chickens you like," said Columbus. "We even cooked some up for ya."

"What do you think?" Peepee said to Teepee, looking for approval. "Should we let them all in?"

"Sure, why not," Teepee said. "Besides, I'm hungry." He looked at Columbus. "Can you spare a couple of pieces for the road?" He said.

Teepee and Peepee enjoyed some of the fried chicken as they led Columbus and his party across the clearing. Columbus, Luis, and Quark walked in front with Teepee and Peepee with the soldiers, friar, and cabin boy behind. As they walked, Columbus became more curious about the hidden doorway that Teepee and Peepee had opened that led to the grassy meadow from the dense jungle.

"When did you make that gateway through the hedgerow?" Columbus asked Teepee and Peepee. "We would never have known it was there."

"We kind of like to keep ourselves hidden," Peepee replied.

"There are some bad hombres out there," Teepee added.

"Like who?" Quark asked.

"Like the Aztecs to the north, the Incas to the south, and the surrounding Mayans, who are going total apocalypto." Said Peepee.

"Clowns to the left, Jokers to the right, and we're stuck in the middle with you," Teepee added.

"We just try to follow the wisdom of our ancestors and not get caught up in everyone else's power struggles," Peepee said. "When one tribe takes over, everybody hopes they'll be better, but they wind up being worse than the last."

"Meet the new boss, same as the old boss," said Teepee.

"Well, you don't have to worry about us," said Columbus. "The last thing we want to do is impose our ways on anyone else. Live and let live; that's what Queen Elizabeth says. We're just here to trade peacefully."

Columbus' conversation stopped when the Guardian's village came into view. It was not a large village. There were about two dozen huts surrounding a large central hall. The huts were oval-shaped and about ten to twenty feet in diameter, with a wooden pole frame with a thatched covering of dried brownish palm fronds. The center structure was much larger and more impressive. It was multilevel and completely made of enormous stone blocks. Even the roof was stone. He could tell from a distance that people had carved intricate designs on the walls. He could also see that the Guardians had set up some kind of welcoming party for them. There was a long stone counter in front of the main hall with woven reed chairs set up on both sides. To the side were wooden tables with tree stump stools surrounded by woven mats and baskets that appeared to contain the local produce. Off to the side was a large mound that was covered with palm fronds. Around the wooden tables stood about twenty of the village's young men silently observing the approach of Columbus and his party. On the table were an assortment of spears, spiked clubs, and wooden shields. That the warriors were not holding the weapons but had them in proximity led Columbus to believe their hosts were welcoming them peacefully but exercising some caution. From inside the huts, other villagers peered out of the entrances at the newcomers.

Once inside the village, Columbus instructed the soldiers and the rest of his party to place the chicken cages and other trading goods in front of the central stone counter and then to back away to a non-threatening distance. Being friendly hosts, Teepee and Peepee offered them seating on the woven mats. The soldiers and cabin boy took a seat on the mats while Luis, Quark, and Friar Juan stayed at the front with Columbus to present their wares. Teepee and Peepee spoke briefly before Peepee left the group and walked into the main hall.

"Are you ready to meet our leaders?" Teepee asked Columbus. Columbus nodded. Seconds later, Peepee and another tribesman adorned in floral robes and holding a large conch shell walked out of the main hall. He blew the conch, and the natives filed out of their huts standing just outside the reception area. Columbus' soldiers watched but did not move forward, having been cued by Columbus not to make any sudden movements.

Then, from the hall emerged six men in white cloaks and feathered headdresses. Three stood behind the counter to one side of an elaborately carved wooden chair, and the three others stood behind the woven reed chairs on the other side. Columbus then noticed the carvings and artwork that adorned the counter, the tabletops, and the large stones that made up the walls of the main hall. They all seemed to have the same design. It looked like some kind of king or deity in a small ship, but instead of being on the sea, the deity appeared to be flying in the air. It appeared to be a recurring theme in the village's decor. Columbus had started to think about what it might mean when the conch shell was blown again.

A tall, mature man wearing a solid jade headdress adorned with quetzal feathers and wearing a cloak made from jaguar skin walked out of the main hall and stood behind the center of the stone counter next to the ornately carved wooden chair. Columbus guessed immediately that he must be the king or ruler of the village. Behind him was a very tiny man dressed exactly the same, but he was less than half the height of the king. Three other warriors came out of the hall and stood behind the king.

The king clapped his hands, and the villagers found places to sit either at the tables or mats around them. Soon some villagers were handing out food from the baskets. There were corn, squash, and sweet potatoes that were baked until soft. Columbus' soldiers were wary at first. Unfamiliar with New World foods, they decided it was better than hardtack after a few bites. They thanked their hosts and began eating. They didn't even seem to mind when curious children would touch their clothes and metal armor.

Teepee and Peepee seated Columbus at the counter opposite where the king was standing. Each of them sat on one side of Columbus with Teepee between Columbus and Luis and Peepee between Columbus and Quark and the friar took the seat next to Quark. The king sat on the carved wooden chair opposite Columbus, and the tiny man dressed exactly like him took the stool next to him. Three of the men in white cloaks, whom Columbus guessed to be advisors or priests, sat on one side of them and the other three sat on the other. The king addressed Columbus.

"I am Dork, the holder of the secrets," the King announced.

"He's like the boss man," Peepee told Columbus.

"It is an honor to meet you," said Columbus. "You are King Dork?"

"I am a keeper of ancient teachings," said Dork. "I do not covet the title of King."

"What title should I use for a man of your position?" asked Columbus. "Sir?"

"No."

"Mister?"

"Fine," said Dork. "You can call me Mister Dork."

"Mister Dork it is," said Columbus.

"This is my assistant, Poopoo," said Mister Dork, pointing to the tiny native sitting next to him. "And these are the knowledge keepers of the village," he said, pointing out the men in the white cloaks.

"I am Christopher Columbus, and these are my associates Luis, Quark, and Friar Juan," he said, introducing his companions. "We have sailed across the great ocean and wish to trade with you for the leaves you call tobago."

"I have come to save your souls," Friar Juan said.

"Later," said Columbus, shutting down Friar Juan. "Do you have this tobago?"

"Yes," answered Dork. "I don't know why you would want it, but we pride ourselves on not being preachy and judgmental. We'll let you have all you want. Peepee has told me about these chickens you have. He says they are delicious."

Columbus stood up, turned around, and grabbed a platter from his wares. He placed it on the table in front of Dork. He took off the cover, revealing stacks of fried chicken pieces.

"Please have some," he said.

Dork looked at one of the knowledge keepers, who reached over, took a piece and bit into it. When he smiled, nodded his head, and made a yummy sound, Dork took a piece as well and ate it.

"It is delicious," he said. "And it is those animals in the cages?"

"Yes," Columbus said.

"May I inspect one?" asked Dork.

"Of course," said Columbus.

Columbus took a large brown chicken out of its cage and handed it to Dork. Dork held it up and looked at it from below. He appeared puzzled by it.

"What's the matter, boss?" Poopoo asked.

Suddenly the chicken began to split into two separate chickens.

"Oh no," said Luis. "It's reproducing!"

"Please don't blow up," Quark whispered under his breath.

Dork held onto the chicken until the energy emitting from it made it heat up. He dropped it down on the table where it smoked briefly before splitting into two separate chickens, which shook off their singed feathers, jumped off the counter, and started pecking at the ground for food.

"Whoa," said Teepee. "Your birds still reproduce through binary fission?"

"I thought that was just a legend," added Poopoo.

"Binary fisss...?" Columbus asked.

"Binary fission." Dork stated. "It's a primordial form of reproduction now relegated to the simplest of organisms."

"Like those tiny things you can't see that change shape," said Poopoo.

"Yah, like Armanis," Peepee added.

"Your birds don't split into two here?" Luis asked.

"No," said Dork.

"How is that possible?" Columbus asked.

Dork leaned over to Poopoo and began whispering some lengthy instructions into his ear. Columbus took this time to look around and make sure everything was still going all right with the rest of his party. His soldiers were behaving themselves so far. They were having fleeting polite interactions with the villagers that included discreet waving and allowing their clothing to be touched. They and the village warriors were still keeping a respectful distance and an eye on each other.

"My men seem to enjoy the food," Columbus said to Teepee while Dork continued talking privately with Poopoo.

"Wait till they break out the balche'," said Teepee. "It's what we drink when we want to party hardy."

"The last time I drank balche', I saw cartoons, man." Peepee said.

"What are cartoons?" Columbus asked.

"I don't know, but I saw 'em!" Peepee said

"Peepee likes to party hardy." Teepee told Columbus.

Columbus decided he needed to warn his soldiers about drinking balche'. He didn't need any liquid courage to start a battle in the village. He called Friar Juan over to him. "Tell the soldiers not to drink the balche'". He told Friar Juan. "And no saving souls until after we load the tobago."

When Columbus looked back in Dork's direction, he noticed that Poopoo and the three cloaked knowledge keepers that were sitting next to him were gone. He pointed in the direction where they were and asked, "Where did they go?"

"I have sent them to prepare a demonstration for you inside our sacred hall," Dork said. "I believe we can show you something much more beneficial to you and the world you come from than the tobago you seek."

"I still wish to trade for tobago," Columbus

"Suit yourself; we hold the knowledge of those who came before, not judgement of those in the present." Dork said.

"That was deep," said Columbus. "I'll remember that."

Moments later, Poopoo walked out of the hall and took his seat next to Dork.

"Boss, we are ready in the sacred hall," he told Dork.

"Excellent," he told Poopoo and then turned his attention back to Columbus. "Very few may enter the sacred hall. You may bring two of your men with you."

"I will bring my advisors Luis and Quark with me," he told Dork and the rest at the counter. "Friar Juan will stay here with the rest of my crew and make preparations to transport the tobago to my ship." He gave a quick glance at the friar to remind him of business before souls.

Dork nodded and stood up. When he stood, the villagers, who had been enjoying the banquet and socializing, fell silent and then noisily got up. They focused all of their attention on their leader, Dork.

"I welcome our esteemed guests into the sacred hall," Dork said, addressing the entire gathering and motioning to Columbus. "In our absence, please enjoy the wonderful offering they have prepared for us."

With Columbus' blessing, the fried chicken was shared with the entire gathering, and Dork, Poopoo, Columbus, Luis, and Quark got up from the counter and walked to the sacred hall.

Though Columbus' previous travels had exposed him to impressive architecture, upon entry to the sacred hall he and his companions were mesmerized. It was dimly lit, with the only light being candles and openings in the upper-level walls for observation. All the stone, the walls, ceiling and floor was carved or brightly painted with the same theme he had seen carved throughout the villages. They all depicted the same man in some kind of craft traveling through the skies. Some with fire or flames coming out of them.

Dork led them to a table in the center of the hall. On it was a wooden tray with a lid. Dork walked around the table and stood behind it. Poopoo, who was much shorter than the table, got on a wooden stool next to Dork. Columbus, Luis, and Quark walked up to the table and stood opposite Dork.

"Your sacred hall impresses us," Columbus said. "The carvings and paintings that adorn it are incredible. What is its meaning?"

"They document the journeys of the ancient gods who gave us the knowledge we keep and hold sacred," said Dork.

"Where did they come from?" Luis asked.

"They flew down from the sky like birds," said Poopoo. "They had great ships that spewed fire and were made of neither wood nor stone. We call them Nekinadnovhcire."

"They brought wonders from the heavens," Dork told Columbus, Luis, and Quark. "Including this, which I will show you now."

Dork removed the lid from the tray, revealing several dozen small, smooth, oval-shaped objects.

"What are those?" Columbus asked.

"They are called eggs," said Dork.

"What do they do?" Luis asked.

"It is how birds and some other creatures reproduce in our world," Dork explained. "Before the Nekinadnovhcire flew down from the heavens, birds and other creatures reproduced through what the ancient ones called binary fission. Each animal would split into two animals. But often the heat from splitting would cause the animals to burst into flames and destroy them both."

"No kidding," said Columbus. "It leaves a mess."

"I considered becoming a vegetarian," added Quark.

"The Nekinadnovhcire saw that this was causing hunger for our people and gave us the egg and taught us how to use it," Dork continued.

"How to use it?" Columbus asked.

"Yes," Dork said.

He clapped his hands, and a man in a white cloak entered with another tray. On it was a bird's nest with three tiny eggs and a clay pot heated by a flame beneath it. He placed it on the table next to the other egg tray and stepped to the side. Dork took the nest from the tray and tapped the tiny eggs that were in it. Seconds later, the tiny eggs started hatching and then the hatchlings separated from the shells.

"This is how birds here reproduce now," said Dork

"But they're so small," said Columbus.

"They'll grow to full size like animals born from a womb." Dork assured him. "And there is one other benefit to these eggs."

Dork took two eggs from the tray that contained dozens of larger eggs and cracked them on the hot ceramic bowl, letting the insides fall into the bowl and discarding the shells back onto the egg tray. He stirred them with a small wooden spoon from the table until they were fully scrambled and cooked. He handed the spoon to Columbus.

"Eat," said Dork.

"Can you eat these eggs?" Columbus asked.

"Yes," said Dork. "You can eat it before the chicken emerges or wait until it grows and eat it then."

Columbus took a wooden spoonful of scrambled eggs and tasted them. He nodded and offered the spoon to Luis, who tasted it as well.

"How do we get our chickens to reproduce with these eggs?" Columbus asked.

"You have to use grafting," said Poopoo.

"What's grafting?" Luis asked.

"It's like when you put the top of one kind of plant on the roots of another kind of plant to make a better crop." Dork explained.

"That's how we got fruit that looks like a pinecone," Poopoo said.

"Even the sacred corn we eat was once grass until we started grafting it," said Dork. "It was the Nekinadnovhcire that taught us how to use grafting to improve plants and animals to feed us better. Now the animals that used to reproduce through binary fission reproduce through these eggs, which we can eat now or what comes of them later."

"Can you show us how to graft these eggs onto chickens?" Columbus asked Dork.

"As keepers of the ancient knowledge we are more than happy to share it," said Dork. "I will have Poopoo consult the notes from the Book of Smart and return with some of your chickens and then we will show you how to graft your world's chickens and our world's eggs together."

Poopoo then set off on his mission to prepare to teach Columbus, Luis, and Quark how to graft eggs and chickens together. "What is the Book of Smart?" Luis asked Dork as Poopoo departed.

"It is an ancient writing that has been deciphered and preserved," answered Dork. "Legend says its opposite lives in another realm."

"Speaking of writing, do you have a way to write this down, Quark?" Columbus asked.

Quark shook his head, and Dork clapped his hands. Soon one of the white-cloaked men that were around the hall appeared and set a quill, a bowl of soot ink, and what appeared to be paper on the table next to the egg tray.

"What is this made of?" Columbus asked, touching the paper.

"The surface of trees," answered Dork.

Just then, Poopoo reappeared inside the sacred hall looking distressed.

"What is the matter?" Dork asked.

"I have bad news and worse news," answered Poopoo.

"What is the bad news?" asked Dork.

"There are no chickens left," said Poopoo. "Everyone thought they were so delicious, they ate them all!"

"And what is the worse news?" Dork asked, alarmed.

"The Mayans have gone super apocalypto and they're coming this way!" Poopoo yelled.

"When will they be here?" Dork asked.

"They could be here tonight," said Poopoo.

"How many tribes?" Dork asked Poopoo.

"Nearly every city-state," Poopoo said. "They are looking for anything to sacrifice to the gods, people and animals. They're even sacrificing plants and virtual assistants."

Dork shook his head and looked at Columbus. "I must apologize," he told Columbus and his group. "We are caught between two empires with a lust for conquest, who have been catching and sacrificing the migratory birds that are a source of food for the people caught between the two empires to their gods to bless their conquests."

"And this has caused those people to sacrifice people and animals to their own gods to bring everything back," Poopoo added.

"The Nekinadnovhcire taught us that the lust for conquest is a vicious cycle." Dork said.

"I speak not only for Spain, but for the rest of Europe, when I say conquest is the last thing on our minds," Columbus said.

"We don't even know what it looks like," added Quark.

Dork nodded and then looked at Columbus. "I apologize, but I must cut our meeting short. If you are not safely out to sea by nightfall, you and your men are in great danger, and they will find our location and destroy us and the ancient knowledge as well."

"We will make preparations to leave immediately," said Columbus. "But please show us how to graft these eggs onto the animals that reproduce by splitting into two and help us carry some tobago back to our boats. You can keep most everything else we brought to trade. There is still some time before nightfall, and I promise we will be at sea before night falls."

"I will take your word," said Dork. "Since there are no chickens and other birds are scarce, we will tell two men of your choosing how the grafting is done, and we will take what tobago we have to your boats. Just keep your promise to be away by nightfall."

"Will do," Columbus said. "I speak not only for Spain but for all people of European descent when I say we would never, ever, ever, break our promises to the native peoples of this land."

"Pinky promise?" said Dork, extending his pinky finger.

"You betcha," answered Columbus, linking pinkies with Dork.

Columbus then told Quark to go watch over the soldiers and send the cabin boy to see him in the sacred hall. He told Quark it was for him to organize the soldiers but after Quark smoked the map, the village people had given him, Columbus did not trust Quark with the job of writing down and saving the grafting process that would allow chickens to reproduce from the eggs Dork provided. When the cabin boy joined Columbus and Luis in the sacred hall, he instructed them to take copious notes. He told Luis and the cabin boy that the success of the voyage depended on them being able to recreate the chicken and egg grafting process that Poopoo was about to teach them. Once he was confident that Luis and the cabin boy knew what they had to do, Columbus went outside to organize his men to load up and evacuate.

Columbus was fortunate that Dork, having been told the purpose of Columbus' visit by Teepee and Peepee, had already collected a supply of tobago leaves before Columbus arrived and had them ready. However, since wheeled carts and beasts of burden were unknown to the village, many villagers were selected by Dork to physically carry the tobago to Columbus' ships and rush back to the village whose entrance was being further concealed to avoid detection by the rampaging Mayans. After Columbus' men shook off the effects of drinking too much balche, the operation ran smoothly. As the sun set, Columbus left the beach with his boats full of tobago, eggs, and a written description about grafting eggs onto fowl meticulously written by Luis and the cabin boy.

Once back on the Santa Maria, the sailors worked feverishly to store the boats and their cargo on the mother ship. The sailors, exhausted, slept mostly on deck as many were too tired to even go below deck after everything was stowed. Columbus, exhausted as well, worked through the night to make his plans for what to do when the Pinta and Nina returned until he too succumbed to sleep. He did not get to sleep for long.

"Ships ho!" There came a cry from the Santa Maria's crow's nest.

"Stop calling me a HO!" said Columbus as he shook himself awake.

The lookout in the crow's nest had sighted ships coming from opposite directions. It was the Pinta and Nina returning to the agreed-upon meeting spot. By the time Columbus made it to the deck, the ships were close enough that they could communicate by shouting. Columbus told Luis and Quark that he wanted to meet with the captains of both the Pinta and Nina, as well as with them immediately. He also asked them to bring some eggs from the ship's storage, the notes on grafting and chickens from Pinta to the meeting. He also told them to limit the sailors' access to the tobago, so they had enough to take back to Europe.

Back in his quarters, Columbus prepared for the meeting. He had the cabin boy move some furniture outside the door. There would only be room to stand around his improvised desk. He laid some maps and other papers out on his desk and waited for his guests to arrive. Finally, Columbus heard voices outside. Not even waiting for a knock, Columbus instructed the cabin boy to open the door. Standing there were Krunch, the Captain of the Pinta; Tennile, Captain of the Nina; Luis, and Quark.

"Please come in," Columbus said to the group. "Sorry, there is no room to sit."

Everyone stood around the oak chest that served as Columbus' table.

"Do we have the grafting notes?" Columbus asked Luis and the cabin boy.

They nodded, holding the scrolls they had written at the village.

"What about the chickens?" Columbus asked. "I don't see any."

"I know," said Tennile. "We have great news. Both Krunch and I found the Fugawi. We traded all the chickens we had, and our holds are full of tobago."

"Oh no," said Columbus.

A look of distress overtook Columbus. He explained to them about the egg and how after grafting chickens and eggs together, chickens would reproduce through the egg and completely transform agriculture as it was known back in the Old World. He further explained that this, combined

with the incessant demand for tobago would be the instrument the no-
bility, and most importantly Queen Elizabeth, needed to maintain their
influence over their subjects and that they would be richly rewarded for
bringing this back to Europe.

They all stood there staring at each other, trying to come up with a new
plan.

"There are chickens back in Spain; we can graft them there," said Luis.

"We can't be experimenting on chickens when we get back to Queen
Elizabeth," Columbus said. "It has to be perfect when we present it."

"How about we stop somewhere along the way, like the Canary Islands,
and get some chickens?" Quark asked.

"Word would still get out that we were experimenting on chickens and
it wasn't preordained." Columbus answered.

"Then go to the Canary Islands and get some canaries," Luis said, trying
to lighten the mood.

"This isn't the time for jokes!" Columbus shouted.

"No, wait, he's onto something," the cabin boy said.

Everyone stared at him. They were too shocked to speak. In a meeting as
important as this, the cabin boy decided to speak up.

"Why not do this egg grafting on a similar creature in a place so unap-
pealing that no one would ever hear of it and once you have it absolutely
perfect, then use chickens and do it so quickly there is no time for it to be
spoken of before you present it to the Queen," the cabin boy explained.

"That just might work, Chips," Columbus said to the cabin boy.

"My name's Pedro," said the cabin boy.

"What place could we go to?" Luis asked. "We cannot stay here, and
there is no place in Europe where word would not leak out about what we
are doing."

"Is there no place in Europe so foul no one ever goes in or out of there?" the cabin boy asked.

"Only Monaco," said Quark, causing Luis, Columbus, Krunch, and Tennile to erupt into laughter.

"What is so funny about Monaco?" the cabin boy asked.

"It is the poorest and most wretched place in all of Europe," said Columbus. "Legend has it Monaco was settled many years ago by exiles from Florence who were judged as being too hopeless to be part of the Renaissance."

"My brother, Captain Tennile and I have sailed past it," said Captain Krunch. "There is no reason anyone would go there. It is completely isolated and inhabited only by the poorest of the poor and ducks"

"Ducks?" the cabin boy asked.

"The wretched refuse were forced to take the ducks with them when they were exiled from Florence according to the legend." Captain Tennile said.

"That's perfect," said the cabin boy. "Ducks are similar to chickens. We can go to Monaco and graft the eggs with the ducks there and transfer the process to chickens once we have perfected it. Then we return to Spain with tobago and chickens that reproduce by eggs and won't blow up."

"But what about the rest of the crew?" Luis asked. "They will surely tell of our plans once we return."

"Not if we sink the Santa Maria," said the cabin boy.

"Sink the Santa Maria?" Columbus exclaimed. "Are you crazy?"

"We don't really sink the Santa Maria," explained the cabin boy. "We pretend it is sinking and transfer everything to the Pinta and Nina and abandon ship. Once everyone else is off the ship, we can take the Santa Maria to Monaco. It can be the base of operations until the grafting works. We just need a place that has animals similar to chickens that we can experiment on where we won't be discovered."

The captains of the Pinta and Nina, Columbus, Luis, and Quark all looked at each other. It was silent for a moment, then they all seemed to nod in agreement.

"That sounds like a splendid plan, Chips," said Columbus. "We will pretend the Santa Maria has run aground, and we had to abandon it. Once everything is transferred to the Pinta and Nina, Chips, and some trusted crew will take the Santa Maria to Monaco with the eggs. We can meet up near Portugal when everything is ready."

"My name's Pedro," said the cabin boy.

"But I was going to put Chips in charge of the grafting experiments in Monaco," said Columbus. "Chips is such a good name for a cabin boy. Every captain wants a cabin boy named Chips."

"So if my name was Chips, I'd get to play God and experiment on all the people and ducks of Monaco until we get ducks and then chickens to reproduce through these eggs you just discovered?" asked the cabin boy.

"Of course, Chips," said Columbus. "You'd be my right-hand man."

"Fine!" said the cabin boy. "I'm Chips. Chips, the cabin boy. Chips, the cabin boy, is ready to experiment!"

"That's great, Chips," said Columbus. "Between people craving tobago and what these eggs will do for the food supply, the royals will pay us dearly."

And thus began the Columbian Exchange that would change all life on Earth and especially on a small part of it called Monaco.

Columbus review

Across

3. New World party drink.
4. Where village people said to go.
8. What Columbus brought to old world.
10. What Mayans went.
11. What Columbus traded.
13. Gave Columbus the egg.

Down

1. Went on rampage.
2. Took Columbus to Dork.
3. How Old World fowl reproduced before egg.
5. Queen that financed Columbus.
6. Tribe with tobago.
7. Process to make chickens reproduce via egg.
9. Mr. Dork's assistant.
12. Where Nekinadnovhcire came from.

CHAPTER THREE

MONACO

It was midnight on the ocean; not a streetcar was in sight. It was a typical night in Monaco with the full moon low in the sky, shining its full light on the grinding poverty and despair the city had known for so long. Only hours before that impoverished despair was contrasted almost perfectly as the sunset behind Tete de Chien simultaneously projected an aura of light around the great Casino Royale of Monaco while throwing even more shade on the dingy beach of Plague Du Larvotto where the people and ducks of Monaco would share what they could scavenge for their meager nightly meal.

Monaco is not only the smallest country in the world, the Vatican is actually much bigger but much of it was built without permits so realtors must report a smaller square footage—it is also the poorest. What began as wretched refuse resettlement has only gotten worse over time. Not only can they afford only two stripes for their flag, they don't even have the funds to buy one. They have to use stolen Indonesian flags because they look the same.

Like the Tower of London after the Great London Fire, the Casino Royale of Monaco stands as a symbol of wealth, power, and oppression over the area's ignited indigence. The casino was an intrusion into Monaco. The casino was the illegitimate brainchild of Princess "Sweet" Peaches of Sardinia, who sought economic gain by using gambling to market the kingdom's namesake fish on the European continent. Princess Peaches approached France with the idea of building the casino there to market sardines, but they wouldn't take the bait. They did not like the idea of people speaking Sardinian in France. Like most of Europe, the French are very protective of their language and even encourage Canadians to stick to one language. Peaches tried Italy next, but they are just as particular about their language, especially the stuff that sounds like Dante, and told her "ciao" as well.

Eventually, "Sweet Peaches" usurped land in Monaco to build the Casino. She reasoned that if a customer lost their entire fortune at the casino, they still couldn't be too angry because there was no way they could be as poor as the people and ducks who lived near the grand casino. The contrasting wretchedness would make the casino look that much more opulent. The only problem was that France, Italy, Germany, and most of the rest of Europe did not want their languages being spoken in morose Monaco. Even Spain had its limits. Though they insisted most of Central and South America speak their language, when California and Texas started speaking English, they asked Mexico to cede that territory to America. Which is ironic because now they speak Spanish there. Kind of like selling a stock too early.

This attachment to language is why both people and ducks in Monaco speak English. Unlike the rest of Europe, the English don't really care who speaks their language. They'll let anyone speak it. Especially if it is harder to understand than when the English speak it. They'll let Australians, New Zealanders, and even encourage Canadians to speak it. As a matter of fact, some say that God created America so there could be one place where people spoke an understandable version of English.

Though the Kingdom of Sardinia is no more and could not have been less, the casino lives on to deflect the world's attention from the suffering. Nothing has formed a stronger bond than the suffering caused in Monaco by the Disflorencia Dispoorencia. When the poor and unworthy of Florence were exiled from the Renaissance, to what turned out to be the cruel secret experiments of the Columbian Exchange, or more aptly, the Columbian Eggschange. Through it all, the destitute denizens and denatured ducks developed a determined devotion to one another as well as a resemblance.

Over time, the people took on some duck-like features and became more squat and triangular in build with wider flattened feet. Slightly smaller heads resulted in hat sizes being reduced by about a centimeter, but no one noticed because they couldn't afford hats. On the other side of the coin, the ducks of Monaco wound up taking on many human-like traits.

The ducks of Monaco are unlike any other ducks in the world. They are much larger, standing a feathery three to four feet tall and more resemble a duck mascot than the rest of the ducks in the world. Most are white or yellow, but they do come in several colors and can resemble a Benetton commercial occasionally. Never much for flying, they have lost that ability altogether with wings that more resemble human arms and hands capable of playing cheap ukuleles discarded after the casino's Grand Prix Luau Nights after each big race.

Besides Casino Royale, the only other time any wealth touches Monaco is through automobile racing. After the disastrous Paris to Madrid Race of 1903, automobile racing promoters began searching for a location where a death race wouldn't be such a bad thing. Monaco was an obvious choice since people rarely complain when cars run over poor people or even poorer ducks, and any litter left would be considered an improvement. It wasn't, however, until 1929 that the first race was held when a promoter organized a colossal event to promote tobacco use, which was one commodity used by the ruling class to influence the masses. Since then, the races have been a regular occurrence.

Though cars screaming through town at 200 miles per hour have made life extremely dangerous, the discards provide some sustenance. Anything left over from any race is scavenged. There is little interaction between the poor of Monaco and race crews, drivers, and spectators. The rich and famous mostly stay at the casino and racing facilities. They often treat the locals with abuse while the locals make use of anything that comes their way. Even if it is being thrown at them amid taunts.

As different as Monaco is, it shares one commonality with the rest of the world. When the sun has set, one question comes to mind. What's for dinner? And like much of the world, the answer is the same. Whatever we can find. Whatever they can find in Monaco goes into the communal pot, where the elders of the community stir the evening soup with tender loving care. Tonight the rusty pot contained the traditional ratatouille composed of algae, barnacles, and small parts from Tag Hauer, Mille, and Omega watches that the drivers throw at the poor to blow off steam when they are frustrated by a car's constant porpoising and underperforming tires.

Hunched over the pot sat Mama Finley, or Chuckles as she was known to the motley ensemble that assembled on the beach of Plague Du Larvatto for what was often their only meal of the day. She was one of a group of elders who tended the pot all day. It was their job. It was also their only job, as nobody outside the casino really has a job in Monaco besides scavenging for the discards of the race car drivers and casino patrons or whatever has washed up on the shore. Mama Finley, like the rest of the people and ducks that would gather for the nightly meal, was dressed in a combination of scavenged scorched Nomex racing overalls and dirty torn pastels with Baindoux embroidering. Next to the simmering cauldron lay stacks of similar damaged designer clothing that served as the communal clothing dispensary. It was basically the Marshalls from hell.

Next to Mama Finley sat Vladdy and Wally, two other elders who were there on the spot of Plague Du Larvotto near the tiny pine and palm grove beneath the cliff that led up to the pathway to the casino. As elders, they could recall a time when the beach they were sitting on wasn't even there. The Plague du Larvotto is really a man-made beach that was constructed when the two old men and old woman were barely in their teens.

Long ago, the shoreline of Monaco was a series of jagged cliffs and hidden caves but one night a fierce Mediterranean storm washed away much of the cliff side revealing the remains of a cavernous dwelling that was hidden by the cliff side which set off a panic among the casino management and patrons. No one spoke of what was uncovered. There were whispers of a ship. The only resolution from the elite class that frequented the casino was that it had to be buried quickly. Overnight, shiploads of stone and gravel appeared along with a convoy of dump trucks and bulldozers to begin a land reclamation project that was covered with sand and secrecy. The impoverished people and ducks were then encouraged to settle in the area by the wealthy of the casino, who figured that if the dregs of society were on the sand, no one would look beneath it.

"Where's Angel?" Mama Finley asked, wiping the dirt and sweat from her brow, which fell into the pot and created a bit more to eat.

"He went out with a boat to get some more to put in the pot," answered Wally. "He took a couple of nets with him."

"I hope he finds something; those Tag Hauer pieces are so hard to digest, especially when the barnacles get stuck to them." Mama Finley said as she went back to stirring the communal cauldron.

Suddenly, a young beige duck named Teemu began cocking his head left and right as if he was listening for something.

"Do you hear something, Teemu?" Asked Torii, a dark-haired girl of about thirteen in chaffed Nomex coveralls who was sitting amongst the group of around a dozen or more people and ducks that sat around the black pot listening to the sound of their meager dinner clinking against the sides of it.

"It sounds like a boat being pulled up the beach," answered Teemu.

"Do you think it could be Angel?" Mama Finley asked.

"Maybe he found something to add to the soup," said Vladdy, his hairy stomach growling excitedly through his torn Nomex coveralls that were only held together by torn remnants of Oracle, Bose, Petronas, and Red Bull stickers.

"Angel, are you out there?" Mama Finley shouted.

The entire group strained for a response. They waited in silence, but soon their patience was rewarded.

"Yes, it's me," shouted Angel. "And I've got a little something for everyone."

When Angel appeared, he was holding a net that appeared to be filled with seaweed and a smaller rubber racing boot that appeared to be filled with tiny fish. As he came further into view, his bright orange feathers were quite the contrast to the dark Mediterranean sky. His wings were more rounded. Much like arms with fingers at the end, elastic enough to even play the ukulele. Golden feathers rounded the crown of his head, giving him the look of a halo, but he was called Angel more for his acts of kindness. One of them, which he performed almost nightly, was going out on the water to find or catch anything to supplement the evening meal. Tonight it was a net full of seaweed and the tiny sardines that filled the racing boot he gave to Mama Finley, who without even a wash, added them to the large black pot.

"This will be the best soup we've had in a long time," said Mama Finley as she stirred the pot with a bent Ferrari diffuser.

"It looks like there might be enough soup for everyone tonight," said Wally.

"That would be a first," laughed Teemu.

"I'm glad I could help," said Angel Duck, showing off his haul. "I've got your back."

"And I've got your quack," replied Mama Finley, continuing to tend the communal pot.

The poor people and equally poor ducks of Monaco have looked out for each other since they were banished to Monaco long ago and the ducks telling the people they have their back and the people replying to the ducks that they have their quack is a familiar call and response.

"It's great when we all can eat," Vladdy mused thankfully.

"But it's not the fullest the pot's ever been," said Torii with an ounce of sarcasm.

"Well, there aren't as many here to feed tonight," said Wally.

"I've noticed!" replied Torii. "I've noticed for a while."

"What do you mean?" Angel asked, sensing that Torii was uncomfortable about something.

"You haven't noticed?" said Torii.

"Noticed what?"

"There's less of us than there were."

The entire group around the pot became silent. Someone mentioned the elephant in the room, and now the cat was out of the bag. "You're right," said Wally. "I never mentioned it before. I was just happy that there was more soup to go around."

"But I still see the same old faces," said Mama Finley. "There's Wally, Vladdy, Grandmama Johnson..."

"Old faces," challenged Torii. "Do you see a pattern?"

"What are you getting at?" asked Wally.

Torii looked around the group as if to give a hint to everyone. It was silent for a moment. The silence was broken when Mama Finley announced, "The soup's ready."

"I've been waiting for this all day," said Vladdy.

Since Vladdy was sitting next to Mama Finley, he just held his bowl up to which Mama Finley filled with the ladle she had been using to stir the pot. Wally, who was also sitting next to Mama Finley, was next. Then, one by one, everyone who had assembled around the pot handed their bowl to Mama Finley. Soon the pangs of hunger that gripped Monaco by day were quelled.

"Everyone got their bowl filled, and there is still some left in the pot," Mama Finley announced happily.

"When everyone shares, everyone eats," said Vladdy.

"Socialism works," said Wally.

"Which is why we're all poor," said Torii.

"Aren't we opinionated tonight?" said Vladdy.

"Someone has to be," Torii shot back. "I mean, look at us. Or what's left of us."

"What do you mean?" asked Mama Finley.

"What I mean is we keep doing what we think is right over and over again," Torii said, getting ready to make a bigger point. "We keep sharing and caring. Watching each other's backs and watching each other's quack. Meanwhile, over at the casino, things just get more and more luxurious and extravagant. And they don't even live in Monaco. They just use it as their playground and leave their trash strewn about and their secrets hidden."

"Watch what you say," cautioned Mama Finley. "We don't want to make things worse."

"How could things get worse?" Torii asked. "Every day, they get more and we get less, and there's more of them and less of us."

"We still see the same old faces," said Mama Finley.

"Exactly!" Torii yelled.

Mama Finley just stared at Torii, as did everyone else. Some of the young ducks looked over at Angel as if they were hoping he would say something to break the silence. One of those young ducks looking to Angel for a response, was Kurri. Angel had always thought that Kurri was cute but had never talked to her much. It would be pointless, he thought. Given their situation, he could offer her nothing. Except of course, scouring the sea each night to find something to add to the communal pot. Angle decided tonight he would add some conversation besides the tiny fish and seaweed he had brought.

"I think I understand what you're getting at," Angel said.

"What do you think I'm getting at?" Torii asked him.

"It's the young who are going away," answered Angel. "The same old faces like Mama Finley and Wally are here every night, but the new faces, the ones who aren't around long enough to remember their names keep disappearing and no one mentions it because they're afraid it might be another persecution or experiment to go along with all the other ones that have happened."

"Yes!" Torii shouted. "But what are we going to do about it?"

"What can we do about it?" Mama Finley asked.

"And how do we know there isn't some logical explanation?" Wally added.

"Like what?" Torii asked.

"Maybe they're leaving for France?" Wally answered.

"France?" Torii shouted. "No one goes there. They're worse off than we are."

"I heard they're so hungry, they eat snails," added Teemu.

"No one wants to set foot in France," said Mama Finley. "That's why they put us here. There's no escape. To get away, you must either set foot in France or be consumed by the most treacherous part of the Mediterranean."

"But the young are disappearing somehow," said Torii.

"It has to be the casino," said Angel. "There's no other way."

"If the young were going to the casino, wouldn't someone have said something?" asked Vladdy. "Did anyone hear anyone say they were going to the casino?"

Everyone was silent. No one in the entire gathering could remember anyone young, either human or duck, saying they were leaving, let alone through the casino. The grim disposition that permeated the Plague Du Larvotto descended into dour dystopian despair. Suddenly Kurri spoke up.

"My younger brother hasn't been around," she said. "I'm so worried. He's not much older than a duckling; could something have happened to him?"

"I'll try to find out," Angel said, seeing an opportunity to offer something to Kurri. "The first place to try is the casino."

"How?" Torii asked. "The casino won't even acknowledge us. No one will."

"We can raise such a ruckus they'll have to acknowledge us," said Vladdy.

"They'll just cover us over like when they made this beach." Mama Finley said. "We'll be covered in sand, like when they wanted to hide what they did before."

"We can't confront them," said Angel. "They're too powerful and well connected. They control everything. We need to sneak in and find out what's really going on."

"I'll help," said Kurri. "I want to find my brother Perry."

"It's too dangerous," said Mama Finley. "I won't hear of it, and neither will any of the elders, human or duck."

The group suddenly fell silent, but noisily got up and finished their meager rations. No one asked for seconds. Mama Finley, Vladdy, Wally, and any other elders always took away what was left in the pot to feed someone or some others who were never present during the nightly meal. No one ever asked who received the leftovers from the communal pot. It was assumed it went to someone or something worse off than they were, and asking could lead to having to help distribute the leftovers. When Mama Finley, Vladdy, Wally and the rest of the elders left with the pot, Angel, Kurri, and Teemu joined Torii and renewed their conversation.

"Well, I guess it's up to us if we want to find out what's really going on," said Torii.

"I'm in," said Kurri. "I'm worried about my brother, and my folks seem in denial that he's missing."

"No one seems to want to face it; they pretend it doesn't exist," said Teemu.

"Well, maybe if we got some information, they might wake up," said Angel.

"So, what's the plan?" Torii asked.

Angel thought for a moment. All their eyes and ears, both duck and human, were on him. He had always been the "go-to" duck, but that usually meant performing some errand or finding something. A perfect example would be the nightly foraging to add to the communal pot. But now he was stepping into a leadership role, which was new to him. He didn't want to come up with something too drastic and wanted to make a good impression on Kurri.

"We need to find out how to get more information before we can make a plan," said Angel.

"So we need a plan to make the plan," said Teemu.

"Actually, we're planning to make a plan to make the plan to make the plan to make the plan." Torii said.

"Can we just get on with it!" Kurri said. "I'm worried about my brother."

It suddenly dawned on Angel why committees don't work.

"Let's just get inside the casino and see what's going on," he said. "That's our first step."

"How do we do that?" Kurri asked.

"We can draw their security out of the casino and slip into the casino behind them," Angel said. "Then we blend in with everyone else at Casino Royale and find out what we can."

"Blend in with Casino Royale?" Torii asked, exasperated. "I'm not old enough or rich enough to be in the Casino Royale, and you're all ducks. How's anyone going to blend in?"

"Statues," said Angel, thinking quickly.

"Statues?" asked Torii.

"Yes, statues," explained Angel. "I've heard that sometimes people in touristy areas color themselves to look like a statue and then not move at all. When they suddenly move, everyone around them gets scared and gives money to the statue person."

"They'll give us money?" Teemu asked.

"No, we won't move," said Angel. "We'll just watch and listen. When we figure out what's going on at Casino Royale, we'll wait until the coast is clear and make a run for it."

"Who is going to act like a statue?" asked Torii.

"I will," said Angel. "No one is going to question if a duck statue suddenly shows up."

"I want to be a statue too," said Kurri.

"No, it's too dangerous," said Angel. "I'll go in alone."

"We need as much information as we can get," said Kurri. "I'm going in too. I just hope it doesn't get too smoky inside there. I'm allergic to cigarette smoke, but I'm determined."

"We'll all go in," said Torii. "Nothing can stop us."

"We can't all go in; we need someone to create a diversion." Angel said as the plan finally came together in his head. "Since we think the Casino Royale is where everyone goes missing, we'll sound an alarm that someone is escaping. Torii will get security to chase her away from the casino. Teemu will help Torii evade their security, and when the security is out of the casino, Kurri and I will sneak in behind them. We'll find their meeting places and blend in as statues. We'll hide in plain sight."

"I'm in," said Kurri as both Teemu and Torii nodded in agreement. "But what if we can't understand what they're saying?"

"If they're making evil plans, they'll be talking in English," said Teemu. "I heard it's politically incorrect to be evil in a language other than English."

"You're right," said Kurri. "And they let anyone speak it."

"It's getting late," said Angel. "Let's all get some rest. Tomorrow we'll find out what's happening at Casino Royale."

Angel got an early start the next morning. He knew he would not be at the communal pot that evening, so he spent the morning foraging for dandelion greens along the grounds between the rocky cliffs and artificial beach. When he gathered what he thought was enough, he placed them in the area where the pot would be later that night along with a note apologizing to Mama Finley for his absence and a vow to get some fish for the following night's meal. After that, he went looking for anything that might make him and Kurri look more statue-like.

Nearly everything discarded from the casino rolled on down to the beach below. For those at the casino, it was easier just to throw something toward the beach than to put it in a trash receptacle. Especially since the paparazzi and gossip columnists were more than willing to rummage through the Casino Royal rubbish but did not want to get near the riff-raff of the Plague Du Larvotto. This meant Angel had plenty to sift through in his search. It ranged in size from the drums of Botox and Ozempic to small jars of Lancaster and Heliabrine cream, in addition to the broken Tag Hauer pieces.

Angel pulled on what he thought was a Nomex balaclava when he noticed something shiny underneath. It was a large jar of glitter. It looked like gold. He wondered why the Casino Royale would have gold glitter when there was plenty of genuine gold inside, but it would look perfect on a duck trying to look like a statue. He grabbed the jar and started toward the meeting spot where Torii, Teemu, and, most important, Kurri would be waiting.

When he got to the meeting spot, it was almost nightfall, and everyone else was already waiting for him. The meeting spot was a small grove of hedges to the side of the Casino Royal. They could hide there and try to sneak through the side entrance. It would be impossible to sneak in through the front. After sunset, expensive cars and even more expensive women always packed the area between the fountain and main entrance. The deliveries came in the rear, just like the rest of the French Riviera, which was usually busy. The side entrance was more for takeaways than deliveries and the only probable place to sneak in.

Angel and Kurri covered themselves with glitter and practiced keeping completely still. Though they were petrified at what was to come, they still occasionally giggled. Teemu and Torii took the time to get a little closer to the side entrance and assess what security or other obstacles they might encounter. When it was fully dark, the four of them got back together and got ready to make their move.

Teemu had found a whistle earlier, which he was going to blow and announce the breakout. At that moment, Torii would run past the side entrance, make sure security spotted her, and lead them on a wild chase. Once security was out of the area, Angel and Kurri would slip behind them, get into the Casino Royale, pose as statues, and listen in on any conversations that might shed light on what was happening to the young of Monaco.

"Synchronize watches," said Angel.

"We don't have watches," said Torii. "We're poor. We eat the pieces we find."

"We're the only ones near this casino without at least a Rolex," Teemu said.

"Fine, I'll count it down," said Angel. "3, 2, 1, go!"

The whistle blew. Teemu announced the jailbreak in English and any other language he had heard a fragment of. Torii ran in front of the Casino Royale side entrance long enough to be illuminated by several flashlights and then ran from the casino followed by everything from uniformed security guards to euro thugs in trench coats. Teemu let out a shout and took off in another direction, taking some of the casino's posse with him. When the side entrance was clear, Angel pointed toward it.

"Be safe," Kurri said as she gave Angel a duckie kiss on the bill and ran toward the entrance followed closely by Angel. By the time he caught up with her, they had made it through the side entrance unnoticed and were in the empty vestibule. To their right, behind a bead curtain that appeared to be made of rhinestones, but could have been actual diamonds, was the casino main floor. Looking at the bottom of the curtain, they could see the Moonstar and Jada Dubai shoes of the people standing behind it. Further right was a door marked Salle de Lecture. Angel opened the door a crack and peered inside. It appeared to be a meeting room of some kind with a meeting table in the center and several chairs around it. It was dimly lit, opulent, and empty.

"Follow me," he said to Kurri.

He opened the door, and she followed him into the room, and he locked the door behind them.

"What do we do now?" she asked.

"Panic."

"I already did that. Give me something new."

Just then, they heard the sound of footsteps in the vestibule. It sounded like a large group had stopped outside the door. Angel and Kurri both looked around the room for a place to hide. There was nothing—not a closet, no drapes, and everything under the table was in plain sight.

"What now?" she asked Angel.

"Did I mention panic?"

"Been there, done that."

Someone tried to turn the doorknob, but it was locked. Both Angel and Kurri breathed a sigh of relief. Then they heard keys jangling and being placed in the lock. The doorknob turned. He whispered in her ear, "It's statue time."

The door swung open. Angel and Kurri froze and hoped for the best. They were standing together, about four feet apart, behind the table with their backs up against the rear wall. Five people walked into the room. It was two men in dark blue business suits, a woman in a lavender Hillary pantsuit, a scientific-looking man in a lab coat, and a French-looking man in a security uniform who was holding the keys and had just let them in. He directed them to sit on the side of the table facing the door. As they were taking their seats, one of the men in business suits noticed Angel and Kurri, who were covered in gold-colored glitter, standing as still as they could, and desperately trying not to blink.

"Are these two statues new?" He said. "They don't fit the rest of the decor."

"Enough with the decoration," said the Frenchman in the security uniform. "Major Tohtstetter will be here for the meeting, and I heard he is not happy about the alarm."

There was an extremely loud knock on the door. So loud that the entire room shook. Then the door opened with such force that it slammed against the backside of the wall.

"Sit!" Major Tohtstetter yelled, and the Frenchman, who was the only one of the five that wasn't sitting, quickly took a seat next to the man in the lab coat.

Major Tohtstetter stepped into the room flanked by two other men. They were dressed in black Hugo Boss uniform jackets, black baggy Hugo Boss cavalry trousers, black leather Hugo Boss boots, and black Stahlhelm helmets on their heads. Between them stood Major Tohtstetter in a black fedora hat and a black leather Hugo Boss trench coat.

"I am here to get your reports," said Major Tohtstettor. "I hope for your sake, our leadership will look upon them favorably."

Those looking at him who were seated at the table trembled. Angel and Kurri tried not to tremble, or blink, or breathe, or move. Major Tohtstetter walked over to the table and leaned over the Frenchman menacingly.

"Who are you, what is your purpose, and what is the status of your operation?" Major Tohtstetter asked the Frenchman.

"I am Manuelle Macaron," said the Frenchman. "I am in charge of the security at Casino Royale."

"Why are we using the French for security or anything here?" Major Tohtstetter asked the man next to him.

"Because they work cheaper, Herr Commandant."

"How cheap?"

"They work for food, Herr Commandant."

"What kind of food?"

"Snails, Herr Commandant."

"Well, I think they're overpaid," shouted Major Tohtstetter. "From now on, give them only half the snails."

"But Major Tohtstetter, France is so poor," said Macaron. "Even the snails are too meager."

"Would you rather be paid in British food?" Major Tohtstetter asked.

"Half the snails will be fine," said Macaron.

"Good," said Major Tohtstetter. "Now I heard an alarm. Was there any kind of escape?"

"No, it was a false alarm. We checked the holds and no assets are missing." Macaron said.

"Fine, I am done with you for now," Major Tohtstetter told Macaron.

Angel and Kurri felt a sense of relief. A false alarm meant that Teemu and Torii must have gotten away. Kurri's sense of relief went away when Major Tohtstetter took a pack of cigarettes from his trench coat pocket and removed a cigarette. He held it for a second, and the uniformed man next to him lit it. Major Tohtstetter took a drag from the cigarette, moved over to the man sitting next to Macaron in the lab coat and blew smoke in his face.

"Who are you, what is your purpose, and what is the status of your operation?" Major Tohtstettor asked.

"I am Dr. Baron Von Farma," said the man in the lab coat, too intimidated to protest having smoke blown in his face. "I am coordinating the manufacture, testing, and distribution of a vaccine we will use to rule the world. The vaccine will make them believe anything they hear enough times."

"That is good news, for your sake," said Major Tohtsetter as he took another drag from his cigarette and blew it into Dr. Von Farma's face and then continued blowing smoke into the face of the woman in the pantsuit seated in the middle of the table.

"Who are you, what is your purpose, and what is the status of your operation?" Major Tohtsetter asked her.

"I am Greta Von Karen, Information Commission President. We have full infiltration and mainstream media control. They will roll up their sleeves like scared little children for the vaccine. They will be told over and over what a wonderful thing it is. Anything else will be misinformation and hate speech and subject to aggressive prosecution from our woke prosecutors and activist judges."

"Excellent," said Major Tohtsetter, blowing more smoke in her face.

The room was filling with smoke, and it was affecting Kurri. She felt like coughing, sneezing, and vomiting at the same time. Angel was having trouble keeping his absolutely still pose. Major Tohtstetter moved over in front of the two men in the dark business suits. He took a long drag from the cigarette and blew it in both of their faces and pointed at one of them.

"You first," he said.

"I am Shein Temuvoffen, I control the design, manufacturing, programming, and labor trafficking for the drones and robots," he said. "Everything will be in place for the event. If they will not take the vaccine willingly, the drones and robots will force them."

"And you," said Major Tohtsetter, pointing at the other business-suited man.

"I am Schultz Dummkopffer, head of the Grand Prix," he said. "We will jet the drivers and crew to California for the promotional events to announce the Newport Beach Grand Prix. Construction of the loop-the-loops and jump ramps over the waterways will be completed early. It will be an exceptional event to introduce the vaccine. We also have an ironclad agreement that the Zero Emission Electric Car Grand Prix will be the signature event of the 2028 Olympics in Los Angeles when we will celebrate full vaccination."

"Leadership will be as pleased with your reports as you will be to stay alive," Major Tohtstetter said as he inhaled again from his cigarette and walked along the table blowing the smoke again in everyone's face. "Do not fail!"

The smoke became too much for Kurri. She could not control her smoke allergy. She sneezed and then coughed.

"That is not a statue," yelled Major Tohtsetter.

One of the men in Hugo Boss outfits grabbed Kurri. Macaron pointed at Angel.

"That's not a statue either!" Macaron yelled.

"No, I'm a statue, honest," said Angel.

But it was to no avail. The other Hugo Boss goon instantly grabbed him. Angel tried to shake free, but the goon's grip was too tight.

"What are these?" asked Major Tohtstetter.

"Ducks from the beach," said Macaron. "Riff-raff just like the people there."

"They're talking," said Major Tohtsetter.

"Monaco ducks talk," said Macaron. "Everybody there is so poor, they're kind of the same. They even share some of the same features."

"Even poorer than the French?" asked Greta Von Karen in the glare of Macaron.

"I don't care what they are!" Major Tohtstetter yelled. "There will be no talking about our plans. Kill them!"

"Wait!" Dr. Farma yelled, pointing at Kurri. "I want this specimen. It will be perfect for my later experiments."

"Will the duck live?" Major Tothstetter asked.

"Let's just say ducks do better in Peking than with me," said Dr. Farma

"Fine, but kill the other one," Major Tohtstetter said.

Macaron and Dr. Farma grabbed Kurri while the Hugo Boss henchmen tightened their grip on Angel.

"Don't let that duck fly away." Major Tohtstetter said.

"I don't think that's a problem," said one henchman. "His wings look more like arms."

"Let's take him on the roof and let him try to fly," said the other henchman.

"Please don't hurt him," Kurri cried in vain as they carried Angel out of the room.

The henchmen carried Angel to the top of Casino Royale. He fought as hard as he could, but they were way bigger, way stronger, and much, much better dressed. It was a long way down. As they tossed him off the roof, Angel thought maybe he could fly. At least he could try. He went flap. He went flap, flap, flap. And he went splat!

When Angel awoke, he was sitting on the warm beach with Kurri. "I guess it was all just a dream," he said to her.

"No Angel," Kurri said warmly. "This is the dream. You're actually a bloody pulp that went splat and is still rolling down a hill."

"Reality sucks," Angel said to himself as his broken and bloodied body continued rolling down the hill.

Angel finally came to a stop on the beach. It was there that Mama Finley and the rest discovered his nearly lifeless body. They picked him up gently and took him to a special place. They knew what he had tried to do for them and prayed he'd wake up.

"Angel, are you alive?"

It was a question they had been asking for more than a day. Mama Finley would ask. Vladdy would ask. Wally would ask. Angel did not respond, but he was breathing. Finally, Angel mumbled. Mama Finley put a little water into Angel's bill and hoped for a word, but they got something better. His eyes opened.

"Angel, you made it," Mama Finley said.

Angel didn't say a word. He just looked around. He could recognize Mama Finley, Vladdy, and Wally, but not where he was. It was like a dark cave. It felt cool and musty inside. Too musty. It was like fresh air was not a regular patron. He lay silent on a makeshift bed of discarded Pirelli racing slicks while they fed him bits of food and tiny sips of water. He still needed a little more time before he could talk. They didn't have to guess his first word.

"Kurri?"

"Just rest, Angel," Mama Finley said.

"Kurri?" Angel said again.

"She's not here," said Mama Finley. "But Torii and Teemu are okay. Everyone is hiding out. They've been looking for your body to make sure you're not still alive. We hid you down here and told them your body washed out to sea. If we stay out of sight, they'll believe that and leave us alone again."

"They'll never leave us alone," said Angel. "They never have, they never will. We are being used for experiments, slave labor, and other things. They have Kurri. I have to go back."

"It's too dangerous," said Vladdy, who along with Mama Finley and Wally had been keeping vigil for Angel.

"It's too dangerous not to go," said Angel. "If we do nothing, we're doomed. It's only a matter of time."

"He's right," said a voice in the cavern Angel had never heard before. "The old can no longer trade their young for continued existence and a peaceful death."

"Who said that?" Angel asked.

"That is Yoduck," said Wally. "He lives down here beneath the sand. He is the wise one who looks into the past."

"When we take what is left in the pot at night, this is usually the last stop," said Mama Finley.

"He sounds like a duck," Angel said, moving his head as much as he could without pain to look around the room for the voice.

"I am a duck," Yoduck said, waddling over to Angel's makeshift bed to be visible.

Angel looked up at Yoduck. He was an old duck, appearing wise and humble at the same time. He had the same golden feathers that surrounded the crown of his head as Angel. The marking that had given Angel his nickname.

"Why haven't I seen you before?" Angel asked him.

"I like to keep a low profile," he said.

"So low he spends nearly all his time below ground," said Mama Finley

"Why?" Angel asked Yoduck. "Why do you stay down here?"

"Up above is the future, down below is the past," said Yoduck. "I don't like what I see up above, so I dwell below in the past."

"Why in the past?" Angel asked.

"So it can't be taken away," said Yoduck. "Like my father and his fathers before him, we have seen our future taken away time and time again. We could never have stopped it. We weren't the ones. So we kept the past alive. We kept it from being taken, and each generation, a new keeper would take over for the one that passed to preserve that knowledge and look deeper into it all the while hoping for the one that could bring back our future."

"Did they ever come?" asked Angel.

"What do you think?" Yoduck said.

"No," said Angel.

"Each generation, there would be someone, and we would ask, are you the one? Are you the one?" Yoduck said. "But there never was. But I'm asking now, Angel, are you the one?"

"I'm just a duck," said Angel.

"So am I," replied Yoduck. "And Mama Finley is just a person, but I have her back."

"And I have his quack," said Mama Finley.

"So are you the one?" Yoduck asked again.

"I can try," said Angel.

"Be or be not, there is no try," said Yoduck.

"I will be," said Angel. "I'll have everyone's back and everyone's quack, especially Kurri's."

"I want you to talk to me as long as you can. Tell me everything you saw and heard inside Casino Royale. Every detail about everyone. Until you can't go on. And then rest and heal and then we'll finally find our future."

For the next, what seemed like hours to Angel, he struggled to stay conscious and tell Yoduck everything. He told him about Von Farma and the vaccine, the Commission and the judiciary, the drones, the slave labor, and the big events. He talked about the Grand Prix. And he talked about Kurri. He talked until he was talking in his sleep.

"Sleep well, Angel," said Yoduck as he wrote his last note. "And wake as the one."

Angel awoke and tried to focus his eyes. He was still in pain, but it was subsiding, or he was just getting used to it. He looked up at the ceiling and could tell he was in a different place. Instead of the sandy earthen walls and ceiling of the tunnel where he had drifted off after talking as long as he could to Yoduck, this new space had walls and a ceiling of ancient and very distressed wood. The bedding below him felt different too. Instead of a foundation of Pirelli slicks, it felt more like older, dried out Goodyear or Bridgestones. He heard some rustling around him, but still did not feel well enough to sit up for a good look.

"Mama Finley? Yoduck?" Angel asked.

"I'm here," said Yoduck.

"I'm here too," said Vladdy.

"Here, where?" Angel asked.

"Inside the ship," said Yoduck.

"We're at sea?" Angel asked.

Yoduck and Vladdy both laughed. Angel decided to face the pain and sit up in his makeshift bed in order to get a better view of his new surroundings. He saw he was in a tiny wooden room that appeared to be hundreds of years old. Hunched over a decrepit old oak chest, Vladdy sat on an extremely rickety old stool with Yoduck standing next to him. Both appeared to be staring into something resembling the small televisions he had seen in advertisements that would occasionally litter the beach.

"We're not at sea," said Vladdy. "We're in the ruins of a ship that's been buried here in the sand."

"This is the ship that was the original laboratory that made us all what we are," added Yoduck. "We're still under the Plague Du Larvotto. We're just further down the tunnel than you were when we last talked."

"What kind of laboratory?" Angel asked.

"A terrible laboratory," said Yoduck. "The history I've kept. But there is no time to tell you now. We must focus on the matter at hand."

"Look what we've got," said Vladdy, pointing at what stood upon the table. "It's a computer."

"I've never seen one up close," said Angel. "How did you get it?"

"We put it together over time from Casino throwaways, but it's more powerful than the computers used by the French Military," said Vladdy. "It has a full 640K of conventional memory and can take 3 ¼ inch floppy disks, not the 8 inch disks the French use."

"I don't even know what you're talking about," said Angel. "How did you learn all of this?"

"Vladdy, Wally, and Mama Finley have become our computer experts; they can even get information off the internet," said Yoduck.

"What is the internet?" asked Angel.

"It's like an encyclopedia," said Vladdy.

"Encyclopedia?" asked Angel.

"A book full of smart things," said Vladdy.

"How did you get this internet?" asked Angel.

"In France they can access it by phone now," said Yoduck. "Computers in France can now be hooked up to something called a phone modem to get on the internet."

"Since we're right on the border with France, we just tap into one of their lines," said Vladdy.

"That's also how we get the electricity to run the computer."

"France has electricity now?" Angel said in amazement.

"Almost a quarter of France has electricity now," Vladdy said.

"Who gave France electricity?" Angel asked.

"America," said Yoduck.

Angel suddenly remembered what he had overheard at the casino. About the event. The Grand Prix. The drones and the Olympics.

"They're planning to do something in America," Angel said.

"I know, you told me what happened at the casino," said Yoduck. "While you slept, Vladdy, Wally, and Mama Finley took turns using this internet thing to research what you told us. We have made a plan."

"I'll do whatever I have to do," Angel said. "I'll be the one."

"I believe that," Yoduck said. "But you still need to heal more before we can send you out again."

"I'd like to see everyone, especially Temmu and Torii," said Angel.

"They've been asking to see you," said Vladdy. "Do you feel well enough to walk?"

"No, but I'll walk anyway," Angel said.

Angel took a deep breath and tried to get his footing under him. He attempted to stand up, but he still could not stand on his own. He made another attempt but still could not get up on his webbed feet. When he looked up at Vladdy and Yoduck, they each put their arms around him and lifted him up.

"Sorry," said Angel as he finally stood.

"There is no shame in needing help to stand up, only in needing help to want to stand up," said Yoduck.

Vladdy and Yoduck helped Angel out of the small room and into what appeared to me the main cabin of a medieval ship. He could see crumbling bunks that looked like they had once been converted into work tables. Some of the ship's wood that made up the walls and ceiling was withered from dry rot, causing sand and dirt to pour in from the beach above and surrounding the remnants of the ancient vessel. Angel had many questions as they proceeded through the hull, but he knew there were more pressing matters at hand and eventually Yoduck, Vladdy or one of the other elders would tell him about the ship and what else lay beneath the beach or at least what they knew.

By the time Angel had exited what remained of the vessel, he was waddling under his own power with Yoduck in the lead and Vladdy closely following Angel in case he stumbled. They were now in the cavern that was just inside the tunnel entrance where Angel had originally been brought after being thrown off the Casino Royale roof by the Hugo Boss-wearing henchmen. He was happy to see Teemu and Torii waiting for him along with Wally and Mama Finley.

"Thank goodness you're alive," said Torii.

"We heard about Kurri," said Teemu.

"I'm glad you're both okay," Angel told them. "We've got to help Kurri wherever she is."

"With that in mind, Vladdy and I still have a lot of work to do," said Yoduck, "Feel free to catch up on things, but make it an early evening. I'm hoping Angel is well enough to travel tomorrow."

Vladdy and Yoduck gave Mama Finley a hug and started back toward the wooden relic. Teemu and Torii had just met Yoduck the day before when Angel was lying in the same bed that was on the floor of the cavern.

They helped him sit down on the same bed and began recounting their adventures from the casino. Mama Finley brought them each some soup for their evening meal since everyone was avoiding the communal pot. The meal was even more meager than before, but they were all grateful. Not just for the soup, but just to be together, which made the topic of conversation constantly return to Kurri. The conversation continued until Angel drifted off mid-sentence.

When Angel awoke, Mama Finley and Wally were standing over him, and Temmu and Torii were gone. Much of the pain was gone too. Angel was still unsure how much time had passed since he had gone splat and rolled down to the beach, but he knew he was healing fast.

"Can you stand up on your own?" Mama Finley asked him.

"Yes," said Angel, standing up rather confidently.

"Yoduck and Vladdy need to talk to you," she said.

Mama Finley put her hand on his shoulder and led him through the tunnel and back inside the remnants of the old ship. She walked him to the doorway that led to the small room where Yoduck, Vladdy and the computer were. She gave him a hug before he entered.

"Good luck," she said. "We're all counting on you. Vladdy and Yoduck have big plans for you, but they can't tell any of us as long as the Casino Royale secret police are out."

"I'll be the one," said Angel. "I'll find the missing, including Kurri."

"I know," she answered.

As he turned and entered the small wooden room, she kissed the back of his head right on the halo marking that surrounded his head's crown. Inside the room, Vladdy was sitting in front of the old oak chest, staring at the computer with Yoduck standing next to him just like when he had awoken there the previous day.

"Have you healed enough to travel?" Yoduck asked.

"Yes, I'm much better," answered Angel.

"Enough to travel a lot?" Vladdy asked.

"But Casino Royale is right here," said Angel. "It's where they disappear, including Kurri."

"It is not safe for you to stay here. and the casino is not the place," said Yoduck. "When you were in Casino Royale you heard about slave labor and experiments for some sinister events between a car race and the Olympics in Los Angeles. With this powerful 640k French computer and cutting-edge French dial-up internet, I could find out that during that time both the Super Bowl and World Cup will be held in Los Angeles."

"Super Bowl and World Cup?" Angel asked.

"Real football and pretend football," said Yoduck.

"They are both huge worldwide events," said Vladdy. "Perfect for the forces of evil to unleash their corrupt plans. That's why you need to be there."

"But what about Kurri?" Angel asked.

"If that is where they are going to strike, that is where everyone they have taken will be," said Yoduck.

"So I'm going to a place called Los Angeles?" Angel asked.

"Close," said Vladdy. "First we needed to find a place where someone would help you. We don't know anyone there; we don't know anyone anywhere."

"So we found the most likely place where someone would help a non-human animal that speaks English," said Yoduck.

"Where's that?" Angel asked.

"A train station," said Yoduck.

"Yes, a train station," said Vladdy. "I was searching through this new internet thing and found a documentary about a bear that spoke English being adopted by a family at a train station in London. There's no bigger bunch of scrooges than the British, so you're sure to be adopted at a train station in America."

"And we have found the perfect location," added Yoduck.

"Near Los Angeles is a place called Anaheim," said Vladdy. "They have a train station there that's practically connected to two sports teams with millions of fans. One is called the Angels, and the other is called the Ducks."

"Angel. Duck. That's you," said Yoduck.

"They'll be fighting to take you home from that train station," said Vladdy. "On top of that, this place called Anaheim has one of the most famous parks in the world where lots of animals can talk. There's even a mouse the size of a person who has his own house and drives a car."

"It must be destiny," said Yoduck.

"This is unbelievably good luck," said Angel. "But how do I get there? I can't fly; a Monaco duck's wings are more like arms."

"We have a plan for that too," said Yoduck.

Angel exhaled and looked at both Vladdy and Yoduck. This was far more than he had expected. He was figuring they would have found a new way to get inside the casino and maybe find Kurri and the rest. But he knew now there was no point in that. Even if he found someone, what could he do? They had all the power. And there was no one who could or would help anyway. Whatever this evil force was, it controlled everything and always has. He could not fight them here; he had to go there.

"They are flying all the Grand Prix drivers on a special airplane over there to get ready for the Newport Beach Grand Prix you heard about," said Vladdy. "That's when they're starting their plan."

"How do I get on the airplane?" asked Angel. "I'll stick out like a sore thumb."

"No, you won't," assured Vladdy. "There is a special bus that will leave from the side entrance of Casino Royale directly to the airplane. The drivers are to take promotional pictures in their racing suits and helmets. We have plenty of those for you; they've left here over the years. Just don't take the suit and helmet off until after the trip. Since drivers are superstitious, they should leave you alone on the flight."

"But look how short I am," said Angel.

"Grand Prix drivers are all extremely short," said Yoduck.

"That's right," said Vladdy. "Tuki Ysunoda is about four feet tall and Hewis Lamilton isn't much taller."

"The short blade will fit in with the rest of the grass," said Yoduck.

"When you get off the airplane, get away from everyone and take off the racing suit," said Vladdy. "At the front of the airport is a giant statue of a cowboy where you can get on a free bus to the Anaheim train station. We wrote a note to wear around your neck that says, to look after this duck and a white toga for you to wear after you take off the racing suit. You'll look more like an angel, and you're already a duck. That should appeal to the fans of either sports team there, and they might take you home. This plan just came together perfectly; it must be destiny. Someone would have to be a genius to make up something like this."

"A handsome genius," added Yoduck. "We're putting the note and toga inside a durse that you can wear on your shoulder."

"What's a durse?" asked Angel.

"It's a bag or purse, but for a duck," said Vladdy. "I saw they were the thing to wear in California."

"I am also putting some other things in this durse for you to take with you," said Yoduck. "They will give you a connection to your home and its past."

Yoduck showed him an old book and chalice. They looked older than the ship remnants that made up the small room inside the tunnel.

"This book and cup came here long ago when people and ducks were originally banished here to live in poverty together," Yoduck said. "The book contains the names of the banished people. I'm not sure what else is in the book. I could not decipher it."

"What about the chalice?" asked Angel.

"I think it is older than the book," answered Yoduck. "I found it with the book. There were some writings with it, but I cannot decipher those either, and I have one more thing for you."

"What's that?" asked Angel.

"It's a small wooden cross with some words carved into it," Yoduck said, showing it to him. "I think it's from the old ship. You can carry it all on the airplane inside your durse."

"When do I get on this airplane?" Angel asked.

"It leaves tomorrow," Vladdy said.

"Will I be able to say goodbye to everyone?" Angel asked.

"No," Yoduck said sadly. "No one must know where you are going. It's too dangerous for you and for us."

Angel felt like crying himself to sleep that night, but he understood Yoduck was right. For the first time in his life, he would be away from home and, on top of that, he could not contact those he grew up with. Even if he could make contact, he had no way to do so. The poor of Monaco had no phones or mail, and Vladdy and Yoduck could only pirate enough internet to find information, not communicate.

When the inevitable morning came, it was easy for Vladdy and Yoduck to awaken him. His sleep had been shallow, if at all. Though they tried to appear smiling and supportive, their demeanor was businesslike and quiet. For the safety of everyone, Angel's departure and purpose needed to remain hidden from the rest. They made sure Angel was fed, washed up, and dressed before anyone else hiding in the tunnel and cavern was up. They had found an extra-small Nomex racing suit with Red Bull emblems. It seems the racing suits with the Red Bull emblems were the smallest suits of any. They also found him a helmet that had ample room for his bill. Finally, they gave Angel the durse containing the note, toga, book, cup, and small cross. Fully dressed, they led Angel to the tunnel exit and made a run for the cover of the small hedgerow near the Casino Royale's side entrance.

While they hid under the cover of the hedges, waiting for the Grand Prix drivers to assemble for the photo shoot and the bus to take them to the airport to arrive, Angel thought about the last time he had been hiding in that same spot. He had been there just a couple of days before with Teemu, Torii, and Kurri. Kurri had given him a kiss on the bill before they snuck into the casino. How could things change so quickly? He thought. They took Kurri away, nearly killed him, and now he cannot contact Teemu or Torii or anyone else. He thought about what it would be like if they were all in a different time and place. They were happy thoughts.

"Angel, wake up," Vladdy said, nudging him.

Angel opened his eyes. He had fallen asleep. When Vladdy pointed to what was going on outside Casino Royale, Angel realized he had been sleeping for a while. Whereas the coast was clear when Vladdy, Yoduck, and Angel made their run from the tunnel to the hedges, the outside Casino Royale was now bustling with activity. There were dozens of Grand Prix drivers dressed up in their racing suits having their pictures taken by what seemed to be an equal number of photographers. Angel was relieved to see that not only were most of the drivers keeping their helmets on when having their pictures taken, they were also all extremely short. The reporters from the news crews that were covering the event towered over them. He noticed that even the showgirls who criss-crossed the area in skimpy outfits to give the event an aura of glamour were not wearing high heels to hide the drivers' inherent shortness. He felt more confident that he could blend in with the Grand Prix drivers during the flight.

Further scanning the crowd, Angel saw something that made his blood boil.There in the middle stood Shultz Dummkopffer, the head of the Grand Prix, who was reporting to Major Tohtstetter in the Casino Royale the night Kurri was taken and he was almost killed. He was talking in a group that included the two men in business suits, the Commission President Greta Von Karen and, worst of all for Angel, Dr. Von Farma. He pointed them out to Vladdy and Yoduck.

"Those are the ones who were meeting in the casino that night," Angel whispered to them. "The doctor who took Kurri is right there. I have to get to him."

"It will do you no good," said Vladdy. "No one will help you here. They almost killed you once. They'll finish the job if you don't follow the plan."

"Life is the balance between impulse and inertia," said Yoduck.

Angel calmed himself. After a while, things started winding down. It appeared that Dummkopffer was trying to get all the drivers to put their helmets on and stand together for a group picture in front of the bus that was going to take them to the airplane.

"Now is your chance," said Vladdy. "They'll probably get on the bus right after these last pictures. Maybe the people you told us about will go there too."

"Maybe they'll lead me to Kurri," said Angel.

"They could, but get to the train station first," said Vladdy. "That is where you'll find someone to help you. You can't do it alone."

"If the penny-pinching British will help a bear, the generous Americans will help you." Yoduck said.

"You can find out more about their evil plan and warn people," said Vladdy. "They might listen to you over there."

When Dummkopffer finally had all the drivers together, Angel knew it was time to make his move. Giving Vladdy and Yoduck as much of a hug as he could without bringing attention to the hedges, he slinked out of the hiding place and inserted himself into the middle of the group of drivers standing around Dummkopffer. The group posed for several pictures and then boarded the bus. Angel was relieved that most of the drivers did not remove their helmets after the photos were taken and kept them on even after they had gotten on the bus. Angel figured that because Grand Prix drivers are so abnormally short, they continually wear their helmets to appear taller. He made a mental note that if anyone during the trip asked him why he would not take off his helmet and visor, he would answer that he wanted to look taller.

Once on the bus, Angel had no problem finding a seat away from everyone else near the back of the bus. Thinking they were real race car drivers, instead of some exclusive inbred club, the Grand Prix drivers all wanted to be at the front. Angel was the only one sitting near the rear of this bus until the group he had recognized from the meeting room in the Casino Royal boarded the bus. Dummkopffer, the Commissioner Karen Von Karen, Dr. Von Farma, and Shein Temuvoffen walked down the aisle and sat together in the very back of the bus.

Angel faced a dilemma. He wanted to sit as close to them as he could so he could overhear more of their plans, but if he was too far away from the rest of the drivers in the front, he might draw attention to himself. Keeping his helmet on would be considered race car driver behavior. Not wanting to be in front would not be. Angel put his faith in his duck hearing. He moved a little closer to the other drivers and strained to hear what he could from the conversation at the back of the bus.

If he missed anything by moving closer to the front of the bus, it wasn't much. It was a quick bus ride. Because the rich and famous wish to fly to Casino Royal to gamble, party, and watch the Grand Prix race, the area between Monaco and France was developed with modern amenities such as an airport and movie theater. Because it was such a nice thing to have in the area, they named it Nice. In less than five minutes, the bus was on the tarmac in front of the boarding stairs to get onto the plane.

The boarding of the airplane was another photo opportunity. Photographers and news crews were all over the tarmac at the Nice airport, along with spectators and supporters. In addition to the drivers departing for the Inaugural Newport Beach Grand Prix, the event signifying the transition away from fossil fuels, the participants would also fly there on the world's first AI-piloted, electric-powered, transatlantic, commercial airliner. As such, Dummkopffer would be posing with the drivers on the boarding stairs before boarding the flight. After the pictures were taken, he was to laud the manufacture of the new, cutting-edge aircraft, and the era it was about to usher in.

The airplane for the trip was the new Hindenburger 420 produced by the World Social Economic Commission. And as such, the entire world had a hand in its production. Nearly every nation, race, sex, and age worked together in the spirit of cooperation and sustainability to produce the groundbreaking aircraft. Women, children, and old men in the Congo, Myanmar, and other countries were joined by old men whose lives found new purpose in joyfully mining and refining the cobalt, copper, and rare earth elements needed for the plane's massive lithium-ion battery. Even better, artificial intelligence would pilot all aspects of the flight. Because there was no human pilot, the chance for human error was eliminated.

Because the electricity needed to charge the Hindenburger 420's massive battery was more than the Nice airport could provide, a coal-powered generator had to be constructed next to where the plane was sitting as it awaited departure. Rushing to charge the plane's battery before the scheduled departure time, the coal-powered generator was running at full speed. Thick black smoke hung over the crowd, and the noise made conversations between journalists and spectators difficult.

The doors of the bus opened, and the drivers got off the bus and stood in front of the boarding stairs that led up to the aircraft entrance. Dummkopffer and his group were the last off the bus. Dummkopffer instructed the few drivers who were not wearing their racing helmets to put them on and stand behind him on the boarding stairs leading up to the plane to pose for pictures. Angel blended in with the rest of the drivers, and the smoke and noise coming from the coal generator helped by creating a distraction away from him.

When Dummkopffer took the microphone to say a few words while the mainstream media snapped their last pictures, it was apparent that the photoshoot was a short, scripted event to generate a few headlines. The spectators were the usual crowd of eco-warriors, who somehow travelled the world from demonstration to demonstration with no visible means to pay for such travels. Some of them had works of art they had looted from museums and painted orange in protest, while others looked for traffic to block, of which there was none. It was hard for them to see and hear Dummkopffer's brief speech, but they managed to cheer when they thought they heard the word sustainable and boo the term fossil fuel. When the woman with purple hair, tattoos, and multiple septum piercings, who was monitoring the coal-powered generator, signaled that the Hindenberger 420's massive lithium-ion battery was charged, Dummkopffer cut his speech short and directed the drivers to board the airplane.

On board the airplane, Angel took a seat away from everyone else but not so far as to draw attention to himself. Unlike on the bus ride, Dummkopffer, Von Farma, Von Karen, and Temuvoffen sat in the front to give off the illusion they were in first class, though there was little distinction between the seats. The Grand Prix drivers kept their distance from Dummkopffer's party, and the rows between them and the drivers were empty. Angel took this opportunity to move to a seat in the empty row directly behind Dummkopffer and his group so he could listen in on any of their conversations. He took the blanket that was on the seat next to him and put it over himself. Hopefully, everyone would think he was sleeping and leave him alone. He also hoped he would not have to get up to use the lavatory. That would be hard for a duck, but if he tried not to think about it, maybe he could make it.

Because of the weight of the battery, the plane had to travel a long way to become airborne, and once it did, it wobbled in the air for a while before it reached airspeed. Because lithium-ion batteries often have less range than expected, the Hindenburger was followed by a gas-powered airplane that contained a mini nuclear reactor like those for data centers and filled with plutonium in case the Hindenburger's battery needed to be charged mid flight. For the first part of the flight, the Hindenburger worked as expected. The flight attendants passed out luxury watches for the drivers, who played with them, even though, being under the age of forty, they could not understand what time was on the watch unless it was digital. The other passengers passed the time watching the latest woke Disney remake. Angel was happy that the trip was uneventful, and he hadn't been noticed, but he wished that Dummkopffer and the rest of the party would start discussing their plans. Unfortunately, to get that wish, the flight would have to become eventful.

While over the Atlantic Ocean, the alarm went off on the plane. The flight planner did not realize that below freezing, lithium-ion batteries lose their power, and since the plane was cruising at 30,000 feet, the outside temperature was about seventy degrees, real degrees not the stupid metric system ones, below freezing. Since Dummkopffer was the trip's organizer, one of the flight attendants rushed over to inform him of the situation.

"The plane is losing power," she told him.

"What's the pilot doing?" Dummkopffer asked.

"There is no pilot," she said.

"Who's flying the plane?"

"Artificial Intelligence."

"Is there a radio on board?"

"It's in the cockpit, but it's locked."

"How do we talk to the artificial intelligence pilot?" Dummkopffer asked.

"There's a button on the door," said the flight attendant. "I'll show you."

Dummkopffer got up and followed her to the cockpit door as the nose of the plane shifted downward and his companions stared at each other in fear. The flight attendant pointed to the button on the cockpit door, and Dummkopffer pressed it. A woman's voice came through the speaker on the door.

"Hello, I'm Amelia, your virtual pilot. How can I help you?" it said.

"The plane is losing power," said Dummkopffer.

"You plan to order flowers," said the virtual pilot. "I can help with that."

"No!" Dummkopffer yelled. "I need to talk to a person."

"I'm sure I can help you just as quickly as a live person," said the virtual pilot. "Who are the flowers for?"

"There are no flowers!" Dummkopffer screamed. "I need a live pilot."

"For a more personal experience, you can speak to me," said Amelia, the virtual pilot, "Or I can give you a link to chat with Wiley, our virtual assistant."

Dummkopffer kept screaming to talk to a live person as the plane's rate of descent increased. Finally, after giving the virtual pilot his name, email address, and birthdate, the virtual pilot connected Dummkopffer to the pilot of the plane with the mini nuclear reactor generator that had been accompanying the flight whose name, coincidentally, happened to be Siri. However, it was a real person named Siri, not the virtual Siri. Otherwise, they might have been in Siri-ous trouble.

Siri contacted Flight Control, who programmed Amelia, the virtual pilot, to level the plane once the altitude was low enough for the battery to warm up and function better. The battery, however, needed to be recharged if the plane was going to reach its destination. It was going to be a tricky operation, and Siri let Dummkopffer know that the flight was still in danger. When Dummkopffer informed his companions, the sense of panic caused them to discuss their plans openly with Angel listening in the row behind them.

"What if we crash? What happens to our plans?" Karen Von Karen asked. "What about the new world order?"

"All must be vaccinated, and we need the drones and robots to make them comply," said Von Farma.

"If we fail The Chip, what will Tohtstetter do to those we've left behind?" Von Karen said. "He works directly for the Party, and they have access to The Chip."

"Keep calm. The Chip will be obeyed," said Dummkopffer. "Siri will charge the plane; we'll be okay."

Siri flew the charging plane above the Hindenburger and prepared to lower the charging cable. Looking down on the Hindenburger, he could not locate its charging port. He called Flight Control and was informed that because the re-charging port needed to be wheelchair accessible it was located on the bottom of the Hindenburger and therefore, in order to be charged, the Hindenburger would have to fly upside down so Siri could lower the charging cable to its charging port. When Flight Control programmed Amelia, the virtual pilot, to make the maneuver, the flight attendant made the announcement to the Hindenburger's passengers.

"Attention passengers, please fasten your seatbelts," she said. "We need to fly upside down for a while in order to recharge the plane's battery."

Dummkopffer and his group became even more panicked. Not just for their mission, but for their lives. They asked Dummkopffer what they were going to do. He got an idea and called the flight attendant over to their row.

"Bring us four parachutes," he told her.

"They were removed from the plane," she said.

"Why were the parachutes taken off the plane?" he asked.

"Because we are flying to California, where they're banned," the flight attendant said. "Using the parachutes if the plane is going to crash could expose you to chemicals known to the State of California to cause cancer or reproductive harm."

"So if we're going to crash, we don't have parachutes?" Von Karen asked.

"Safety first," said the flight attendant. "I have to put on my seatbelt now. We're about to flip."

The flight attendant left to make sure everyone had their seatbelt fastened and then put hers on. Moments later, the plane flipped over, and the Omega and Richard Mille watches the Grand Prix drivers were playing with fell down to the ceiling of the plane.

Above the Hindenburger, Siri could now locate its charging port. He lowered the charging cable from his plane and hoped the magnet from the charging port would attract and connect the cable to the port. It took Siri several minutes to line the two vessels up, but eventually the cable connected to the charging port, and the mini nuclear reactor on Siri's plane began recharging the Hindenburger's battery.

Inside the Hindenburger, flying upside down was taking its toll. The blood rushing to everyone's heads combined with a sense of impending doom made Dummkopffer, Von Farma, Von Karen, and Temuvoffen reveal their inner secrets and last testaments. Angel struggled to make sense of what he overheard. Blood was also rushing to his small, feathery head. From what he overheard, he could make out that they were all part of a powerful secret organization bent on world domination and that it involved drones, a vaccine, climate change, censorship, an all-powerful chip, and Germans. Angel realized there was no way he could memorize all of this and started looking in the seat pocket for something to write with when suddenly the plane jolted.

Up above, Siri could sense that the charging cable had come loose. Siri had charged the Hindenburger somewhat, but it still needed more, so he lined it up for another charge. As the cable and port were connecting, the wind flipped the charging cable, connecting the positive current to the negative, causing a short, which charged the plutonium in the reactor beyond critical mass. Siri lost control of his aircraft, and it came crashing down on Sanctuary Island in the Gulf of America, destroying the island with a nuclear explosion.

Because the Hindenburger had drifted south of its flight path while being recharged, it was now flying over Mexico. Flight Control didn't know if the Hindenburger had enough battery charge to reach its final destination, but they couldn't land early for fear of a collision because the airspace below them was in designated cartel flight paths. No longer able to be charged, the plane flipped right side up for the rest of the journey.

Because of the crash risk, Angel could keep his helmet and visor on without question. He could also take advantage of the Hindenburger making an emergency landing. When the plane finally landed, inflatable slides were deployed, and the passengers exited the plane and tumbled down to the tarmac. In the confusion of all the emergency vehicles circling the runway, Angel was able to sneak into a luggage transport and hide between two suitcases. When the luggage handlers weren't looking, he jumped onto the conveyor belt and tumbled down onto the baggage claim carousel. He jumped up and ran out of the baggage claim and there to his left, just like Vladdy said, was a nine-foot tall statue of the cowboy John Wayne. A shuttle van pulled up in front of the statue, and Angel ran toward it.

"Where does this go?" Angel asked the driver.

"To the ARTIC," the driver answered.

"I need to go to the train station," said Angel.

"There are trains there," said the driver.

Angel was confused. Was it really going to the Arctic? He didn't have cold-weather clothes, but he had no choice. He had to get away, and it had trains. Angel jumped inside the van.

Monaco review

Across

3. The wise one.
5. Santa ship buried under Monaco beach.
7. French city with electricity.
8. Princes who built Monaco casino.
9. Grand Prix driver height.
11. discarded coveralls worn by Monaco's poor.
13. A.I. pilot.
14. Monaco casino.

Down

1. Memory of French computer.
2. Grand Prix started to promote.
4. Overrated Monaco race.
6. Hugo worn by henchmen.
10. Starving French are force to eat.
12. Language they'll let anyone speak.

CHAPTER FOUR

ORANGE COUNTY

 He had been standing there for a couple of hours wearing the durse and white toga he had put on after ditching the racing suit. He resembled both an angel and a duck, as Vladdy and Yoduck had planned. The shuttle van had taken him to the ARTIC, otherwise known as the Anaheim Regional Intermodal Transit Center, a train and bus station which to Angel resembled a gigantic igloo. It was, except for the airport where he had gotten on the shuttle van, the biggest building Angel had ever seen. It was much bigger than the Casino Royale, and thinking of the Casino Royale and what had happened to Kurri made him even more determined to find someone who could help him. However, he was still too shy to speak up. He just stood at the end of the great hall, in front of the stairs and escalators that went up to the shops and restaurants, trying to make eye-contact with anyone who walked past.

No one made eye contact. He was in California, where no one makes eye contact unless they want to start something or they're panhandling.

Anyone you meet can be a panhandler in California. It's like a second job for most everyone there. With gas prices, utilities, and rent double most other states, it is not uncommon to see people in designer suits begging. Some people even rent children to use while panhandling, which makes them even have to panhandle harder because the state legislature voted children rented for the purpose of begging must be paid a living wage. Therefore, Californians refrain from talking to each other. That's what texting is for. So it was no surprise that the first person to speak to Angel was not from California. It was a woman in her forties who was walking with her husband when she accidentally bumped into Angel.

"I'm sorry," she said. "I was looking for my daughter Judy, who's on break from school, and wasn't looking where I was going."

"I wasn't looking where I was standing," said Angel. "By the way, my name is Angel."

"Pleased to meet you, Angel. I'm Mrs. Brown, and this is my Husband Mr. Brown," she said. "Are you familiar with this station? It's quite different from Paddington Station in London, where we're from."

"No, I'm not familiar with it at all," Angel said. "I just got here and have no place to stay. Can you help me?"

"We once tried to help a talking bear we found at Paddington Station," she said.

"Did it turn out well?" asked Angel.

"No," she said. "He was later arrested by the Metropolitan Police for reposting a meme on the internet that caused someone distress, and he's serving three years in prison."

"Do you think you can help me?" asked Angel.

"I'm sorry, but we're British and too cheap to help anyone anymore," she said. "Oh, I think I see our daughter Judy now. Cheerio!"

She and her husband scurried off, and Angel was alone again. He scanned through the sparse crowd inside the massive igloo-shaped station trying to make eye contact with someone in hopes his next conversation might be more productive. Everyone looked away when their eyes met Angel's eyes except for two men sitting on a bench in the hall in front of the escalators and staircase. The young men were wearing flannel shirts, baggy chino pants, long white sweat socks, and white tennis shoes. One wore a backward Dodgers cap and the other a backward Kings cap.

"Are you mad-dogging us, Homes?" the one with the Dodger cap asked as they both got up to confront Angel.

"I'm not a dog, I'm a duck," replied Angel.

"You're a weirdo," said the one in the King's cap.

"Can I stay with you?" asked Angel.

"This dude's got some bad juju, Teepee," said the one in the Dodgers cap.

"There's something wrong with his head, Peepee," said the one in the King's cap.

"Inside and outside, Teepee," said the one in the Dodgers cap.

"I need help," said Angel.

"No schizz, Sherlock," said the one in the King's cap. "I'll call 1-800-HELP-THE-WEIRD-UGLY-DUCKLING; maybe they'll send somebody."

They both laughed and walked away. Angel hung his head. Another conversation had gotten him nowhere. He was wondering if he would ever find someone to help him when he got the feeling that someone was looking at him. When Angel looked up, he realized he was right. Someone was looking at him.

He was a man of about forty with a moustache and medium length combed back dark brown hair wearing an orange track jacket, khaki pants, and bright white tennis shoes. He stared at Angel with a beaming smile and gave him a thumbs-up. Then, he pointed at Angel and said, "Bingo!"

"Bingo?" said Angel.

"Yes, bingo," said the man. "I'm with the team."

"I need help," said Angel.

"That's why I'm here," said the man. "I'm here to take you with me. When I saw you, I knew you had to be the one."

"You know I'm the one?" asked Angel. "Do you know about my mission?"

"Bingo!" said the man. "Your mission is my mission. We're in this together."

"My name is Angel."

"Bingo! I guessed that," he said. "You're Angel the Duck. Angel Duck! It's perfect. I knew you were the one."

"I am?"

"Of course. It's obvious."

"What's your name?" Angel asked.

"Everyone calls me Bingo," he said. "It's because I say that word a lot. Instead of yes or right on, I just sort of say bingo. Seems to work."

"Pleased to meet you, Mr. Bingo," said Angel.

"Just Bingo, that's what everyone calls me," he said. "Where's your luggage?"

"Just this," said Angel, pointing to the durse.

"Bingo, that's the way to do it," he said. "You traveled light, so we can get going right away."

"Where are we going?" Angel asked.

"To meet the team. That's who sent me," said Bingo.

"What team?" Angel asked.

"Both teams," said Bingo. "I was expecting two of you, but you have it covered perfectly all by yourself. We'll go meet the Angels tonight before their game and the Ducks before their homestand starts next week."

"Okay," said Angel.

Angel was confused. He didn't exactly know what Bingo was talking about, but he had no other option but to play along. Bingo said he was the one, just like Yoduck had. Did Bingo really know what his mission was? Yoduck and Vladdy didn't say they had any way to contact anyone in America, but when Bingo started walking toward the exit, he followed. He at least had a chance that someone might help him.

"You know you didn't have to show up in costume," Bingo told him as they walked toward the exit. "You could have gotten dressed in the locker room with the players."

"I could have?" Angel asked, trying to play along.

"I understand," said Bingo. "With studios using CGI instead of hiring live actors, it's hard for people like you to find work, so you come as prepared as possible to show what a better job you can do."

"Uh, bingo," said Angel.

"I like that," Bingo said.

Bingo led Angel through the great hall and pointed to a giant granite and pink brick arena with a giant sign over the entrance that read THE HEAVEN CENTER, which was visible through the station's immense glass facade. Angel waddled as fast as he could to keep up as Bingo led him out of the station's giant glass doors and into the parking lot. They walked along a street until they were walking through another parking lot. Along the way, Bingo pointed to a giant stadium that was bigger than the train station or the arena they were walking toward that had a gigantic triangular sign in the parking lot that read THE BIG POND.

"That's where we'll meet your other team," Bingo said. "The Ducks are just starting off their season, and the Angels are just finishing theirs. Unfortunately, the Angels didn't make the playoffs this year. It's like they've always got something else on their mind."

"I know how that can be," Angel said.

"Do you like hockey or baseball better?" Bingo asked.

"I'm not sure," said Angel, trying to hide his ignorance on the subject.

They continued through the parking lot as the sun was setting. As they entered The Heaven Center arena, Bingo flashed a card that let him pass through security, but it was apparent that everyone knew him. Some even pointed their fingers and said, "Bingo" as he passed. Angel marveled at the size of the ice rink and the thousands of seats surrounding it. Bingo led Angel through a long corridor to a door that his card unlocked. Bingo flung the door open and stepped inside.

"Meet your new mascot!" He shouted.

The room suddenly fell silent. But then, noisily got up. Inside, about a dozen men were putting on their hockey uniforms. Some were already dressed except for their shoulder pads and jerseys, while others were still getting their knees and ankles taped. No one had laced up their skates yet. Sitting on a bench in the middle of the room were two veteran team captains named Phil Errup and Bobby Ferapples. Phil was light-skinned with dirty blond hair, while Bobby had a darker complexion and brown hair. That was the extent to which their features differed. They were both tall and athletic and had old-time hockey faces. The kind players had before the fights interrupted the games. Back when the games interrupted the fights.

"Here's Angel!" Bingo announced as he pulled Angel into the room.

Everyone stared silently at Angel for a moment. A few of the play-ers clapped quietly to show Angel some moral support. Phil and Bobby looked at each other quizzically and then looked back at Angel and Bingo.

"Two mascots for the price of one?" said Bobby.

"Bingo," said Bingo, pointing at Bobby.

"Why don't you introduce him around?" said Phil.

"Bingo," said Bingo, and he began taking Angel from locker to locker to introduce him to the team and staff.

"Something doesn't seem right about that new mascot," Bobby whis-pered to Phil now that Bingo and Angel were out of earshot.

"I know what you mean," said Phil. "He seems a little too short to be a mascot. He's almost as short as a Grand Prix driver."

"And there's something wrong with that costume; his head isn't shaped right," said Bobby.

"Is it even a person in there?" asked Phil. "Is it an android?"

"It could be anything," said Bobby. "We know they're planning some-thing big."

"Do they know about us?" Phil asked. "Are they trying to infiltrate us?"

"I don't know," said Bobby. "They haven't been able to find us out, but nothing lasts forever."

"We've got to check him out, away from Bingo," said Phil.

"I've got an idea," said Bobby. "You go over to Bingo and that mascot and make some conversation to keep them busy, and I'll tell Doc what's going on. I'll have him come up with some way to occupy Bingo, and you bring the mascot back here and we'll give him the once-over."

"You don't think Bingo's in on something?" Phil asked.

"Bingo's an idiot, but he's not evil," said Bobby. "He could be getting played though."

"Anything's possible," said Phil.

Phil got up and walked over to Bingo and Angel. He backed them into a corner and started telling them a story about a previous team mascot. He was making up the story as he went along, but he knew they would keep listening politely as long as he kept talking, which he planned to do until Bobby sent Doc over.

Doc was the team doctor and had been with the team for years before Bobby joined the team and had been the one who had recruited Bobby to sign with the team. He and Bobby were very close, so Doc didn't mind at all when Bobby interrupted him while he was examining another player's injury. Doc was ready for a cigarette break, anyway. He removed an unfiltered Chesterfield from a pack in one carton he kept in his medical bag, lit it up, and took a few drags while Bobby told him about the new mascot and his concerns. Doc nodded and agreed to keep Bingo busy while Bobby and Phil checked out the mascot to see if someone was trying to infiltrate the team or if there was even a person inside the costume. Bobby told Doc he thought there was a possibility the new mascot could actually be some cutting-edge robot sent to spy on their operation.

Doc assured Bobby that he could keep Bingo occupied for as long as Bobby and Phil needed to vet the new mascot. Since Doc had been with the team for so long, his duties were far more reaching than dealing with injuries. He had authority over most team functions. He told Bobby they could use the x-ray room, a room with medical imaging equipment Doc used for early injury detection, to check out the mascot. Once Doc got Bingo involved in an errand that would keep him busy and away for a while, he would return to the x-ray room and help assess the mascot. As they completed their plans, Doc commented to Bobby that it was a good thing that they were already eliminated from playoff contention because they still had two games to play and with all this drama making it hard for him and Phil to concentrate it was a good thing there wasn't a lot riding on the game. Bobby commented back that there might be a lot more riding on what might be going on with the mascot.

Doc hurried over to where Phil had Bingo and Angel cornered. He took a moment to study Angel before interrupting Phil's story. Looking at Angel, he agreed Bobby had a point. Angel didn't look like someone in a costume.

"Bingo, I need you to do something right away," said Doc. "Phil will help our new mascot get situated while I show you what needs to be done."

"Can't it wait?" Bingo asked. "I've got to get Angel ready for tonight's game."

"No, it can't wait; it's important," said Doc, taking Bingo by the arm.

Phil reached behind Angel and gave him a push in Bobby's direction. Bobby saw this and motioned for them to follow him. He walked over to the X-ray room, opened the door, and invited Phil and Angel in. Phil pushed Angel through the locker room toward the X-ray room. A few of the other players and staff that were in the locker room nodded at them as they walked past, but most went about their business getting ready for the upcoming game. When they got in the X-ray room, Phil closed the door behind him and quietly locked it.

"Angel, this is Bobby Ferapples. He's another team captain," Phil said as he pushed Angel toward Bobby.

"How long have you been wearing that costume?" Bobby asked Angel. "I'm sure you could use a break."

Bobby lifted Angel up and sat him on the X-ray table. It wasn't hard because Bobby was so much bigger than Angel. Bobby and Phil started looking for a way to take the costume off of Angel. They jostled him around the table and pulled at his feathers looking for a hook, or buckle, or zipper, or anything found on a costume but found nothing. Underneath the feathers appeared to be skin.

"I'm not exactly wearing a costume," said Angel.

"You're not wearing a costume?" Bobby said, bewildered..

"I'm really a duck," said Angel.

"Ducks don't talk," said Phil.

"This one does," said Angel. "I'm from Monaco; all the ducks in Monaco talk."

"Monaco?" said Bobby. "There's nothing in Monaco. I mean, there's that casino where the richest people in the world hang out and the Grand Prix, but other than that it's just a wasteland. No one lives there."

"Ducks live there, and people too," said Angel. "We live together and help each other."

"How come no one's ever heard about it?" asked Phil.

"Because we're poor and forgotten," said Angel.

"Sounds like a sob story to me," said Bobby.

"And in every sob, is an S-O-B!" Phil said menacingly. "Who sent you?"

Suddenly, there was a knock on the door. Both Phil and Bobby let go of Angel and stared at the door. They both remained silent as someone outside the door tried to turn the doorknob, which was locked. They heard the door unlocking, and it opened to reveal Doc with a nearly finished Chesterfield in his mouth.

"Bingo will be busy until the game starts," said Doc. "What did you find out?"

"There's no costume," answered Bobby. "He claims to be a duck."

"A talking duck?" Doc said.

"I'm from Monaco," said Angel.

"There's no one in Monaco, except that rich casino and the Grand Prix," said Doc. "Let me examine him."

Doc hunted through his medical bag until he found a pack of unfiltered Chesterfields. He lit it using the one he had in his mouth and discarded the old cigarette. Then he took a stethoscope and a small flashlight out of the bag. He examined Angel.

Angel held still during the examination. He knew if he moved, Bobby and Phil would force him to comply. Doc checked him with the stethoscope and looked in Angel's eyes and ears with the small flashlight. Bobby took Angel's durse, opened it, took a quick look inside and sat it down on the table next to Angel.

"This can't be," he said. "I can't find anything synthetic. It's biological," said Doc.

"They've created a bio-robot; we need to destroy it," said Bobby.

"Before it destroys us!" Phil said as he grabbed Angel by the neck.

"Don't kill me!" Angel pleaded. "The Germans almost did!"

Bobby, Phil, and Doc froze. Their eyes were wide open. Their mouths were wide open, and their flies were probably open too. In stunned silence, they stared at Angel.

"What did you say?" asked Doc.

"Please don't kill me," Angel said, almost crying. "The Germans almost did. They threw me off the roof and took Kurri for experiments. They're planning something terrible with drones and vaccines, and it involves the Grand Prix and all kinds of other things."

"He knows what the Germans are planning," Doc said.

"It's too much of a coincidence," Bobby said. "This is right out of The Art of War. They tried to kill you, and you just happen to know their plans. It's a little too convenient."

"Yah, how'd you get Bingo to bring you here?" asked Phil.

"Nothing, he just pointed at me and said bingo," said Angel

"He does that a lot," said Doc.

"He's an idiot," said Bobby. "He brought back a robot spy. "

"I'm a duck," said Angel. "I need help; they'll destroy us."

"We should destroy you," said Phil.

"I've got an idea," said Doc. "We scan him for a tracking device. If we find one, we incinerate him. If we don't, then we find out what he knows."

"We'd better do it quickly," said Bobby. "We've got Montreal tonight, and the puck drops in an hour."

Like clockwork, Doc put Angel through a series of x-rays and ultra-sounds. He also scanned Angel for any radio frequencies that could emanate from him. Doc also scanned Angel's durse. Afterward, Doc confirmed that Angel was not bugged or transmitting their location.

"If he's transmitting, it's something that has yet to be invented," said Doc. "We'll take him through the tunnel to HQ."

"That will take time," said Bobby. "Phil and I wouldn't be able to get on the ice in time for the game."

"Are we a scratch tonight?" Phil asked.

"No, I can take Angel myself, and I'll have the equipment staff help," said Doc. "And speaking of equipment, I have a gift for Angel."

Doc opened up a large cabinet above the room's hand-washing area. He took a large orange duffel bag out of the cabinet and unfolded it in front of Angel. It displayed the logo of the Angels hockey team.

"You'll need a bag big enough to hold your stuff," said Doc. "But for now, it can hold you."

Doc pointed his finger at Bobby and Phil. Then he pointed his finger at Angel and then at the orange duffel bag. Bobby and Phil got the message. They grabbed Angel, stuffed him into the bag and zipped it up. Inside the bag, they could hear Angel pleading not to be taken to the Germans.

Once he felt himself being picked up inside the duffel bag, Angel quieted down. He thought that the odds of Doc taking him to the Germans were not as great as the odds of them just killing him if he made a scene. Angel noticed how their mood had changed when he had mentioned the

Germans. He thought maybe they might help him or maybe they might kill him. Either way, he got a free carry bag. He kept quiet as he was carried in the bag for what seemed an hour.

Thump! He felt the duffel bag drop to the floor. Being zipped up inside the bag was not a pleasant experience. The entire trip inside the bag wasn't either. That is probably the reason people don't travel inside their luggage even though it would be much more economical. Angel was dropped a few times during the journey, but only a foot or so each time. He felt like he was carried or pushed on a cart for the whole time, and he could hear voices talking quietly outside the duffel bag. Someone unzipped the duffel bag, and Angel looked out. It was a dark room. He heard footsteps walking away and a door close. He lay still and closed his eyes and fell asleep until singing awakened him.

"Wake up, you sleepyhead, get up, get out of bed," a woman's voice sang and continued. "Wake up, you sleepyhead, wake up. Get up; it's time to go. Let's go, go for the show. Wake up, you sleepyhead, wake up. Angel is a sleepyhead. He likes to sleep all day, but we've got lots of things to do, so don't sleep the day away. Wake up, you sleepyhead, get up, get out of bed, wake up, you sleepyhead wake up."

Angel shook himself and rubbed the sleep out of his eyes. The room was dimly lit, and he could smell cigarette smoke.

"I'm going to turn the lights up," he heard Doc say. "Let me know if it gets too bright."

The room got brighter as Doc turned up the dimmer switch. Angel sat up. He was still sitting in the duffel bag.

"You didn't kill me," Angel said.

"I knew we forgot something," Doc said to the blond woman in a lab coat next to him.

"I'll get the ax," she said as panic overtook Angel.

"Psyche!" they both yelled in unison.

Angel stared up at them in silence. They both started laughing. Angel didn't know what to think.

"Relax, we're not going to kill you," said Doc. "At least not right now. We just didn't know what to make of you."

"We still don't," said the woman in the lab coat.

"This is Dr. Pussy Ryder," said Doc, taking another puff from his cigarette. "She's a doctor, veterinarian, zoologist, and robotic engineer. She also blurts out songs and rhymes."

"I got bored being in school all the time," she said. "I started making up songs and now I can't stop."

"Pleased to meet you," Angel said.

"Pleased to meet you," said Dr. Pussy Ryder. "Since I started working with Doc and both of the teams, I've seen a lot of things; but this is the first time I've ever talked to a duck."

"Well, in Monaco, ducks and people talk all the time," said Angel. "We live together and help each other out. We have their backs, and they have our quacks."

"We've never heard of that," said Dr. Ryder. "The world knows nothing about Monaco except for the Casino and Grand Prix."

"It's like no one knows on purpose, like it's being hidden," said Angel.

"What do you think they are hiding?" Doc asked.

"Look at me," said Angel. "How did I come to be? I heard about terrible things that happened over hundreds of years."

"I know," said Doc. "There are sinister forces everywhere."

"That is why it is so important that you tell us everything," said Dr. Pussy Ryder. "Everything about Monaco and everything about the vaccine, Grand Prix, and Germans."

"Especially about the Germans," said Doc.

"I bet you're hungry," said Pussy Ryder. "What do you normally eat?"

"Not much. Monaco is very poor," said Angel. "Usually, it's barnacles or Tag Hauer watches that the Grand Prix drivers throw at us."

"Is there anything you won't eat?" she asked.

"Foie Gras," said Angel.

"How about sweet corn?" she said.

"Wonderful," said Angel.

"Just relax and tell us everything you can," she said.

"Especially about the Germans," said Doc, crushing out his cigarette.

Angel told them everything. He told them about the struggles in Monaco and the young people disappearing. How fearful Mama Finley and Vladdy were about the past and how different life was at the casino. Doc and Pussy Ryder wanted every detail about who he saw inside the casino, if he could remember any names, what their plans were, and what they looked like. Doc even sketched some drawings from his descriptions. He told Angel they would show him pictures after they did some research to see if he could identify anyone he might have seen — anyone they thought might be involved.

After about an hour, they told Angel to relax. He told them he did not want to relax and was prepared to keep going until he found Kurri. They said they needed to meet with some others and would have more information to help identify people who had been planning at the casino and what they might have been planning. Since the room had barely any furniture, they had a small couch brought in for him to relax or even stretch out on. Although they said he was welcome to sleep in the duffel bag again if he wanted. Since he said he had been living among people, they assumed he knew how to use a bathroom and told him to call someone if he needed to go. He understood that though they appeared to be on good terms; he was not free to leave. But he didn't wish to. He might have found some people to help him.

Angel relaxed on the couch and ate the sweet corn Pussy Ryder had brought him. It was the best meal he had enjoyed that he could remember. While he was sitting there, he kept trying to recall more about what he saw and heard that night at the casino. Was there one detail that could save Kurri?

The time passed slowly, but it passed. After several hours, there was a knock on the door. Doc and Pussy Ryder opened the door and entered the room.

"Let's go, let's go, it's time to hit the road. Get up, you duck, it's time to truck. Let's go, let's go, let's go," she sang as she entered the room.

"That singing is an annoying habit she has," Doc said to Angel as he lit up a cigarette.

"Are we going somewhere?" Angel asked.

"We've got some people to meet," she said.

"Where are they?" Angel asked.

"Just down the hall," she said. "Follow me."

She turned around and started walking down a long hallway. Angel and Doc followed her. She stopped at a door about fifty feet down the hallway and opened it.

"Come on in, Angel," she said, inviting him into the room.

Angel stepped into the room followed by Doc. It was set up like a typical corporate conference room. In the center was a rectangular table that seated about a dozen. The chairs were comfortable, but not too fancy. The walls were barren and concrete. It was apparent that the room was below ground and strictly business. There were no frills or decorations on the walls. There was just a projector affixed to the ceiling that projected a screensaver of California landmarks on the wall.

An attendant directed Angel to a seat at the end of the table closest to the door and then quickly left. He recognized Bobby, Phil, Doc, and Pussy Ryder, but the rest of the people seated at the table were new to him. After everyone sat down, Doc stood up and spoke to Angel first.

"Hello Angel," he started. "You're already familiar with some people here, but let me introduce you to everyone else here."

He got up from his seat and stood behind the people he was about to introduce to Angel.

"This is Skeeter Bytes and Daisy Chane. They are associates of Mr. Smurdley. Basically, his right-and left-hand persons, and this is Mr. Smurdley. He is the boss and owner of both teams."

When Doc finished his introduction, he sat down, and Mr. Smurdley, who was seated at the head of the table flanked by both Skeeter Bytes and Daisy Chane, stood up and looked at Angel. He had a rugged look about him. He was tall and fit, appeared to be in his late sixties, and was dressed in conservative business attire.

"Sorry we have met under such unusual circumstances," he said to Angel. "But I am still pleased to meet you."

"Pleased to meet you, sir," said Angel.

"Bingo was supposed to meet a mascot for the Angels hockey team and a mascot for the Ducks baseball team," Mr. Smurdley said. "When he saw you, he must have thought..."

"Uh, Bingo," said Angel.

"Yes," said Mr. Smurdley. "He must have thought to himself, bingo, they've hired one mascot for two jobs."

"So that's why he brought me here?" said Angel.

"Yes, and we thought you might be a spy or even some kind of android," Mr. Smurdley explained. "So we had to be cautious. We've fully examined you, the things you had with you, and completed some research on our own. From the things I have seen in my life, I know nothing is impossible. Including talking ducks hidden from the rest of the world. It is apparent that terrible things have happened and that the ancient relics you had with you are authentic and they all need to be investigated, but the plans you have told us about require our immediate and full attention."

"I understand," said Angel.

"Especially what the Germans are up to," said Doc.

Mr. Smurdley paused for a moment. He looked at Daisy and Skeeter and pointed to each of them. He was making sure they both were ready.

"Since time is of the essence, I am going to be blunt," he said, directing his speech toward Angel. "The Angels and Ducks are a front."

"A front?" asked Angel.

"A front," said Mr. Smurdley. "Yes, they're real professional sports teams. They've even won world championships, but that is not their primary focus."

"Then what is?" asked Angel.

"Fighting the forces of evil," said Mr. Smurdley. "There are evil forces out there that seek to destroy or enslave all that is good. We fight those forces wherever they are."

"Especially Orange County," said Doc. "We've been carrying on the fight for decades."

"When did you start?" asked Angel.

"During the Really Big War," said Doc, "after the Germans destroyed the fleet, there was nothing here to fight them except cowboys. We stopped the Germans and have been fighting evil doers ever since."

"Evil is more than one country or one war," said Mr. Smurdley. "It is constantly trying to conquer free will if not constantly opposed."

"That is why the leader of the cowboys started the baseball team," said Doc.

"Evil has no trouble finding recruits; it can use greed and lust," said Mr. Smurdley.

"The leader of the cowboys decided to use sports to recruit heroes for good, so they started the Ducks and later the Angels," said Doc.

"That's how we get the best and brightest to fight doers of evil," said Mr. Smurdley.

"And Phil too," said Bobby, adding some levity.

Angel looked at Phil and Bobby. He hadn't noticed it before. Each had a black eye and swollen lips. It was like each of them had been hit in the face a few times.

"What happened?" Angel said to them. "You look hurt."

"We figured we could get here earlier if we got thrown out of the game," said Bobby.

"But it's kind of hard to get thrown out of a hockey game," said Phil.

"It's okay to get into a fight," said Bobby.

"You just get like a time out," said Phil.

"So we started a riot," said Bobby.

"How did you do that?" asked Angel.

"I went over to their bench and started teasing them about Mama France dumping them for some island in the Caribbean," said Bobby.

"The entire team attacked him," said Phil.

"That's so cruel," said Pussy Ryder. "You know French Canadians have abandonment issues."

"Did you get attacked too?" Angel asked Phil.

"No, I walked into a glass door on the way home," he said.

"Anyway," said Mr. Smurdley, trying to get the conversation back on track. "Most of the Angels and Ducks are part of our mission, but I don't think I have to say that nothing we discuss here leaves this room. With that said, Daisy and Skeeter have some things to share."

"Hello Angel," said Daisy, double-checking the laptop in front of her. "I have some pictures to show you."

Daisy Chane possessed the ability to be both on and off fleek at the same time. A woman in her mid-thirties, she had the hair and makeup of a model but dressed like a sister wife. She and Skeeter Bytes handled the research that helped the team's players identify and neutralize or otherwise deal with the world's bad actors when they weren't competing against the world's top baseball and hockey players. Since both Daisy and Skeeter wanted to be Mr. Smurdley's go-to person, it was not uncommon for them to show each other professional discourtesy. She pressed a key on her computer, and a picture of a middle-aged woman with short brown hair and black eyeglasses appeared on the wall of the room.

"That's her," Angel shouted. "The woman in Casino Royale and on the plane. She's on some commission."

"The European Commission," said Daisy. "Her name is Greta Von Karen. She has control of the media and judges in Europe and more. Any dissent regarding their agenda can get you slammed in the media or dragged into court for a hate crime. She is their censor."

Daisy continued her presentation until she had identified and informed everyone at the meeting about the rogues' gallery Angel had seen at the Casino Royale and at the airport. There was Schultz Dummkopffer, the head of the Grand Prix. Schultz, who in reality could neither operate a wrench or automobile and became head of the Grand Prix by moving up the bureaucratic ladder of Global Media Corporation, a shadowy international holding corporation that controlled much of the world's broadcasting, publishing, and information services. Daisy described him as the porcelain poster boy. The biggest turd that floated to the top of the bowl.

Next, she gave a briefing on Shein Temuhoffen, who she described as dirtier than an Eskimo's panties. He was a shadowy figure whose shadow even had its own shadow, and that shadow could be linked to every major hub of human trafficking, slave labor, and covert manufacturing that encompassed everything from cheap clothing and electronic gadgets to munitions for the illegal arms trade.

During her briefing on Von Farma, Angel had trouble keeping his cool. He was the one who had taken Kurri and he let everyone at the meeting know that. It did not help when Daisy informed the meeting that Von Farma was not only involved in the development, manufacture, and dispensing of pharmaceuticals, he was on the board of several national and international boards that controlled vaccination programs on an international level.

Daisy finished her briefing with some information on Major Tohtstettor. There was little official data available about Tohtstettor. Most of it was rumors that he was the sadistic enforcer for a new world order controlled by an entity known as The Chip. The identity and origin of the Chip were unknown. It was even speculated that The Chip might even be rogue artificial intelligence. All that was certain is that Angel had heard someone from the flight refer to The Chip. When Daisy finished, she turned it over to Skeeter, who said, "And now for the real show," in an effort to bolster his importance.

He pressed a few keys on his computer, and a map of Orange County, California, was projected on the wall. Using a laser pointer, he highlighted the city of Anaheim and, in particular, the train station between the stadium where the Ducks played baseball and the arena where the Angels played hockey.

"This is where we are," he said.

Then he moved the laser pointer south on the map to a beach city called Newport Beach. He circled the laser around an area of the shore where a peninsula formed a bay with islands inside the bay. He zoomed in on that area and superimposed an overlay of a roadway that ran around the bay and connected one of the islands to the mainland with what appeared to be a pontoon bridge.

"And this is where they will strike," he said.

"Newport Beach, that's the Grand Prix they were talking about," said Angel. "That's why they flew all the Grand Prix drivers here."

"It's going to be a big event, and now we think we know why," said Skeeter. "They are going to conquer and rule the world, not with an army, but with a vaccine."

"There is something in that vaccine that will make people easier to control and conquer," added Daisy.

"They said that at Casino Royale," said Angel.

"But why are they doing it here?" asked Bobby. "Why start in Orange County?"

"Because they know if Orange County falls, America falls, and with it the rest of the world," said Doc. "The Germans remember the ass whipping they got in Orange County by the cowboys during the Big War. They're here for a rematch."

"You bet the Germans are involved," said Pussy Ryder. "And Major Tohtstettor is running the show."

"You bet," said Phil. "My daddy always told me if you want a job done right for cheap, hire a Mexican, but if you want to subjugate the world, hire a German."

"But what are we going to do about it?" asked Mr. Smurdley. "How do we stop it?"

"Destroy the vaccine, robots and drones and neutralize Major Tohtstettor and the rest," said Skeeter.

"Duh!" Daisy said. "I think he was looking for details."

"I was getting to that genius," Skeeter snapped back at Daisy. "Look at the map."

Skeeter gave a rundown of the racecourse. The first thing he pointed out on the map were the areas where spectators would gather such as the grandstands near the loop-the-loops on the Balboa Peninsula, the ramps where the cars would jump the channel between the Balboa Peninsula and Corona del Mar and the Death Race through the Fashion Isle Mall. Skeeter speculated that drone-assisted vaccination kiosks would be stationed in those areas to vaccinate the tourist population that traveled in for the race.

Skeeter then pressed some more buttons on his computer, and the map zoomed in on Lido Island, a small island in Newport Bay. He highlighted a network of pontoon bridges being built that connected Lido Island to the Balboa Peninsula saying that while the ramps, loop-the-loops, and path through the mall that were under construction were part of the raceway, the pontoon bridges were not and appeared to be designed to move freight and not spectators.

"That is the likely staging area for the drones." said Daisy.

"I was gonna say that," said Skeeter.

"Well, I beat you to it, ha ha," said Daisy.

"Well, I have more, ha ha yourself," said Skeeter. "Lido Island is a notorious haven for degenerate gamers. If you're part of an evil empire staging drones for world domination, you might as well do it where you have a population of tech-savvy, vice-ridden, commie-bastard, fuzzy-headed dope suckers to prepare them for their godless mission."

"Okay, we have an idea of where they plan to stage the drones," said Mr. Smurdley. "What about where they're making the drones and the vaccine?"

"On that we're not sure," said Skeeter. "Given the facilities and slave labor needed, I doubt it is near the race area."

"But at least we know where to infiltrate their operation in order to find out," said Daisy.

"And how would we do that?" asked Mr. Smurdley.

"I have an idea," said Pussy Ryder.

"Let's hear it," said Mr. Smurdley.

"I'm sure we have some people that could pass as gamers," said Pussy Ryder. "Have them hang out on Lido and maybe they'll hear something or even get recruited."

"We have some swamper pitchers on the Ducks that kinda look like fuzzy headed dope sucker hippie freaks," said Bobby. "Put a Hawaiian shirt and pair chomp stompers on them and they'll fit right in with the Lido gamers, but if they're recognized as players it could blow the cover off our whole operation."

"We can't take that risk," said Phil. "The Ducks baseball team has been fighting evil for sixty-five years and the Angels hockey team for over thirty. We'd have to start all over."

"I don't care," said Mr. Smurdley. "I have friends in Corona del Mar. We must stop this evil plan even if we blow our cover after six decades."

The room got quiet. Everyone took a moment to think about what Mr. Smurdley, the owner of the Ducks and Kings, had just said. He was the keeper of the cowboy legacy from the Really Big War and willing to risk it all to stop the conquest by vaccine. The silence lasted only a moment before Pussy Ryder broke it.

"And I have another idea," she said.

"I'm all ears," said Mr. Smurdley.

"If you are willing to risk each team's cover being blown, then why not invite them in?" she said.

"I'm not sure what you mean," said Mr. Smurdley.

"If Angel could fool them by passing himself off as a Grand Prix driver, then a Grand Prix driver could fool them by passing himself off as Angel."

"Now I'm not sure what you mean," said Bobby.

"If the Grand Prix drivers are about the same size as Angel, why not make an Angel Duck costume and use a Grand Prix driver as the mascot for the last Angel and upcoming Duck's games? The Grand Prix will love the publicity, and we'll get access to the drivers to find out what they know."

"That's perfect," said Mr. Smurdley. "Instead of trying to find Von Farma, Temuvoffen and the rest, we let them come to us."

"I'll take it one step further," said Pussy Ryder. "Maybe I can channel my inner Mata Hari and seduce one driver to work for us."

"Ew!" Daisy said. "I know they're celebrities, but they're so short."

"Well, I like short guys," said Pussy Ryder. "They're the right height to please me, and I can set my beer down on their heads. Plus, I know how to get them."

"How's that?" asked Daisy.

"I challenge them to a game of basketball and let 'em win," said Pussy Ryder. "Works every time."

"Why don't we bring some psyops into this?" said Skeeter.

"Like what?" asked Mr. Smurdley.

"Major Tohtstettor, Von Farma, and the rest all saw Angel at Casino Royale," said Skeeter. "Angel can haunt them. Kind of like I know what you did last summer, but when they think they've caught Angel, it's their Grand Prix driver dressed as a mascot."

"They'll think they're going crazy and might make a slip," said Daisy.

"I was gonna say that," said Skeeter.

"Beat you to it again," said Daisy.

"Who is going to approach them with the Grand Prix driver as a mascot idea?" Pussy Ryder asked.

"I think we need someone who doesn't have a clue about our operation in case they get suspicious," said Bobby.

"I think we need someone who doesn't have a clue that I'm really a duck," said Angel.

"I think we need someone who doesn't have a clue," said Doc.

"Are you all thinking what I'm thinking?" asked Mr. Smurdley.

"Bingo!" they all replied.

After the meeting, Doc took Angel back to the room with the couch where he had been before the meeting. They both sat down on the couch. Doc searched around his pockets until he found a cigarette and lit it.

"Besides being a cowboy who fought the Germans, my granddad was a doctor too," Doc said.

"So it runs in the family," said Angel.

"He smoked unfiltered Chesterfields too," said Doc. "Back then doctors used to endorse smoking. There was a commercial that said nine out of ten doctors who smoke chose Camel cigarettes. Then, nine out of ten doctors died of lung cancer."

"Then why do you smoke?" asked Angel.

"Because I don't smoke Camels," said Doc. "It ain't the cigarette, it's the brand. My dad and granddad smoked Chesterfields. Didn't hurt 'em one bit."

"So they lived a good long life?" asked Angel.

"Damn near made it to sixty," said Doc. "It doesn't get much better than that."

There was a knock on the door, and it opened. It was Pussy Ryder. She was holding the durse that Angel had carried with him from Monaco. Dr. Ryder was in a good mood and broke into a dance. She did a two-step, quickstep and a Bossa Nova, then a little Fosse Bearvester, and Willie Wonkentino.

"Umpa gumba dippity doo, I have a little present for you," she sang as she twirled the durse in front of Angel.

"What is it?" asked Angel

"I did a little research on the book and cup you had in your bag," she said. "These are authentic relics; they should be in a museum."

"Well, I'd like to keep them with me for now," said Angel. "It's my connection to Monaco."

"I understand," she said. "Even though the book was written by hand, we used a special program to scan and translate it. Then we used artificial intelligence to write a summary of the book so you can get a quick idea of what it's about. Besides Latin, a lot of it is in Yiddish, just like the ancient scrolls. It must be over two-thousand years old."

"How's everything else going?" asked Doc.

"Things are already happening," she said. "Bingo just set up the Mascot promotion with the Grand Prix drivers. He was a little flustered about you sending him on a wild goose chase, but he got over it when Mr. Smurdley told him that everything changed because of the promotion and that he would be a big part of it."

"Small brain, big ego, that's Bingo," said Doc.

"Later today I'll go with Bingo to meet the drivers during their practice session today at Boomers and see if we can find a driver who we can get working on our side," she said. "You and Angel have a busy day planned too."

"What are we doing?" he asked.

"Mr. Smurdley figured if we were going to switch between Angel and a Grand Prix driver as a mascot Angel should be able to operate a car, and the only place to teach him in secret is the hangar, so you're both headed over there. Since there's no game tonight, Phil and Bobby will be there too. They're bringing a couple of pitchers from the baseball team to get them ready to pretend to be gamers on Lido Island. Oh, and since it's an off-night for both teams, Uncle Robert will be there coordinating."

"Sounds like a busy afternoon," said Angel.

"It's just getting started," said Pussy.

Pussy and Doc left shortly thereafter, and Angel soon found himself alone on the couch with his durse containing the book and cup. Pussy had to get ready to go to Boomers with Bingo to meet the Grand Prix drivers, and Doc left shortly after Pussy, saying he had some things to get done before they took Angel to the hangar for his driving lesson. Angel figured he would pass the time until Doc returned by getting acquainted with the things in his durse that Vladdy and Yoduck had given him to take along on his journey. He was interested in the book summary that Pussy had mentioned. Angel wasn't sure about what artificial intelligence meant, but if it was a way to find out what was in the book without learning a bunch of languages, he was going to do it. He could barely read English. There are few options for practicing reading among the poor people and ducks of Monaco. There are no libraries or schools, and the only reading material available to the poor of Monaco are Tom Ford, Tory Burch, Ralph Lauren or similar catalogs discarded from the casino. Catalogs that are not in English are not typically littered from the casino because the Spanish, Italians, and the like don't want the truly unwashed reading, let alone speaking, in their language.

Angel focused on the cover page of the summary. It was titled Ancient Book of Stupid A.K.A. Bukh Fun Narishkeytn, and below it was a disclaimer that the interpretation could not be precise because most of the book was handwritten in double ancient Neolithic Yiddish. Angel soon became tired of trying to fully comprehend the summary and skimmed over it making mental notes of questions to ask Pussy later about things mentioned in the book like French bulldogs, texting, microaggressions, and pierced septums and what he should do if he encountered a texting French bulldog with a pierced septum accusing him of microaggressions.

Having exhausted his mind trying to comprehend the artificial intelligence summary and wondering if artificial intelligence itself would be in the book, Angel turned his attention to the ancient cup. He put the summary back in his durse and took out the cup, held it by the stem and admired it from top to bottom. He thought about its history and the troubles that must have surrounded it during its multi-millennial history. The evil plots through the years that were hatched or carried out in its presence and the emotions felt by those who had previously handled the chalice as those scenarios played out.

That brought him to his own emotions and situation. He was now a player in yet another plot that was unfolding in proximity to the ancient chalice. When he thought about the others involved, he noticed something strange happening with the cup. If he thought about the new friends he had made, such as Bobby, Doc, and Pussy, the chalice warmed his hand slightly. When he thought of Kurri, the chalice grew even warmer, but it was a pleasant warm and it seemed to send a satisfying vibe through his body. However, if his thoughts turned to those he viewed as adversaries, those he had encountered in the casino and airplane, the chalice rapidly heated until it became uncomfortable, even painful to hold. Then he said it. The name of the person he hated so much. The one who had taken Kurri. He grumbled, "Von Farma." The cup erupted with intense heat, nearly burning Angel but still managing to singe a few of his feathers. He quickly dropped the chalice back into his durse, saving himself from injury, but he could smell the durse's fabric beginning to smolder. Thinking quickly, he turned his thoughts back to his friends Bobby, Doc, and Pussy, and the chalice slowly began to cool. His mind raced. He had to tell someone about the chalice. He could not ignore it. But who should he tell? Doc would be back shortly to take him to the hangar, but Doc might act impulsively and take the chalice. Angel decided he would wait until Pussy returned from meeting the Grand Prix drivers at Boomers and tell her. He figured that since she had taken an interest in the book and chalice, she would have a more measured approach. Angel plucked out his singed feathers and put them in his durse to show Pussy when she returned. He set the durse down on the couch next to him and rested until Doc returned.

It wasn't long before Doc returned and announced that he was going to drive him to the hangar for his driving lesson, but for the sake of secrecy he would have to carry Angel in the duffel bag Angel had awakened in earlier. Angel agreed and got inside the duffel bag. It wasn't a long trip to Doc's car, and Doc only dropped the bag a couple of times, but Angel got a little concerned when he heard the trunk being slammed over him. Fortunately, Angel was not kept in the trunk for the entire trip to the hangar. Once Doc thought that the coast was clear, he stopped the car and took the duffel bag out of the trunk. He laid it across the back seat of the car and unzipped it so Angel could get some fresh air.

Along the way, Doc told him the history of the hangar and what the teams used it for. He told Angel that the hangar was one of two that were built during the Really Big War for cowboys to use to defend Orange County against the German invasion, and it is still used today by the Ducks and Angels against evildoers. He also mentioned that the other hangar had mysteriously burned down, but they were satisfied that it was not an attempt at sabotage. Although he did mention that he thought it might have something to do with the land's value. When Doc announced they were nearly there, Angel sat up to look out the window.

"It's enormous," said Angel.

"That's Costco," said Doc. "The hangar is on the other side of the street."

Doc continued driving along Tustin Ranch Road until he got past the crowded shopping center and turned onto a dirt road that led to the hangar. Driving up to it, the height of the hangar amazed Angel. Doc noted that it might be hard to keep using the structure as houses and apartments are built closer and closer to it. Doc pulled off the dirt road that surrounded the hangar and drove across a strip of dirt and weeds to the side of the hangar. He pressed a button on the remote that was sitting on the console, and a well-hidden door opened, and Doc drove into the hangar.

The hangar was massive. About the size of two soccer fields inside. The inside was empty except for a few cars that had driven in earlier and a handful of people who were waiting. Angel recognized Phil and Bobby, but there were three others that he was not familiar with. The group met Doc and Angel, and Doc introduced them.

"Angel, this is Ellis Prezlee and Lee Mialone," he said. "They are pitchers on the Ducks, but they are going to be posing as gamers on Lido Island."

"Pleased to meet you," said Angel.

Ellis and Lee looked and dressed similarly. They were both tall and lean with long hair and goatees, with Lee's being fuller and Ellis' goatee being more scraggly. Both were dressed in khaki shorts, Hawaiian shirts, chomp stomper shoes, orange camo MindsEye beanies, and HD Vision wraparound glasses held together with a Band-Aid in the middle. Then Doc turned his attention to an Asian man in an orange polo-style shirt who had just arrived at the hangar and was walking towards them.

"And this is Uncle Ben," he said. "He is the unofficial coach and manager of both the Ducks and Angels. Though you won't see him at the games. He runs the show. That means team practices, logistics, and any special programs we have going."

"Pleased to meet you," Angel said to Uncle Ben.

"Aw, why are you wearing the same clothes?" said Uncle Ben, guessing that Angel was still wearing the same toga from when he was discovered at the train station. "Are you trying to dress like kimchi? I got you a duck uniform in kiddie size."

Uncle Ben showed him a baseball uniform in a child's size and held it in front of Angel to get an idea if it would fit. Then he showed Angel some other clothing items he had gotten.

"Do you wear boxers or briefs?" asked Uncle Ben.

"What do you mean, boxers or briefs?" asked Angel.

"Underwear," said Uncle Ben. "What kind of underwear do you wear?"

"I don't wear underwear; I'm a duck," said Angel. "I barely wear clothes."

"Aw, but you're talking duck," said Uncle Ben. "You talk, you wear underwear. I don't care if you're a panda. Talk then wear underwear."

"I think boxers," said Doc stepping in.

They helped Angel get dressed. Angel had a little trouble with his webbed feet getting caught in the underwear, but he made do. Uncle Ben looked Angel over, gave a thumbs-up sign and then pointed to an area of the hangar where an electric Grand Prix car was sitting. He told Angel and Doc to wait by the car, and he would give Angel his driving lesson after he taught Ellis and Lee how to talk and act like Lido Island Gamers. As Doc and Angel walked toward the car, Uncle Ben looked over Lee and Ellis.

"Haiyaa, why are you dressed like that?" he asked.

"We're supposed to pose as gamers," said Lee.

"You're supposed to pose as Newport Beach Lido Island gamers," Uncle Ben said. "They don't play MindsEye in Newport. It's not their game."

"What do they play?" asked Ellis

"Robot Wars," Uncle Ben exclaimed. "Droids, drones, bots, all fighting."

"How do they talk?" asked Lee.

"Very simple," said Uncle Ben. "They say Look, Jane. Look, look. See Dick."

"See Dick?" said Ellis

"Yes," said Uncle Ben. "They say, look at Dick. Get Dick. Go and get Dick."

"They seem to like Dick a lot," said Ellis.

"Yes, they like Dick," said Uncle Ben. "And Jane. They like Dick and Jane. That's how they talk."

"Like Dick and Jane?" asked Lee.

"Dick and Jane are little kid books," Uncle Ben explained. "Gamers don't grow up talking; they text. They learn to talk like little kids learn to read. Simple words like in Dick and Jane books. Go Spot go. Look, Jane, look. Go get Dick."

"I get it," said Ellis. "We should talk like little kid books."

"Yes," said Uncle Ben. "Now repeat after me. I will get Dick."

"I will get Dick," said Ellis with great hesitation.

"So weak," said Uncle Ben. "Say it like you mean it!"

"I don't," said Ellis.

"Haiyaa," said Uncle Ben.

Standing by the car, Doc and Angel watched as Uncle Ben coached the pitchers to pass as Newport Beach gamers. Doc smiled, shook his head, and lit up an unfiltered Chesterfield.

"This might take a while," he said to Angel.

Over at Boomers, the excitement was palpable. It wasn't every day that the park was filled with celebrities, such as Grand Prix drivers. None of them was driving yet because the Formula E electric cars that they drove in the Grand Prix were not as fast as the karts at Boomers and in order to get used to the faster speed it was decided that the drivers would get acclimated to the higher speeds on the Bumper Boats and the Magic Tea Cups ride before practicing in the carts. The media were there getting pictures and interviews, and there were signs all over advertising the Newport Beach Grand Prix and Health Fair. In the middle of it all, Greta Von Karen and Schultz Dummkopffer were helping direct the festivities. Pussy spotted them as soon as she and Bingo arrived, and they made a beeline straight toward them. She was the first to introduce herself.

"Hi, I'm Dr. Pussy Ryder," she said, extending her closed hand out for a fist bump. "I'm here representing both the Ducks and Angels for the mascot promotion."

"I'm Greta Von Karen," she said, bumping fists with Pussy. "I represent several parties connected to the event."

"I'm Schultz Dummkopffer, President of the Grand Prix," he said, extending his hand toward Bingo. "And you must be?"

"Bingo," replied Bingo, completing the fist pump.

"We are so excited to partner with you," Dummkopffer said to Pussy and Bingo. "This could be about more than sporting events. We can use this to change the world."

"Bingo," said Bingo.

"We can completely change the way people live," Von Karen said.

"Bingo," said Bingo.

"Life on Earth as we know it," said Dummkopffer.

"Double Bingo," said Bingo.

"There are so many others who want to be a part of this," said Von Karen. "This could be the biggest thing ever."

"Double Bingo plus!" exclaimed Bingo.

"We have a group of government and industry leaders who wish to partner in this, and they can be at the game tomorrow," said Greta Von Karen.

"Tell us who they are," said Pussy Ryder. "We can reserve a luxury box and hold a press conference at the last hockey game tomorrow and then promote it more during the next baseball homestand."

"The mayor of Los Angeles and the governor of California are all in and can be there tomorrow," said Greta Von Karen.

"Mayor Nero and Governor Gettyoyl can be there?" said Pussy Ryder.

"Absolutely," said Dummkopffer. "We also have Dr. Baron Von Farma, a leader in world health and medicine, and Shein Temuhoffen, a world leader in technology, manufacturing, and robotics eager to join."

"That's great; the more the merrier," said Pussy Ryder.

"Bingo," said Bingo.

"All of us will work together for a greater purpose," said Greta Von Karen. "We would like to continue this partnership beyond the Newport Grand Prix."

"We're all in," said Pussy. "With the World Cup and Olympics on the horizon, Southern California is the place to be for promotions."

"We cannot wait to get things started," said Greta Von Karen.

"Neither can we," said Pussy. "Just so we can get started right away and help every stakeholder, tell us everything you have planned and everyone we'll be working with."

Greta Von Karen and Schultz Dummkopffer both looked at each other. They were silent for a second. Then, Dummkopffer smiled, or at least came as close as a German can to smiling, and nodded. Greta made her pitch.

"We will cure the world," said Greta Von Karen.

"Of what?" asked Pussy.

"Everything," said Schultz Dummkopffer."

"Everything?" asked Pussy. "I'm not sure what you mean."

"Every disease, every ailment, every unbeneficial condition, we can cure it," said Greta Von Karen.

"How?" asked Pussy.

"A vaccine," said Schultz Dummkopffer.

"A vaccine that cures everything," said Greta. "A chemical solution that when administered will cure everything."

"The final solution," said Schultz Dummkopffer.

"Developed in Germany, so it is of the highest quality," said Greta Von Karen.

"German engineering is the best in the world," said Schultz Dummkopffer.

"And German social engineering is even better than that," said Greta Von Karen.

"So we've seen," said Pussy. "How do you plan to roll out this vaccine?"

"At the Grand Prix," said Greta Von Karen. "It will also be a health fair where everyone will be vaccinated."

"What if they don't want to be vaccinated?" asked Pussy.

"We will convince them," said Greta Von Karen. "It is for their own good."

"What if they don't come to you?" asked Pussy.

"We will come to them," said Greta Von Karen.

"How?" asked Pussy. "You would need so many people."

"No people," said Schultz Dummkopffer. "We use drones and robots."

"It is fully automated; no one can escape," said Greta Von Karen.

"Whether we roll them or fly them, they will vaccinate them," said Dummkopffer. "Have you heard the slogan for the event? It is auto racing, auto vaxxing, auto this world. Do you think it is a silly and funny slogan?"

"Yes, it's alright," said Pussy.

"We didn't think of it," said Dummkopffer. "We're German; we don't understand silly, funny, so we had to hire someone."

"Who'd you get?" asked Pussy.

"We needed something quick and cheap, so we hired a Mexican," said Von Karen.

"Bingo," said Bingo.

"Are you sure just vaccinating people with drones is legal?" asked Pussy.

"It will be perfectly legal," said Von Karen. "We have the full support of Mayor Nero and Governor Gettyoyl."

"That's right, the mayor of Los Angeles and governor of California," said Dummkopffer. "They do everything great. Everything they do turns out great. This will be the best thing ever. And it's great for the Angels and Ducks because healthier fans can come to more games. Right Bingo?"

"Bingo," said Bingo.

"Well, I'm so excited, I can't wait to get started," said Pussy. "I'm going to see what the drivers are up to and leave you all to firm up the plans for the game."

Pussy left the group to meet some drivers. Along the way, she noticed the drivers had all moved away from the Magic Tea Cups and Bumper Boats to the Go-Cart area to practice. Since the Bumper Boats appeared to be empty Pussy decided it would be an excellent place to make a call directly to Mr. Smurdley and inform him about what she had just learned about drones being used for mass inoculations of a mystery vaccine during the Newport Grand Prix, World Cup, and Olympics. She entered the ride area and found an empty boat on the opposite side of the ride's entrance. Pussy took a quick look around and dialed Mr. Smurdley's personal emergency number and gave him every detail about the conversation she had just had with Greta Von Karen and Schultz Dummkopffer. She warned him that Bingo was alone with them to firm up the plans for the game promotions before she had to cut the call short when someone came and sat inside her bumper boat. It was a Grand Prix driver in his racing suit who looked very sad. Pussy deleted the recent call record from her phone and put it away in her purse. She tried to make eye contact with him, but he just looked over the water, taking no interest in the few other boats that were occupied.

"Why so glum, sugarplum?" she asked him.

"Nothing," he said.

"Why are you practicing on the go-kart track?" she asked.

"They won't let me."

"Why not?"

"You must be over forty inches tall to use the go-karts at Boomers," he said.

"But other Grand Prix drivers are practicing in go-karts." she said.

"They stacked Rolex and Tag Hauer watches in their shoes until they were tall enough," he said.

"Why didn't you do that?" she asked.

"My Richard Mille watches are too thin," he answered.

"A big boy like you doesn't need to put watches in his shoes," she said, moving closer to him. "How about a game of basketball?"

"I don't think they have a basketball court at Boomers," he said.

"There's a court just past Culver Drive; we can go there and play," she said. "I can take us in my car."

"Okay, I guess," he said.

"What's your name?" she asked.

"Hewis Lamilton," he said.

"Hewis Lamilton!" she squealed like an excited schoolgirl. "I've heard so much about you. You're a real big-boy driver. I'm so thrilled to meet you. There are literal chills going down my spine."

"What's your name?" Hewis asked her.

"My name is Pussy," she said, licking her lips. "Pussy Ryder."

"Pleased to meet you, Pussy Ryder," said Hewis.

"I'm with the Angels and Ducks sports teams," said Pussy. "I'm not sure if you heard, but we are looking for a Grand Prix driver to pose as our mascot for our cross-promotion with the Newport Beach Grand Prix. Since you're so famous, you'd be perfect. I'm envious of your success. I would love to be a Hewis Lamilton."

"I would love to be a Pussy Ryder," said Hewis.

"Maybe we can form a mutual admiration society," she said with a wink. "We can discuss working together on the way to the basketball court."

Back at the hangar, Angel was finally getting his driving lesson. Uncle Ben had finally gotten Lee and Ellis to speak Newport gamer lingo to his satisfaction and even exclaimed "fuiyoh" after some of their responses. Uncle Ben had added a few more names to their vocabulary, such as Bruh, Dude, and Boss to go with Dick and Jane. After Lee could say some simple gamer phrases, Uncle Ben felt confident enough in their skills to focus on Angel's driving lesson and gave each of them a remote control transmitter. He told them to pretend they were controlling the car Angel was learning how to drive in order to practice looking and talking more like Lido gamers. He finally turned his attention to Angel, who was behind the open wheel of a formula-type electric car. It wasn't exactly like the ones that would be used at the upcoming event, but it was as close as they could come to get Angel up to speed. Which he was not.

"Haiyaa!" Uncle Ben cried. "Why do you drive so slow? You're boring me."

"Push the pedal down like I showed you," Doc called out to Angel.

"You're not making pho," said Uncle Ben. "Go faster."

Doc's cell phone rang as Angel continued to putter around the makeshift track inside the hangar. He dropped a lit Chesterfield cigarette from his hand, crushed it out on the hangar floor, and answered his Motorola Dynatac 8000x. It was Mr. Smurdley calling. He had just gotten

Pussy Ryder's call about her meeting with Schultz Dummkopffer and Greta Von Karen, and he told Doc to get everyone together for a morning meeting to get ready for the dignitaries she said would be at the game. He also wanted Lee and Ellis to start posing immediately as gamers on Lido Island so they might find out something before that meeting.

As soon as he got off the phone, Doc called Lee and Ellis over to him and gave them their assignment. They both wanted to pitch during the upcoming homestand, but this was more important. They knew that the Angels and Ducks always play to win, but they also knew that the most important triumphs are against evil. Once they left, Doc told Uncle Ben about the call from Mr. Smurdley. Uncle Ben shook his head. He was going to be two pitchers short for the baseball team's upcoming homestand. He made a mental note and then turned his attention back to encouraging Angel to drive faster.

"Haiyaa!" he screamed at Angel. "Drive like wok hei, drive like Gordon Ramsay makes ramen! Go too fast!"

After about half an hour of practicing with the remote controls, Lee and Ellis left the hangar and headed over to Newport Beach. Along the way, they picked up two large plastic fishbowls, a few rolls of duct tape, aluminum foil and a lot of cash. They figured they would fit in better with the droid robot gaming motif if they wore the fishbowls like space helmets and wrapped the foil and duct tape around themselves. The cash was in case they needed bribe money. After they got off the Pacific Coast Highway, they parked the car at Lido Park and walked across the Via Lido bridge onto Lido Isle. They didn't want to park on the Isle because of the prevalence of car vandalism on fossil fuel vehicles by the woke vagrant gamers that called the dingy back streets and alleyways of Lido Isle home.

They continued walking along Via Lido Soud toward the Yahtzee Club District. The district was the gaming hub of Lido Isle, having gotten its start with the illegal gambling and dice games that surrounded the speakeasies and brothels that haunted the San Remo neighborhood. At the time, people called the brothels doghouses instead of cathouses, because of the working girls' appearance. It is said that Via Dijon, the street that housed those ladies, was so named because they couldn't cut the mustard in other L.A. area brothels such as those on Skid Row. As a matter of fact, the expression "I'm in the doghouse" can be traced back to the husbands of that time who would access the unsightly ladies' services after being cut off from spousal privileges because of real or perceived misdeeds.

Not that Lido Isle was not appreciative of these ladies' contributions. As they continued toward the Yahtzee Club District Lee and Ellis walked past statues dedicated to the ladies who helped establish the District such as Legless Lefty, Stump, and Mrs. Ed who not only plied their trade but saved all of Lido by putting out the Great Dumpster Fire of nineteen twenty-seven. These revered statues were in stark contrast to the derelict factories they passed along the way. The crumbling shells of the Midway, Neversoft, and Visceral Games plants lined were a sad reminder of the glory days of American Gaming production when patriotic engineers rolled up the sleeves on their blue collar shirts, put on their hard hats and churned out classics like Space Invaders, Pacman, and Mortal Kombat. The sight of it made Lee and Ellis think about what it must have been like back in the day.

"It's incredible to see these old factories," said Lee. "You can almost hear the hum and clanking of machinery."

"Actually, I think I hear machinery at work in those factories," said Ellis.

"Can't be, the lights are all out," said Lee. "It's completely dark inside those abandoned factories."

"Those old factories don't sound abandoned," said Ellis. "I definitely hear machinery at work."

"But how can they work without lights?" asked Lee.

Ellis shook his head and then noticed lights and activity up the road. Across from the lights and activity around the Yahtzee Club District were lights and construction equipment on the beach and over the channel to the peninsula. As they got closer, they saw a construction crew creating a roadway that led to a pontoon bridge connecting Lido Isle to the Balboa Peninsula.

"This must be one of the bridges they told us about," said Ellis.

"It looks like it's nearly done, and there are others," said Lee.

"Those factory sounds are making sense," said Ellis.

"But how are they working without light?" asked Lee.

Finally, they arrived in the Yahtzee Club district and stopped at a place called The Bot Spot. The Bot Spot was the major hangout for gamers on Lido Isle because it featured what Uncle Ben had told them were the favorite games among the locals. Before going in, Lee and Ellis took a look around the district to see if there was a better place to pose. There was Minecrafters, which looked like a giant sandbox that had a few blockhead-ed gamers in swimsuits holding plastic buckets and tiny shovels standing in front, and Nite Fort, where gamers could build their own fort while gaming. After looking around, it appeared that Uncle Ben had called it right and The Bot Spot, whose games featured all manner of battling drones, droids, bots and autos, was by far the most popular joint in the district. They took a deep breath and entered.

The Bot Spot looked like a science fiction B movie poster on the outside, but the inside was decorated with lava lamps, black light and black velvet paintings of Gort, Hal 9000, Bender, Optimus Prime and robotic dogs playing poker. Next to the windows facing the street was a section resembling the Spaceballs diner, while the rest of it was rows of Atari 520 computers with neon graphics where gamers were locked in mortal robo-combat. Lee and Ellis sat down in one of the booths on the diner side. They didn't have time to eat while getting from the hangar to Lido Isle, so they figured they might as well order something while they got acclimated to the gaming establishment.

"I'm hungry, but it's so dark, I don't think I can read the menu," said Ellis. "I hope I can see the food."

"Ask for pasta; it will reflect the black light just like the paintings," said Lee.

"Really?" said Ellis.

"Yes, certain things absorb the UV light and that energy gives off light," said Lee. "That's how the paintings glow."

"Maybe they can make the food glow," said Ellis.

"That's it," said Lee. "That's how those factories we passed sound — like they're working but look abandoned. They're using black light. They coat what they're working on with something that absorbs UV, and then they can see it. That's where they're making everything, and they're going to use the bridges to move it fast. This isn't just where they'll stage things; this is where they're making things."

"What do you think they're making?" asked Ellis.

"The drones or at least some parts," said Lee, "maybe they're doing the vaccine too."

"I don't know, but I'd sure like to get a look inside," said Ellis. "Do you think we can break in?"

"Maybe we can get invited," said Lee. "I've got an idea."

"What's that?"

"Gamers love free food," said Lee. "Let's order a bunch and get real generous. If they're doing something in those factories, maybe they'll bring us along to keep the snacks coming."

"Let's try out our gamer talk and see what happens," said Ellis.

Lee and Ellis got a couple of menus and used the glow from the black velvet paintings to read them. The menu was filled with local favorite gamer snacks. When Lee had made his selections, he tried using his local gamer lingo to order food.

"Look, look," said Lee, holding a menu close to the glow of a black velvet painting. "This looks good."

"What looks good?" asked a waitress with short curly blond hair and a name tag that said Jane.

"Butter balls look good," said Lee. "Jelly grips look good. Ghost pepper Tide Pods look good."

"How many do you want?" asked Jane.

"Lots," said Ellis. "Lots and lots and lots," said Ellis.

"Do you want to share?" asked Jane.

"Yes, yes, yes," said Lee. "We will share. We will share, share, share."

"I will bring lots of butter balls, I will bring lots of jelly grips, I will bring lots of ghost pepper tide pods," said Jane.

Jane left to get their order, and not long after she had set it on the table, hungry gamers invited themselves over to Lee and Ellis' table to share their food. Three of them crammed into the booth with Lee and Ellis. One was next to Lee and two were next to Ellis. The two next to Ellis were almost identical and resembled a cross between Data from Star Trek and Matrix agents. The one sitting next to Lee seemed to be the leader of the group and was dressed more casually. He sported a lavender Hawaiian shirt and Candy Crush trucker cap.

"Look!" he said, pointing to a pyramid of golf ball-sized butterballs on a platter. "Will you share?"

"Yes," said Lee. "Who are we sharing with?"

"This is Bruh, this is Dude," he said, pointing to the other two gamers. "I am Dick."

Dick reached over to the butterball platter, took a butterball off the top and popped it into his mouth and sucked on it like a gumball. As he rolled it around in his mouth, melted butter rolled down the corner of his mouth. Lee knew he had to introduce himself and Ellis, but he was stuck for gamer names. In desperation, they flew out of his mouth.

"I am Boss," said Lee. "That is Spot."

"Will Boss share more?" Dick asked. "Will Spot share more?"

"Yes," said Lee. "Boss and Spot will share more."

Dick then took one of the jelly grips. Jelly grips are large blobs of fruit-flavored petroleum jelly that gamers consume by the handful and are a popular snack at climate protests. Bruh and Dude followed suit, sucking the jelly out of their semi-closed fists.

"Can you share games, Dick?" Lee asked.

"What games are good?" asked Dick.

"Drone games are good, droid games are good, robot games are good," said Lee.

"War games are good?" Dick asked.

"War games with robots are best," said Lee.

"We can go and see," said Dick. "Can you share more snacks?"

"Yes, Dick," said Lee. "Show us a good game. We will share more snacks."

"The game is not here," said Dick. "We must go."

"We will get more snacks," said Lee. "Then we will go."

Lee gave Ellis most of his cash, and Ellis left the booth to find Jane and put together a large to-go order. While waiting for the resupply of snacks, Dick and his two companions freely helped themselves to the food that was already on the table. One of the Data-Matrix hybrids that came with Dick started two-fisting the jelly grips and stuffing them into his mouth until he could barely close it. Then he managed to push in two ghost pepper Tide Pods in and mashed them together in his mouth. The heat from the ghost peppers ignited the petroleum jelly in the jelly grips, causing his head to burst into flames, which was exacerbated by the cheap flammable hair gel he had used to slick back his hair. He face-planted on the table smoldering lifelessly. Dick continued consuming the butterballs and jelly grips that were on the table while the other Data-Matrix hybrid started pressing his burnt companions back hoping to find a reset button until Ellis and Jane the waitress returned to the booth with two large plastic bags containing the take out order. Lee got up and took the bag from Jane.

"Go, Dick, go," he said. "Go to a good game."

"Come, Boss, come Spot, we will go to a good game," said Dick.

"We have snacks," said Ellis.

Dick scooped up what was left of the butterballs and put them in his pocket for later. He hesitated for a moment to see if the two who came to Lee and Ellis' table with him were coming, but one seemed intent on finding the reset button on the smoldering motionless other, so he continued to the gaming area without them. Lee and Ellis put on their fishbowl helmets and followed him with the snacks. Dick led them past the rows of Atari 520 computers to the back of the building. There they stopped at a staircase that was hard to see without the light of the computer screens they had just passed. They followed Dick down the staircase, leaning against the wall for balance while they carried the snacks with them. When they got to the bottom of the staircase, the lighting was a little better, and they could read the sign on the door Dick had stopped in front of. It said, "DANGER-ELECTRICAL ROOM-IMMINENT SHOCK-DEATH." Dick opened the door revealing a tunnel.

Lee and Ellis wanted to say something about the tunnel but realized they had to keep up the Dick and Jane gamer lingo. When they came to a point where the tunnel split into two directions, they realized that there was an entire network of tunnels below Lido Isle. They continued to follow Dick until they came to what looked like an access door about three feet high. As they got closer to the door, they could hear noise on the other side of the wall. It sounded like cheering, swearing and metal clanking. Dick opened the door, crouched down, and went inside. Lee and Ellis removed their fishbowl helmets, held on to the bags of snacks and followed.

Lee and Ellis were stunned. Dick had led them into what could best be described as a black light underground fight club glow party. In the dark room, a crowd of gamers surrounded a half-scale boxing ring. The gamer spectators, mostly young males, were visible by their glow in the dark face paint, white trucker caps, glow stick eyeglasses, and fluorescent chomp stompers. Some were even wearing neon Hawaiian shirts. Neon images of syringes, spacemen, and computer components, especially chips, illuminated the dark walls. Inside the small boxing ring, two silver humanoid robots speckled with glow-paint were locked in combat. One robot was armed with a Roman short sword and large shield, and the other was armed with a trident and net. The robot with the sword kept trying to move in close, but the robot with the net kept it away by poking at it with the trident all the while waiting for an opportunity to throw the net. Outside the ring, two gamers in white Compaq caps controlled the robots as they jockeyed for position inside the ring. The robot with the trident cast its net over its opponent, who shook it off its head but could not shake it off its large shield and got its feet tangled in the net. It fell to the mat, and its opponent pounced quickly, pressing the prongs of its trident against the fallen humanoid robot's neck region.

The gamer crowd roared, gave the thumbs-down sign, and began chanting, "Chalked, chalked, chalked." A spotlight illuminated the middle of the ring, and a man entered the ring and stood in the spotlight in front of the two humanoid robots. It was Shein Temuhoffen. Lee and Ellis recognized him from their previous briefings.

"The net is a success," Shein Temuhoffen loudly announced to the crowd. "Now we need to test it! Who will volunteer? We need someone to come into the ring and try not to get caught in the robot net and vaccinated."

The room suddenly went silent. None of the gamers appeared keen to take a chance at being jabbed with a mystery vaccine by a robot. Lee and Ellis glanced at each other, but each decided not to draw attention to themselves by volunteering. It was important for Temuhoffen to test the robots' ability to vaccinate unwilling victims, so he sweetened the pot.

"There is a prize!" Temuhoffen proclaimed. "If you can avoid being caught by the robot, you win a Nintendo Wii."

Suddenly, there was a surge of volunteers among the gamers. They swarmed around the ring apron trying to get into the ring. One gamer outmaneuvered the others and got through the ropes, plopping into the ring at Shein Temuhoffens feet. Temuhoffen helped him up onto his feet. To Lee and Ellis' surprise, it was Dick.

"We have a volunteer!" Temuhoffen shouted, introducing him to the crowd. "Do you have a name?"

"I am Dick," he answered.

"Are you a gamer?" Temuhoffen asked him.

"Yes, I am a gamer," said Dick.

"We have a gamer who's a Dick," said Temuhoffen. "Do you want a Wii, Dick?"

"Yes, yes," said Dick.

"Well, every gamer wants a Wii, Dick," said Temuhoffen. "Do you think you can get the better of the robot and not be injected?"

"Yes, I will go and go," said Dick, pointing at the robot with the trident.

"Good to see you're confident, but that's not the robot you'll be facing," Temuhoffen announced. "Bring in Hello Nursie!"

On cue, Major Tohtstettor and his two henchmen pushed through the gamer crowd to the ring apron. Soft lights illuminated the ring. Tohtstettor and his henchmen pushed the gamers watching away from one side of the ring and positioned a ramp large and sturdy enough to support a refrigerator up against the ring and unhooked the ropes on that side. Onto the ramp drove a small medical services van. It was much smaller than a real medical services van, about the size of a kiddie fire truck ride one would find in front of a grocery store or inside a mall. It was decorated with cartoon characters in nurse uniforms holding syringes with a cute goat's face and the words "HELLO NURSIE" all over the white van. It drove up into the ring. Once the Hello Nursie mini medical van was in the center of the ring, the defeated robot was removed and the robot with the trident walked triumphantly on its own down the ramp. Major Tohtstettor and his two henchmen in their black Hugo Boss attire reattached the ring ropes, and Shein Temuhoffen made his next announcement.

"Introducing Hello Nursie, the family-friendly health services van that will change the face of healthcare," Temuhoffen told the crowd. "Look what it can do!"

The Hello Nursie mini medical van suddenly began to change shape. The outer shell panels shifted and split open. Its wheels retracted. The rear half of the van split down the middle, forming legs. The front portion of the van unfolded, revealing a chest and torso. Ratchet-like arms sprung from the sides, and a head resembling the cartoon goat with a nurse's hat emerged from inside the robot chest. In a second, the Hello Nursie mini medical van had transformed into a humanoid scary nurse robot wielding a syringe with one ratchet arm and pulling a net from its chest compartment with another.

"Let's get ready to robottttttttttt!" Temuhoffen yelled. "In one corner we have Nurse Ratchbot!. In the other corner we have Dick!"

"No, no," said Dick. "I will not go."

"Then you won't have a Wii, Dick," said Temuhoffen.

"I will go," said Dick.

"Let the games begin!" Temuhoffen declared.

With the ring of a bell, Nurse Ratchbot stepped toward Dick. Lee and Ellis watched from the crowd as Dick ran from one side of the small ring to the other trying not to let the robot get a good shot with the net.

"Don't try to get away," Nurse Ratchbot said to Dick. "Accept the vaccine. It will protect you from everything. Disease, depression, even bad luck. You wouldn't want to have an accident, would you?"

Nurse Ratchbot swung one of its ratchet arms down, hitting the mat and shaking the whole ring to emphasize to Dick that he might have an accident if he didn't get the vaccine. Dick continued to feign and dodge to get the robot off balance. Finally, Nurse Ratchbot backed Dick into the corner and unfurled the net over him. Tangled up, Dick fell, and the robot pinned him forcefully to the mat and thrust the needle into his butt and vaccinated him.

"No Wii?" asked Dick as he lost consciousness.

"Success!" Temuhoffen declared. "We'll finish the best game ever. The first gamers at the programming stations will get extra snacks and a free GTX 480 graphics card!"

The room emptied quickly as the gamers rushed to get to the programming stations in order to get the coveted graphics cards. While there was still a crowd in the room, Lee and Ellis had a word with each other.

"Do you think he really got vaccinated?" Ellis asked Lee.

"It's possible if they wanted to test everything," answered Lee.

"We might find out what's in the vaccine if we can get him out of here," said Ellis.

"Let's try. I think it's worth the risk," said Lee.

By the time they got to the ring apron the crowd of gamers had mostly filtered out leaving only Shein Temuhoffen, Major Tohtstettor and his two henchmen in the ring with the nurse Ratchbot robot that was now folding back up into the Hello Nursie mini health services van. They were congratulating each other on the successful test and trying to move the Hello Nursie van out of the ring and down the ramp when Lee called out to Dick, who was still unconscious on the floor of the ring.

"Can you go, Dick?" Lee asked.

"Move, Dick, move," said Ellis.

"Who are you?" Major Tohtstettor asked Lee and Ellis.

"We are Boss and Spot," said Lee using his Lido Isle gamer lingo. "We like Dick. We want to get Dick up."

"Can they help him?" Temuhoffen asked Tohtstettor.

"Yes, they can make sure he is okay," said Tohtstettor. "But he must not leave the building. The chip is inside him."

"You can help your friend Dick," Shein Temuhoffen told Lee and Ellis. "But he must stay here."

"We will get Dick up," said Lee.

"We will have Dick stay here," said Ellis.

Shein Temuhoffen nodded and went back to moving the Hello Nursie van out of the ring. As they did so, the lights slowly dimmed until the room was once again lit only by black light, and it was difficult to see. When Temuhoffen, Tohtstettor, and his henchmen took the Hello Nursie van outside the room through a larger entrance, Lee and Ellis saw their chance. They dragged Dick to the small access door where they had originally entered from and went through the tunnel back into The Bot Spot and out a side exit onto Via Lido Soud. As they hurried toward their car, shouting and whistles erupted from inside The Bot Spot. Lee and Ellis realized the commotion meant Tohtstettor had discovered that Dick had gone missing.

They knew they had to get across the bridge quickly. Until the pontoon bridges were complete, it was the only bridge off the island and the first place Tohtstettor would secure if he was setting up a perimeter. The noise from their search was also awakening Dick.

"What is it?" Dick asked as he woke up.

"We must go, Dick," said Lee. "Go, Dick, go."

"Are you The Chip?" Dick said. "I will go with The Chip."

"We are The Chip," said Lee, thinking quickly. "Go with us. Go, Dick, go."

"I will go with The Chip," said Dick.

To Lee and Ellis' surprise, Dick began running along with them. The faster Lee and Ellis ran, the faster Dick ran. They scampered across the bridge and made it to the car just as Major Tohtstetter's henchmen made it to the bridge. Fortunately for Lee, Ellis, and Dick, the henchmen did not see them cross the bridge in the darkness, and instead of crossing the bridge, they stopped on the bridge to block any traffic that might come. By the time they got to the car, the run had made Dick more alert, and he looked at Lee and Ellis quizzically.

"You're not a chip," Dick said to them.

"Good night, Dick," said Ellis, knocking him out with a punch to the jaw.

They dropped Dick in the trunk of their Chevy Impala and drove off, careful not to turn on the lights until they were almost to Newport Boulevard. They immediately called Doc, who directed them to meet him at an empty clinic that was just past the hospital on Newport Boulevard. While they waited in the lot, they heard Dick pounding against the inside of the trunk.

"I'll be back," said Ellis.

Ellis got out of the car, walked around to the trunk, opened it and sent Dick back to slumberland with another right cross. About fifteen minutes later, Doc pulled into the parking lot. Lee and Ellis carried Dick to the door of a medical office in the deserted medical complex. Doc unlocked the door, and they brought him inside and laid him on a bed in an examination room while Doc turned on all the equipment and lit up a Chesterfield cigarette.

"Why did we come here? Don't you have all this stuff at the stadium?" asked Ellis.

"We don't know what they put into him," answered Doc. "There may be some way to track him. As a matter of fact, I'm gonna scan him before I take a blood sample. Did he get jabbed anywhere else?"

"Just the butt," said Lee.

Doc handed his cigarette to Lee and flipped Dick over. He took a universal scanner out of his jacket pocket and held it over Dick's butt. The light on the scanner turned from red to yellow. Doc held the scanner steady until it beeped.

"That vaccine has a chip in it," said Doc.

"He kept mentioning the chip, like he wanted to follow it," said Lee.

"We need to find out what's in that chip," said Doc. "I'm gonna cut it out of him and then take a blood sample to see what else we can pick up from the vaccine then see if he might work for us."

"He won't work for us," Lee said. "Those gamers don't even know they're working for them. They think they're playing a game."

"Then we've gotta find a place to dump him," said Doc.

"Dump him?" asked Ellis. "Like dead?"

"No, no," answered Doc. "He'll be fine, but we have to cover our tracks. We can't alert the Germans. We need to make it look like after he wandered away something bit him on the ass to account for the missing chip."

"Like a dog?" said Ellis. "Those stupid little dogs old Chinese women push around Irvine in strollers are always trying to bite someone's ass."

"We need a more substantial bite out of the bum of a beach bum," said Doc.

"What about sharks?" asked Lee. "The channel is full of giant mirror-back sharks. Every other day, they're dragging tourists off Pirates Cove Beach. I heard it's the top destination for depressed tourists."

"It's also number one on the bucket list of people with a short bucket list," added Ellis.

"A shark bite would be a suitable cover," Doc said. "The Back Bay and San Diego Creek are full of sharks, even all the way to The Spectrum. I'll cut out the chip and then make the wound look like a shark bite. Then I'll wrap the chip up in foil so they can't track it and have it analyzed. You can dump him on the beach. Make sure he's wet, so it looks like he went in the water. Avoid any closed-circuit cameras. I'll delete everything from the cameras around the medical office. Also, don't forget we have a meeting with everyone before the hockey game. Now let's get moving; they might be trying to track that chip already."

"It's gonna be a long night," lamented Ellis.

Orange County review

Across

3. Anaheim train station.
4. Orange County hockey team.
7. Kicked German ass in the really big war.
8. Location of the Hangar.
11. Where Grand Prix drivers practice.
12. California Governor.

Down

1. Gamer club district on Lido Isle.
2. Orange County baseball team.
5. Beach with Grand Prix.
6. Isle of degererate gamers.
9. Los Angeles Mayor.
10. Grand Prix driver Hewis.

CHAPTER FIVE

MORE ORANGE COUNTY

Morning came quickly. Doc was running on coffee and cigarettes when he arrived at the corporate-looking conference room where they had held the previous meeting. He was the first to arrive and the last who felt like being there. It had been a long night but after analyzing Dick's blood sample and the chip that had been in the vaccine he had groundbreaking news for the group which he guessed would be larger than what was at the previous meeting because of the extra chairs at the meeting table. Since there were three more chairs, he figured that Lee, Ellis, and Uncle Ben would arrive soon. He felt like having a cigarette but didn't. Mr. Smurdley was the one person he would not smoke in front of. He sat down at the end of the meeting table and waited, enjoying the closest thing to a rest he had experienced in a long time.

Mr. Smurdley arrived next along with Skeeter and Daisy. Mr. Smurdley, in business attire, sat at the head of the table flanked by Skeeter and Daisy as normal. While Skeeter and Daisy took their laptops out of their cases and assembled any papers they needed, Mr. Smurdley addressed Doc.

"I want to thank you for what you are doing," he said. "I know it isn't easy."

"I'm honored to do it," responded Doc. "Old-timers like us who have been through the battles of the past know how important the Ducks and Angels have been to keep the forces of evil at bay and if it takes all night and day, that's what has to be done."

"I was talking about not smoking during the meeting," said Mr. Smurdley.

Skeeter, Daisy, and Doc smirked. They were used to Mr. Smurdley's deadpan humor. Soon, the others arrived. Lee, Ellis, Phil, and Bobby arrived together. It was apparent that Lee and Ellis could have used more sleep. Next to arrive was Pussy, who to the chagrin of the tired Doc, Lee, and Ellis, entered singing and dancing.

"Spy, Hewis, spy," she sang to the tune of Fly Robin Fly. "Spy, Hewis, spy. Spy, Hewis, spy. The mascot that will drive."

Behind her entered Angel, shaking his head. She had been singing like this since she had met him that morning to take him to the meeting. He had tried to talk to her about The Book of Stupid and the chalice heating up in his hand, but she kept breaking into song. A tired Doc looked up at Mr. Smurdley and rolled his eyes.

"If she keeps singing, I will smoke," he said.

Mr. Smurdley tried to call the meeting to order. Since everyone had important new information, side conversations kept breaking out. Finally, Mr. Smurdley had to raise his voice, which he normally never had to do.

"We need to get started!" he said forcefully. "We have a lot to do to get prepared for tonight, so let's get it started. You've all already given a full report to Skeeter, Daisy, and me. What I want is a quick summary of what you've done since our last meeting and how it fits into what we need to do during the Angel's last hockey game of the season tonight and the Duck's homestand at the Big Pond this weekend."

He paused for a second and made eye contact with everyone around the table. Then he looked at Pussy Ryder. Since she seemed the most excited, he called on her first so that she would calm down and the meeting could proceed quickly.

"You first, Dr. Ryder," he said to her. "And no singing."

"I've got our driver mascot, and he's willing to work for us," said Pussy. "It's Hewis Lamilton. He's a well-known Grand Prix driver. We spent yesterday together, and he is motivated. He doesn't like how the Grand Prix is being taken over, and he thinks Major Tohtstettor might be behind the disappearance of some drivers."

"Tohtstetttor is the one we got away from last night," said Lee. "He's gonna be all over everybody."

"We've got to keep him off our tails," said Mr. Smurdley.

"That's who we should aim our mascot switch at," said Pussy. "If he thinks people have gotten away from him, he's gonna go crazy when Angel pops up."

"And everyone else will think he's crazy when he tells them their Grand Prix driver is really a duck," said Doc.

"They'll think he's overcooked his rice and gone mushy," said Uncle Ben.

"How do you plan to do this?" Mr. Smurdley asked Pussy.

"Angel can of course be in on it, but I still don't feel comfortable enough for Hewis to know about our operation. Right now it's just him and me, and we're trying to save the Grand Prix."

"So he doesn't know much, just like Bingo," said Mr. Smurdley.

"Bingo knows nothing," said Bobby.

"He knows his name," said Phil.

"Bingo," said Bobby, doing his best Bingo imitation.

Mr. Smurdley saw the conversation digressing, so he gave everyone the stare, which quieted everyone. He called on everyone after Pussy and got their summary. The most significant was Doc, who, despite prompts to keep it to a summary by Mr. Smurdley, explained the vaccine analysis in detail. The chip at the center of the vaccine was not only the smallest microchip ever deployed; it engaged in direct neural stimulation to a level beyond anything previously documented. It could make recipients compliant and obedient to a central authority. This was highlighted by Lee and Ellis reporting that Dick was motivated to run by something he called The Chip, Angel having heard references to The Chip on the airplane, and the rumors that Major Tohtstettor was the enforcer for an entity known as The Chip. Doc further noted that Dick's blood sample revealed the presence of spike proteins that would not only make the brain more susceptible to the mini microchip, it could cause infertility and shorten life spans.

Skeeter and Daisy were the last to report. They told the group that the mini microchip and blood sample were presently undergoing further intensive testing inside the hangar. They were hoping to reverse engineer the spike proteins and chip to deduce their method of production and, hopefully, that could lead them to where they were either being manufactured or stored. Until then, the only way to track the vaccine would be what they could find out during the Grand Prix promotions at the

Duck and Angel games before the actual Grand Prix. Before the meeting adjourned, Mr. Smurdley stood and looked around the room.

"We've got our work cut out for us," he said. "The Ducks and Angels have competed against the best while fighting against the worst for decades, but this is the greatest threat to humanity since the Cowboys stopped the Germans during the Really Big War. We have to stop this vaccine ourselves. Freedom hangs in the balance. Industry, the media, and government are the forces behind this. There's no authority to tell. They're all in on it. We have to destroy it ourselves, no matter the risk."

Pussy walked Angel back to the room down the hall where he had been staying. Besides the couch, he now had a small bed in the corner. The serious way the meeting ended had put a damper on Pussy's singing, and she just sat quietly on the couch next to Angel. Angel picked up his durse from the floor and took out the chalice.

"I tried to tell you about this earlier, but you wouldn't stop singing," he said.

"About the cup?" she asked.

"Yes."

"What about it?"

"It reacts to what I'm thinking," Angel said. "When I think of good people like you and Doc and the people and ducks back home, it feels warm and nice. But, when I think of bad people like Von Farma, it gets hot, burning hot."

"Show me," she said.

"Okay, I have an idea," he said. "You hold the chalice and I'll think of good people and ducks."

He handed her the chalice and started thinking. He thought of the new friends he had made and the old friends back in Monaco. Pussy held on to the chalice. She didn't really feel anything but played along with Angel to humor him.

"I think I feel something," she said.

"Now I'm going to think about Tohtstettor, Von Karen, Temuhoffen, Dummkopffer, and Von Farma."

Pussy dropped the chalice. Her hand was burning. It felt as if the cup was on fire. She looked down at the smoldering cup and checked her hand to make sure it wasn't blistered.

"I've never felt anything like that," she said breathlessly. "The heat, the power, we have to take it somewhere and study it."

"I have to keep it with me," said Angel. "I feel like I need it with me. Like it was meant to be. I remember when Yoduck gave it to me along with the book. He said I was the one."

"Do you want to carry the book with you too?" she asked.

"I can't read it," he said. "I can barely read the summary you made, and that's in English. I'd like to use the computer thing you have to see what it says about things."

"You mean the A.I. program?" she asked.

"Yes, for a book about stupid things, it's kind of smart," he said.

"Ancient words usually are," she said. "A wise man once said that wisdom cuts through time while its winds carry folly."

"We could keep the book here and use your A.I. with it, but I want the cup with me," he said.

"Then we have to give a matching durse and cup to the Grand Prix driver mascot," she said. "You both have to look the same to confuse them. Let me take a picture of the chalice and durse. I'm sure I can get something similar."

For a hockey team that had been eliminated from playoff contention, The Heaven Center was bustling with activity. Between the annual Fan

Appreciation Night and promotion for the upcoming EV Grand Prix and Health Expo, a full crowd was expected despite the team's losing season. All around the Heaven Center arena were signs advertising the Grand Prix. The path from the train station to Heaven Center Arena as well as the path from the train station to The Big Pond stadium was lined with advertisements.

Inside The Heaven Center, everyone was taking their places for the big night. Phil and Bobby were in the locker room getting dressed for their last game of the season. It wouldn't be easy competing at the top professional level while the fate of the world hung in the balance, but fortunately they were playing a Canadian team again, so it wouldn't be that difficult of a game. In professional hockey, playing a Canadian team is almost considered a bye as no Canadian team has won a Stanley Cup in over three decades, with teams from such winter wonderlands as Southern California, Florida, and Las Vegas winning ten cups over that period. Since becoming woke, Canada has sucked at hockey, but it wasn't like no one saw it coming. The name Toronto comes from the Mohawk word to-choke-o, which translates to disappointment on ice. The one thing that could make the play rough for Phil and Bobby was that instead of Toronto, they were playing Calgary, which, like their previous opponent Montreal, doesn't really want to be in Canada and could have an attitude. That means throwing hands instead of looking for a safe space like the Vancouver team would do.

Angel waited with a napping Doc in the x-ray room adjacent to the locker room. He was being kept ready in case there was an opportunity to switch him with the Grand Prix driver acting as mascot. Doc was just trying to get some shut-eye after his long night analyzing the chip and blood sample taken from Dick. As he watched Doc sleep with an unlit cigarette in his mouth, Angel stared into his durse at the chalice, trying to think of anyone or anything that might heat it up. Pussy had provided a pretty close recreation of the durse for Hewis Lamilton to carry around during his mascot duties. He knew that Hewis, Pussy, Mr. Smurdley, and of course Bingo would be meeting with Dummkopffer and the rest in the VIP suite. While he waited, he tried not to dwell on anything that might affect the chalice.

In the VIP suite, Mr. Smurdley, Pussy, and Hewis waited for Bingo to bring Dummkopffer and the rest to the suite to begin the festivities. Hewis was dressed up in an Angel Duck dual mascot costume created to look like Angel. Skeeter and Daisy had been in and out of the suite all day. They were working behind the scenes to make sure all the logistics regarding the promotion were running smoothly in addition to gathering any intelligence that might uncover the vaccine and mini-microchips' whereabouts. As such, they would not be officially introduced to Dummkopffer and were blending in as common Heaven Center staff.

The suite was impressive, as are the main VIP suites for professional sports teams. It could hold over one-hundred and had separate areas for dining, meeting, relaxing, and viewing the game high above center ice. The dining area featured an extravagant buffet.

"Are you ready for your big debut?" Pussy asked Hewis.

"Yes, I'm ready," said Hewis.

"You're not too hot in there, are you?" asked Mr. Smurdley. "I know you've got your racing suit on under the Angel Duck costume so we can promote the Grand Prix."

"I'm fine," said Hewis. "The ice keeps things cool in this place."

Daisy came into the suite to announce that everyone was coming and then stepped back out. Seconds later, Bingo opened the suite door with a large crowd visible behind him.

"Heeeeeeere's Bingo!" he shouted as he held the door open for an enthusiastic crowd that filled the entire suite. At the front were Schultz Dummkopffer, Karen Von Karen, Shein Temuhoffen, Baron Von Farma, Mayor Cubana Nero, and Governor Craven Gettyoyl. As Pussy introduced the group to Mr. Smurdley, local news crews and assorted national media had the cameras out and were taking it all in. Every celebrity and politician longing for face time was basking in the moment's energy. It was not until the ANGELS ON ICE pregame ice skating show started and people quieted down to watch through the suite's window wall overlooking the ice that they could even hear each other speak.

"It's an honor to meet you, Mr. Smurdley," said Governor Gettyoyl. "California is proud of its sports teams."

"The honor is mine, Governor Gettyoyl," said Mr. Smurdley.

"Soon to be President Gettyoyl," said Mayor Nero.

"My commitment is to the people of California," said Governor Gettyoyl. "I wouldn't run unless I was sure the state was in expert hands."

"I could take over your job," said Mayor Nero.

"You've got the hot hand," said Governor Gettyoyl. "Maybe I should run for president. We can make that big announcement at the Grand Prix."

"Bingo," said Bingo.

"You would be a great global president," said Von Karen. "So much better than the non-collective there now. You would have the world's media behind you."

"And the global economic collective," said Temuhoffen.

"So you're both moving up," said Mr. Smurdley.

"Like a pyramid scheme," said Governor Gettyoyl.

"Of course, you've both done so many great things," said Pussy, trying not to throw up in her mouth.

"We'll be aligned in our vision," said Von Farma.

"And the vaccine will put everyone on the same page, so to speak," said Von Karen.

"Yes, Governor, I mean soon to be President Gettyoyl," said Dummkopffer. "Many of your policies align with the climate policies of the Grand Prix. Such as electric vehicle racing."

"A Gettyoyl Administration will bring an end to fossil fuels," said the Governor. "No more gas cars."

"Speaking of cars," said Pussy. "Is everyone ready to be introduced along with our driver mascot between the periods?"

"More than ready," said Dummkopffer. "To lead the people."

"It's like their ships have come in," laughed Temuhoffen.

Dummkopffer, Von Karen, Von Farma, Mayor Nero, and Governor Gettyoyl laughed along with him. Pussy glanced at Hewis and then at Mr. Smurdley. She felt that there was something cryptic in Temuhoffen's inside joke, but she wasn't sure what.

"Please help yourselves to some food," said Mr. Smurdley, pointing out the extravagant buffet set up in the suite.

"Sounds great," said Mayor Nero. "What politician doesn't want to feed at the trough?"

Dummkopffer, Von Karen, Von Farma, Nero, and Gettyoyl made a bee-line for the buffet. Pussy guessed that Mayor Nero and Governor Gettyoyl probably had rubber pockets so they could steal soup. She waited until everyone was out of earshot before she spoke to Mr. Smurdley and Hewis.

"What do you think he meant by ship coming in?" she asked.

"Since we're not in on the joke, maybe we should take it as a clue," said Mr. Smurdley. "I'll run it past Skeeter and Daisy and see what they think. I've got to touch bases with them right now."

Mr. Smurdley went in search of Skeeter and Daisy. This left Pussy and Hewis alone, but it wasn't for long. Within seconds, Major Tohtstettor and his two Aryan Hugo Boss poster boys were standing right in front of them.

"You two seem to spend a lot of time together," Major Tohtstettor told them.

"This is Hewis Lamilton, the Grand Prix driver and Angel Duck mascot for the promotion," she said, pointing to Hewis. "I'm Dr. Pussy Ryder, the promotion coordinator."

"I know who you are," Major Tohtstettor said. "I am Heinrich Tohtstettor in charge of security, and I don't think I like this relationship."

"Well, I don't think I like yours," countered Pussy. "Oh, that's right; you don't have any relationships. Never mind."

"I don't think you are funny," said Tohtstettor. "You know why I don't have a sense of humor?"

"You're German?" said Pussy.

"I don't have a sense of humor because I'm watching everyone, especially you," said Tohtstettor.

With that, Tohtstettor left the suite with his two Hugo Boss-clad henchmen, staring several guests up and down on the way out. Pussy looked at Hewis quizzically.

"What was that about?" Pussy asked Hewis.

"He does that to everyone," said Hewis. "All the drivers hate him. It just makes me want to help you even more. Especially since they want to go all-electric. It will ruin the Grand Prix. Look at me. If I weren't a Grand Prix driver, I'd just be a little man with nothing going for him."

"I think you'd be great at anything," said Pussy. "You beat me at basketball."

"I wouldn't be surprised if he and his goons were watching us play," said Hewis. "That guy is everywhere. Do you think if Mr. Smurdley complained about him to Dummkopffer and the rest, Tohtstettor would back off?"

"It might arouse their suspicions," said Pussy. "We need to discredit Tohtstettor first."

"How would we do that?" asked Hewis.

"I have a plan," Pussy said. "Follow me."

Pussy led Hewis through the Heaven Center to the Angels' locker room. The attendant recognized her and nodded when she asked if Doc was inside. She asked Hewis to wait outside for a moment while she talked to Doc. Pussy went inside the locker room and walked through the now empty locker room to the adjoining x-ray room. The locker room was empty because the team had gone out on the ice when the Angels on Ice pregame show had ended. Inside the X-ray room she found Doc and Angel.

"We need to do something about Tohtstettor," she said.

"Did he approach you?" asked Doc.

"He came on pretty strong," said Pussy.

"He's been making the rounds," Doc said. "He and his goons were shadowing Daisy and Skeeter. Uncle Ben put Lee and Ellis on the injured list for the Ducks homestand so their pictures won't be in the program in case Tohtstettor recognizes them."

"I've got our other mascot outside," said Pussy. "He thinks if Mr. Smurdley complains to Dummkopffer and the rest, they'll tell him to back him off, but I think we need to discredit Tohtstettor first."

"I agree," Doc said. "I know how the Germans work. Dummkopffer and the rest don't give Tohtstettor orders; he has the power of life and death over them and gives them the orders. His orders come directly from this chip thing we've heard about that's behind everything. Until those above

Tohtstettor lose confidence in him, even Mr. Smurdley's complaints won't have an effect."

"That's right," said Angel. "He blew smoke in their faces. He's the enforcer of whoever or whatever is behind this."

"And we need to take him down quickly," said Doc. "This isn't our first rodeo with the Germans. It won't be long before he figures out our cover."

"Then we need to make the mascot switch now," Pussy said.

Together, they decided on a plan. During the intermission between the second and third periods, Hewis was supposed to be introduced as the new Angel Duck Mascot along with Dummkopffer, Mayor Nero, and Governor Gettyoyl. After being introduced as the new mascot, Hewis was supposed to rip off his Angel Duck costume, revealing himself as a Grand Prix driver to start the Grand Prix Promotion. They would try to get Tohtstettor alone and have Angel confront him about trying to kill him at Casino Royale. Angel would run away toward where Hewis was being introduced during the intermission. On the way to the rink, someone would help hide Angel, and Tohtstettor would look like a fool when he tried to apprehend Hewis in front of the Mayor and Governor.

"Is the Grand Prix driver gonna know about this?" asked Angel.

"We can't tell him," said Pussy. "He thinks he's helping to save the Grand Prix from Tohtstettor and the rest. I feel terrible about not being fully truthful with him, but I can't be. It's too dangerous. He doesn't even know about Angel."

"What's he gonna think when Tohtstettor grabs him and says he's really a duck?" asked Doc.

"He'll think Tohtstettor's a nut, we all do," Angel said.

"Angel's got a point," said Doc, lighting up a cigarette.

"I'll work on a way to get Tohtstettor away from his goons," said Pussy. "In the meantime, just keep out of sight here until I need you."

"You got it," said Doc. "I just hope none of the players get injured and need me."

Pussy left the locker room and walked down near the ice. Along the way, she ran into Skeeter and Daisy. After making sure Tohtstettor and his goons weren't around, she filled them in on her mascot plan, and they looked for an opportunity to get Tohtstettor on his own. When she saw Tohtstettor coming toward the three of them, she suddenly got an idea.

"Tohtstettor's coming," she whispered to Skeeter and Daisy. "Play along with me. I'm gonna make a scene. If he thinks we'll turn against each other, he'll try to exploit that and maybe talk alone."

Pussy suddenly looked at Skeeter with pure hatred. She waited until Major Tohtstettor was almost upon them. Then she pointed at Daisy and began screaming at Skeeter.

"Is it her or me?" she wailed.

"What?" said Skeeter.

"I thought you were with me," Pussy continued yelling. "Not this ugmo ho!"

"Back off, skank witch!" Daisy growled, picking up on Pussy's cue. "Get your own man!"

"You're gonna do me like this, after you did me like that?" Pussy roared.

"If he did you, it was in your dreams," said Daisy. "We'll leave this nightmare to her dreams!"

Daisy grabbed Skeeter by the arm and dragged him away. Pussy stood there pretending to sob uncontrollably, hoping that Major Tohtstettor bought her act. She felt a gentle tap on her shoulder.

"Why so upset?" Tohtstettor said. "I apologize if I upset you earlier."

"It isn't you; it's something else," she said.

"Maybe I can be of help," he said.

"It's okay," she said. "I just hate them so much. I just want revenge."

"I think I can be of help," he said. "Sometimes those you thought were friends are really enemies, and those you thought were enemies are really friends."

"Things are not always as they seem, that's for sure," she said.

"I could tell you stories," he said.

"No, I could tell you stories."

"Then do."

"Not now," she said. "I need a bit to collect my thoughts. I'll meet you at the beginning of the second intermission at the top of Section 207. Just us. I have some things to tell you."

"I'll be there, just us," Tohtstettor said. "You'll be surprised who your friends really are."

Pussy turned and headed straight for the ladies' room. If she had been hoping to be alone, she was out of luck. Like most arenas, there was a line to get into the ladies' room. In the end Pussy used that to her advantage, figuring she could get lost in the crowd in front of the ladies' room and not be spotted by Tohtstettor's henchmen while she called Doc and arranged for Angel to be in position for her meeting with Tohtstettor. During the call, she also told Doc to discreetly inform Mr. Smurdley, Skeeter and Daisy about what was about to go down. Once she got out of the ladies' room, she wandered around the Heaven Center pretending to sob.

On the ice, they were midway through the second period of a large fight sporadically interrupted by a hockey game. The Angels were in a bad mood about missing the playoffs again, and Calgary was in a bad mood because, like every other Canadian team, they would soon be swept out of the playoffs by a warm-weather American team. Bobby and Phil were racking up the penalty minutes, but sitting in the penalty box was their first chance to relax since Angel came into their lives. So far, the game was a scoreless tie as the players seemed more interested in finding the penalty box than the net.

Pussy waited until there was less than a minute left in the second period before starting toward section 207. About a hundred feet from the meeting spot with Tohtstettor, she found an empty seat and tried to blend in. She did not want to be spotted by Tohtstettor until Hewis was on the ice with Mayor Nero and Governor Gettyoyl to kick off the Grand Prix Health Fair Promotion.

When the period ended, Pussy noticed a commotion at the Angel team bench. Most of the players had left the ice for the locker room at the end of the period, but Doc and another player were there with a gurney and were attending to a player who appeared to have taken ill. Looking closer it appeared that the stricken player was Bobby and Phil was with Doc trying to get him on the gurney while staying out of the way of The Mayor, Governor, and the costumed Hewis who were being led past the Angel bench onto a carpet that had been unfurled on the ice. Mayor Nero, Governor Gettyoyl and Hewis managed to get out onto the ice where they were to be introduced to the crowd by Bingo, who was waiting for them.

Just then, Pussy noticed Major Tohtstettor arriving at the top of section 207. He was alone as agreed upon. Pussy got up and rushed over to meet him. As she got within ten feet of Major Tohtstettor, seemingly out of nowhere, Angel appeared and punched Major Tohtstettor hard in the thigh.

"Burn in hell, Tohtstettor!" Angel screamed.

"You!" Tohtstettor screamed, recognizing Angel from Casino Royale. "I should have killed you myself!"

Tohtstettor rushed at Angel, and Angel ran away down the steps toward the Angels' bench, where Doc and Phil had just loaded Bobby on the gurney and were trying to take him to the top of section 207. Behind them on the ice, Bingo had just introduced Hewis in his Angel Duck costume as the new duel mascot of both the Angels and Ducks and Hewis was about to emerge from the Angel Duck costume in his racing suit to promote the Grand Prix and Health Fair. With Major Tohtstettor in hot pursuit, Angel dove under the gurney to evade him. When Tohtstettor tried to push the gurney aside to find where Angel had gone, Phil punched him, knocking him down.

"We've got an injured player here!" Phil yelled.

Tohtstettor shook it off, got up and ran around the gurney. He looked down and saw a large duck in the rink next to a man with a microphone. His blood boiled. He rushed onto the ice, and to the shock of the crowd, tackled the duck. As he tried to bodyslam the duck, a small man in a racing suit flew out of the costume and fell to the ice. When Major Tohtstettor stood there holding a mascot costume above him and with a battered Grand Prix driver below him, the deathly silent crowd booed. As the crowd booed louder and louder, Bingo looked up at them and pointed.

"Bingo," he said.

The boos of the intermission did not give way to third period cheers. The uninspired play of both teams was enough to get the crowd chanting "meh." When Calgary lost on a fluke goal at the end of the period, it just looked like they were just starting the Lord Stanley maple syrup playoff choke early.

Angel and Doc had waited out the third period together in the X-ray room. After getting Pussy's phone call, Doc had gotten word for Bobby to feign illness while he smuggled Angel into section 207 with the help of Skeeter and Daisy. After Angel dove under the gurney while Tohtstettor was chasing him, Bobby pulled him back under the gurney mattress hiding him. Tohtstettor then mistook Hewis Lamilton in the Angel Duck costume for Angel and pummelled him. It had all gone according to plan.

With the disgraced Tohtstettor detained by Heaven Center Security and Mr. Smurdley having called an emergency meeting with Dumkopffer, Von Farma, and the rest to discuss his concerns about Tohtstettor, all the conspirators were able to slink away at the game's end. Pussy left with Hewis to console him, Bobby and Phil showered and left with the rest of the team, and Skeeter and Daisy left with Mr. Smurdley after his emergency meeting. The Angels' season was over, but there was little time to rest. The Grand Prix Health Fair promotion would continue throughout the Ducks homestand and the Grand Prix Health Fair itself was soon to follow.

The next morning, Angel was awakened by Pussy in his room. She came in singing something about Tohtstettor getting his comeuppance, but Angel was too groggy to follow the words. He got out of his bedding, sat down on the couch, picked up his durse, and stared at the book and chalice inside.

"It must have felt good to hit Tohstettor last night," said Pussy. "It was good to knock him down a notch."

"Do you think they'll get rid of him?" asked Angel.

"Not yet," Pussy replied. "Remember, he's still the one in charge."

"Even after Mr. Smurdley complained?" said Angel. "Doc told me Mr. Smurdley had an emergency meeting with Dummkoppfer and the others after the game."

"Mr. Smurdley told me he thinks Tohtstettor is still the one relaying The Chip's orders to everyone else," said Pussy. "He also thinks Mayor Nero and Governor Gettyoyl are part of the plot. Only the ones giving Tohtstettor his orders can get rid of him, and we can't find where they're hiding everything with Tohtstettor on our tail."

"So what do we do next?" asked Angel.

"We have to knock down Tohtstettor again," said Pussy.

"What do we do?" asked Angel.

"I'm sure he'll approach me at the baseball game tonight," she said. "Let's see if he falls for the same trick again."

"I'd rather burn him with this," Angel said, taking the chalice out of the durse.

"Maybe you'll have a chance later," she said.

"I'll make sure I have it the next time we see Tohtstettor," Angel said. "I'd also like to use your A.I. with the book. Maybe it can help?"

"I'd like to do that, but we have to get ready for the game tonight," she said.

Pussy waited with Angel until Bobby and Phil arrived to take him over to The Big Pond for the Duck's baseball game. Since the hockey season was over, they were free to help in whichever way they could. There was a team shuttle that ran between The Heaven Center and The Big Pond, so Phil and Bobby used that to transport Angel, but they still had to put him in the duffel bag for the trip to keep him hidden. They waited until they got to the X-ray room, which, like the X-ray room in The Heaven Center, was also next to the locker room, before letting the duck out of the bag.

"I guess we both got a chance to punch Tohtstettor last night," said Phil.

"I would have liked to have got him with this," Angel said as he pulled the chalice from his durse.

"That looks ancient," Bobby said. "Where did you get it?"

"The elders gave it to me when I left Monaco," said Angel. "It has special powers."

"Sure it does," laughed Phil.

"No, really," said Angel.

Just then, Doc walked into the X-ray room with Uncle Ben. Each was carrying a medium-sized suitcase, which they set down just inside the doorway. Doc opened a medical supply cabinet and took out a carton of

Chesterfields while Uncle Ben walked over to Phil and Bobby and put his hand on each of their shoulders.

"Ready to play baseball now?" Uncle Ben asked them. "We're short-handed. I'm down two pitchers."

"Our season just ended. I haven't touched a ball in months," said Phil.

"Ahhhh, take one for the team," said Uncle Ben.

"Sorry, Charlie," said Bobby. "I've been taking one for the team since the duck showed up."

"Why isn't the duck practicing driving?" Uncle Ben asked. "If he has to drive, he'll wind up crispier than Peking duck! Haiyaa!"

"Calm down, Uncle Ben," said Doc after he got a cigarette out of the carton. "Until we get rid of Tohtstettor, Angel is gonna be too busy for anything else."

Doc opened one suitcase and started putting things away. Uncle Ben opened the suitcase he brought in and did the same thing. Bobby and Phil watched them, unsure if they needed to help.

"What's with all the new stuff?" asked Bobby.

"We're moving our operation over here," said Doc. "Now that hockey season is over, they've got concerts scheduled at the Heaven Center."

"Haiyaa!" Uncle Ben cried. "Asian gangsta rap concert tonight. Don't mess with Wong; he has a 4.9 GPA. What's your crib, bro? Stanford Piru! Take cover! Drive by calculus! Do you bang? No, I sing SHE BANG, SHE BANG!"

"Do you need any help setting up?" Phil asked, trying to ignore Uncle Ben's rant.

"No," said Doc. "You just stay ready to help Pussy. I just heard from her. Tohtstettor is on the warpath. He and his goons have been harassing everyone. She's afraid he might scare off our other mascot."

"After he tackled him?" asked Phil. "I figure that would make him want to help us more. "

"But he doesn't know about us," said Doc. "He thinks he's saving the Grand Prix from completely ditching fossil fuels. When he finds out we haven't been straight with him, he could turn against us."

"To think I was looking forward to a vacation when the season ended," mused Bobby.

The sun was just setting when the pregame festivities began. Though Mayor Nero, Governor Gettyoyl, and other dignitaries were on the field, and there were dozens of signs throughout the stadium advertising the Grand Prix and Health Fair, the pregame festivities were devoted to Diversity, Inclusion, and Equity. It's also known as D.I.E. This was at the insistence of both Mayor Nero and Governor Gettyoyl, who had made it a centerpiece of both their administrations.

To start things off, Mayor Nero introduced the deaf singer, who performed the Black National Anthem in sign language accompanied by a morbidly obese man in a rainbow tutu who did an interpretive dance of the song or lack thereof. Governor Gettyoyl then introduced the ceremonial running of the bases by the legless migrant children where, even though he generously gave them a head start, he was able to beat them to home plate and win the trophy. However, he did break off a small piece of the trophy and gave it to the children, except for the 13% that had to be withheld for California state income tax. Finally, to cap things off, both Mayor Nero and Governor Gettyoyl selected one of the legless children who also had no arms to throw out the first pitch.

As the game started, Pussy stood in the outfield section overlooking the tunnel and bullpen. She thought it would be the easiest place to be spotted if Tohtstettor was looking for her. It was also convenient that there was a promotion during the seventh-inning stretch. Hewis, dressed up in the Angel Duck costume would drive out of the tunnel next to the bullpen in a Grand Prix car and circle the bases while Mayor Nero, Governor Gettyoyl, Schultz Dummkopffer, and Bingo got the crowd excited about the upcoming Newport Grand Prix and Health Fair. As she stood there looking out onto the field, a brilliant idea popped into her head.

She walked down the steps to an open seat, crouched down to be out of view, called Doc and told him to get Angel ready.

She walked back up the steps to the walkway above the section and stood looking over the railing, making sure no one was around her so she would be more visible. It wasn't long before she saw Tohtstettor and his Hugo Boss-clad henchmen approaching. This time she was not going to wait for him to come to her. She walked straight toward him with a scowl on her face, not even looking at the two goons that flanked him.

"Are you crazy?" she yelled. "You attacked a mascot. You should be locked up right now."

"You pulled a fast one," snorted Tohtstettor. "Where is the real duck?"

"The real duck?" asked Pussy, pretending to be shocked.

"The real duck that talks," said Tohtstettor.

"The real duck that talks?" Pussy asked mockingly.

"The one that was at the Casino Royale!" Tohtstettor shouted.

"A talking duck you saw in a casino?" She asked, glancing at his henchmen. "Are you on drugs?"

"Don't play games with me," said Tohtstettor. "He is here and I will find him."

"Listen to me," she told Tohtstettor. "Ducks don't talk. Ducks don't gamble in casinos. And I don't work with crazy people. You have one chance left. I have some big information. If you want to hear it, you'd better be in the tunnel next to the bullpen. I've got to be there getting the Grand Prix driver ready for the seventh-inning presentation. Be there alone, apologize to the driver, and drop the crazy or I have nothing to say to you."

With that, she turned from Tohtstettor and walked away. She knew that Tohtstettor and his henchmen would not force her to come with them in a crowded stadium. She just hoped her supposed information would still tempt Tohtstettor enough to show up alone in the tunnel next to the bullpen.

She was familiar enough with the stadium to disappear into one of the maintenance rooms and use a service elevator to make it to a storage room underneath the grandstands on the other side of the tunnel from the bullpen. In it were Uncle Ben and Hewis, who were waiting for Pussy to bring them out to the tunnel for the seventh inning.

"Look who's finally here," said Uncle Ben as Pussy came into the room.

"Did you see Tohtstettor out there?" asked Hewis.

"Yes, I told him to apologize to you," said Pussy.

"That will be the day," said Hewis.

"I think we can knock him down again, and maybe even knock him out this time," said Pussy.

"I'm up for it," said Hewis.

"Good," said Pussy. "We'll be using a decoy duck."

When the seventh inning started, Doc, Angel, Uncle Ben, Pussy, and Hewis took up their positions in the tunnel near the bullpen. Hewis was dressed up in the mascot costume and sitting in the Grand Prix car waiting to drive the car out onto the field and get out dressed as the Angel Duck after the Mayor and Governor had officially invited the crowd to come to The Grand Prix and Health Fair the following weekend. Uncle Ben, who was supposed to drive the Grand Prix car back to the tunnel, was distracted by his starting pitcher's velocity and getting what few pitchers he had available ready in the bullpen.

"Haiyaa, his pitches have no MSG!" Uncle Ben yelled at the bullpen as he got in the Grand Prix car. "Get someone ready."

The Ducks pitcher got the side out, but not before two more runs scored. When the players cleared the field, Bingo introduced Dumfopffer, Mayor Nero, and Governor Gettyoyl, who all said a few words and then a few more and a few more and a few more. While they were talking and talking and talking, Major Tohtstettor approached Pussy who was waiting for him in the tunnel. Before he got close, Doc tripped him from behind, and when he fell, Angel, who had been hiding with Doc, ran up and kicked Tohtstettor in the head.

"You tried to kill me, now I'm here to kill you!" Angel cried as he kicked Tohtstettor a second time.

"I will kill you if it's the last thing I do!" Tohtstettor yelled back.

Tohtstetttor got to his feet and lunged at Angel, who dodged him and ran away from Tohtstettor. As he ran down the tunnel toward the field, he saw that Tohtstettor's henchmen were blocking the access to the field and felt that Tohtstettor was gaining on him. He ran past the Grand Prix car that was preparing to drive out onto the field and took a quick turn in front of it and looked back at Tothstettor. He had the Grand Prix car between him and Tohtstettor, but Tohtstettor was onto his maneuver. Tohtstettor stopped chasing Angel and stood behind the Grand Prix car to block Angel's path back to the grandstands. Tohtstettor motioned for his henchmen to close on Angel with the younger looking henchman in a black Hugo suit and Hugo sunglasses approaching on one side of the Grand Prix car and the older looking henchman in a black Boss suit and black Boss sunglasses approaching on the other. Angel appeared trapped, but as they were almost upon him, the Grand Prix car door opened and

Angel jumped in. The Grand Prix car drove through the tunnel onto the field, nearly running over Tohtstetter's henchmen, who leapt aside at the last millisecond.

The car raced across left field toward home plate, where Governor Gettyoyl was trying to awaken the crowd he had put to sleep. The Grand Prix car slowed as it came to home plate and circled the bases. As it did, Governor Gettyoyl pointed to it and then to the scoreboard, which was advertising the Newport Beach Grand Prix and Health Fair. "Electric vehicles and mandatory vaccines!" he shouted. "Whether you like it or not, it is the future!"

After circling the bases a few times, the Grand Prix car drove to center field and started doing donuts. Tohtstettor and his henchmen, who had followed the car out onto the field, approached cautiously. After about ten donuts, the car came to a stop, and the Angel Duck mascot got out and started dancing for the crowd while the PA system blared out "Stayin' Alive" by the Bee Gees. As he danced, the Grand Prix car seemed to drive itself back to the bullpen tunnel while Tohtstettor and his henchmen closed in on him. By the time the Angel Duck mascot noticed Tohtstettor, it was too late. Tohtstettor threw him to the ground, and his henchmen joined in the pummeling, drawing boos from the crowd. Just like before, Hewis' costume was ripped off, revealing him in his race suit. Seeing that he was once again a Grand Prix driver, Tohtstettor and his henchmen stopped the pummeling only to be tackled by security themselves.

Once again, Mr. Smurdley called an emergency meeting with Dummkopffer, Von Karen, and the rest to press for Tohtstettor's removal, and this time things were different. Because it was the second time Tohtstettor had assaulted a mascot at a pro sports game, and the argument could not be made that Tohtstettor thought he was thwarting an attack on the mayor and governor. Dummkopffer and Von Karen informed Mr.

Smurdley that their superiors had instructed them to remove Tohtstettor and coordinate with the team's security for the duration of the promotion. They also told him they were working on a deal with the district attorney for the assault charges to be dropped against Tohtstettor in exchange for their cooperation to deport him back to Germany.

Now that Tohtstettor was out of the way, Pussy, Skeeter, Daisy, and Mr. Smurdley felt more emboldened to get more information about the location of the vaccine and the drones and robots that were to dispense it. Pussy accompanied Hewis to every Grand Prix driver practice and promotion. When the Grand Prix cars were unattended, Doc would scan them for microchips. Mr. Smurdley even pretended to be interested in investing in the vaccine and asked to see how and where it was produced. Everyone else took turns following Dummkopffer and any dignitaries he brought to the Ducks games during the homestand. Each night the mayor and governor made their speeches, and Hewis drove the Grand Prix car around the field, got out, and danced.

Though the team was playing well and the promotion was going smoothly, when the home stand ended they still did not know the location of the vaccine or the robots and drones. To make matters worse, Von Farma and Temuhoffen had dropped out of sight. Especially painful for Angel, they did not know where the slave labor, including Kurri, that was producing everything was located. With only a few days until the Grand Prix, Mr. Smurdley made a decision. Lee and Ellis would go back to Lido Isle, but this time they would bring Phil and Bobby, burglary tools, and night vision equipment. If they couldn't bluff their way into the factories they thought might be secretly working under black light, they would break in and sabotage what they could. In addition, everyone was to meet in secret the next day to plan what to do if the vaccine, drones, and robots could not be found before the event.

Pussy did not have to wait until the meeting to find out what Lee, Ellis, Phil and Bobby found when they went back to Lido Isle. Mr. Smurdley called her early that morning as soon as he had heard from Bobby. The Bot Spot had been damaged by fire the night before and was closed. The tunnels had been blocked off, and when they broke into the factories they thought were working under black light, they found them empty. Mr. Smurdley figured that they knew someone was onto their plans, had covered their tracks, and that it was now a dead end. There was nothing there anymore. Mr. Smurdley said he was considering sinking the pontoon bridges in case that was how they planned to move the vaccine, drones and robots during the Grand Prix.

While talking to Mr. Smurdley, Pussy had a crazy idea. She decided to see Major Tohtstettor. Since he was still in jail awaiting deportation, he would not be hard to find, and if she said she was there to tell Tohtstettor that Hewis Lamilton had forgiven him, she had the perfect cover. Mr. Smurdley agreed it was worth a shot, so Pussy headed straight over to the Anaheim Detention Center. She didn't need a reservation; she was a doctor after all.

Pussy went through an abbreviated security screening after showing her Ducks and Angels credentials, and someone led her into a small room with a few folding chairs. A couple of minutes later, two deputies escorted Major Tohtstettor into the room and then left.

"Have you come to gloat?" Tohtstettor asked.

"I've come to extend an olive branch," said Pussy. "I wanted to let you know that the Grand Prix driver forgives you. He understands you were under a lot of stress and may have been seeing things."

"In Germany we would say so ein Schwachsinn," said Tohtstettor.

"What's that mean?" asked Pussy.

"It means that's bullshit," said Tohtstettor. "You and I both know I wasn't seeing things. The talking duck from Monaco is here. You know what is going to happen."

"Tell me what you think will happen," said Pussy.

"So ein Schwachsinn," Tohtstettor said again. "Like you don't know what is going to happen. All of you are such contradictions. So goody, goody. So dedicated to fighting evil, but always lying through your teeth. I'm the one on the side of evil, but I'm truthful, and you think you're going to fight evil by standing there and lying to me."

"I'm not going to stand here and lie to you," she said. "Let's sit down."

She sat down on one of the folding chairs in the room. She motioned to the one next to her.

He sat down in the folding chair next to her and shrugged his shoulders.

"I'll be honest with you," she said. "But first you need to be honest with yourself."

"Honest with myself?"

"Yes, how can you claim to be honest with everyone else when you're not honest with yourself?"

"What are you getting at?" he asked.

"What do you think will happen when you get deported back to Germany?" Pussy said. "Are you expecting a parade? They'll kill you the minute you get there."

"They will not. There is loyalty," he said.

"You'll be dead before you can say Ernst Rohm," said Pussy. "You don't care who leads. The Fuhrer was an Austrian, the Kaiser was Queen Victoria's grandson, and who knows who or what The Chip is. The point is, you just want to be the baddies and look stylish doing it. Deep down you're all barbarians and you want to act like barbarians but in an orderly fashion. You want to be brutes in Hugo Boss suits, wearing jackboots, and a Mercedes-Benz Glashütte watch."

"There is nothing wrong with being stylish," he said.

"Karl Lagerfeld had a really stylish coffin," she said. "After they're done with you, there won't be much left to put in one."

"What can you do for me?" asked Tohtstettor.

"Von Karen has control of the politicians, but I am a doctor," she said. "We can delay the deportation for a psychiatric evaluation. If you tell them you attacked a talking duck, they'll give you psychological treatment before deporting you. You can walk away from the clinic and find a new leader to be a stylish baddie for."

"And what do you want from me?" asked Tohtstettor.

"Where's the vaccine, drones, and robots?" she said.

"How do I know you'll do your part?"

"I'm a goody, goody, remember?"

"And I'm a baddie."

"But a stylish one."

"Maybe we'll go up against each other again in the future?"

"I can't wait," she said. "Now where's the vaccine?"

Inside the Heaven Center, everyone except Pussy was assembled in the same meeting room where they had met before. Lee and Ellis had just told them about how Lido Isle had been scrubbed of any trace of activity surrounding the vaccine or robots and how none of the gamers, even ones they remembered from when Dick got vaccinated, could remember a thing. No one even remembered Dick, who had vanished. With no new information about the location of the vaccine or robotics and time running out, Mr. Smurdley announced his decision to Lee, Ellis, Bobby, Skeeter, Uncle Ben, Doc, Daisy and Skeeter.

"The Grand Prix and Health Fair are just a couple of days away, and the consequences of people getting that vaccine will be catastrophic," Mr. Smurdley began. "Not just for those getting the vaccine, it is catastrophic for the entire country and even the world. And those perpetrating this monstrosity have control of the media and political establishment. We can't warn the authorities; they're part of it. If we can't destroy the vaccine and everything else before the Grand Prix, we have to prevent them from getting it to the Grand Prix site. For decades, the Angels and Ducks have fought the forces of evil to stop destruction. Now, to save the world as we know it, we're being forced to resort to destruction. I see no alternative but to sink the pontoon bridges and make Balboa Boulevard impassable."

Mr. Smurdley sighed and looked over at Skeeter and Daisy. They looked at each other and motioned for the other to go first. For the first time, they were not competing with each other. Finally, Daisy decided to go first. She clicked on her computer, and an image of Newport Beach Bay appeared on the wall that showed the Newport Beach Grand Prix race course and the newly built pontoon bridges.

"I hate to say it," said Daisy, "but there is no way to do this without a hell of a lot of explosives."

"I'm not sure if I can do this," said Ellis. "If something went wrong, innocent people could die."

"The alternative is doomsday," said Doc.

"There's got to be the FBI or Army to go to," said Ellis.

"There's nobody else; we're just like the Cowboys!" Doc yelled back.

Just then, there was a knock on the door, and it opened. It was Pussy Ryder. She bounded into the room excitedly singing, "Whoomp there it is, whoomp there it is."

"I've been trying to call you," said Mr. Smurdley. "Why haven't you answered?"

"I didn't want to use my phone," she said. "I didn't want to be tracked. As a mattter of fact, I even showed my doctor I.D. at the jail so there would be no record of me signing in there. Tohtstettor told me everything."

"Everything?" asked Doc.

"Everything," she said.

"Where's the vaccine?" asked Mr. Smurdley.

"On the ship," she said.

"What ship?"

"The hospital ship," said Pussy. "There's a large hospital ship next to the Emmy oil platform off Huntington Beach. They figured someone was on to what was going on at Lido Isle, so they moved everything there. The vaccine, the drones, the robots, and the slave labor. Everything is on that ship."

"On a hospital ship?" asked Skeeter.

"It's not really a hospital ship," said Pussy. "It's just going to look like a hospital ship."

"Is Kurri on the ship?" Angel asked excitedly.

"There's a good chance," said Pussy. "Everything is being done there from the vaccine to the bots."

"They can't get a ship that big into Newport Beach Bay; the channel isn't big enough," said Doc.

"That's why they put ramps in for the jump between Balboa Island and Corona del Mar," said Pussy. "It gave them an excuse to dredge it out so a big ship could get through there."

"What about the pontoon bridges?" asked Mr. Smurdley.

"Those aren't for moving the vaccine and bots," said Pussy. "The pontoon bridges are to hold spectators. No one can get off those bridges without being vaccinated."

"Unless they swim," said Bobby, "which they can't because of the sharks."

"Why would he tell you this?" asked Uncle Ben.

"We made a deal," said Pussy. "He knows if he gets deported back to Germany he's a dead man, but I swung a mental health hold until after the Grand Prix and some time in an institution. He can probably get away from the institution, but he'll be locked up pretty tight until after the Grand Prix with no visitors."

"How much did you tell him about us?" asked Mr. Smurdley.

"Nothing," she said. "He has his suspicions, but I confirmed nothing. Oh, and there's the biggest thing."

"What's that?" asked Daisy.

"The Chip is on the ship," she said.

"Is this another one of your rhymes?" asked Uncle Ben. "Please don't sing; you sing like Rachel Ray's orange chicken."

"No, it's not another rhyme this time," said Pussy.

"That was a rhyme," said Doc.

"Okay, no more rhymes," said Pussy. "The big news is that Tohtstettor said The Chip is there. On the ship, overseeing everything."

"Did he tell you who The Chip was?" asked Daisy.

"Is it even a person?" asked Skeeter.

"Whatever it is, we have to destroy it," said Doc. "Otherwise we'll go through the same thing during the World Cup and the Olympics."

"If The Chip is a person, we can't just execute him," said Skeeter.

"Why not?" said Doc. "We can't turn him over to the authorities. The media and politicians are on their side."

"And what if Tohtstettor is lying?" asked Mr. Smurdley. "Taking over that ship is a tremendous risk."

"What choice do we have?" asked Pussy. "We can't blow the pontoon bridges with spectators on them, and if we miss this chance, the vaccine and robots are still out there."

"We have no choice," said Mr. Smurdley. "We've got to take that ship, and we've only got a couple of days to figure out how."

After the meeting, Pussy followed Doc and Angel back to Angel's new quarters inside the Big Pond baseball stadium. It was a small apartment inside the stadium that was used by coaches or scouts if the hours they were putting in got to be too much to commute home. It was the best Angel had ever lived. He had a bed of his own, a desk, chairs, a couch, a bath, and best of all a refrigerator full of sweet corn. Doc let Angel and Pussy into the apartment and then left for his office in the X-ray room. Angel and Pussy sat down on the couch, and Angel opened up his durse and stared down at the book and chalice.

"If Kurri is on that ship, do you think she's still okay?" asked Angel.

"I don't know," said Pussy. "There's so many things about this we don't know."

"Would the book help?" asked Angel.

"It will tell us what's stupid, but I'm not sure that will help," she said.

"Wouldn't knowing what's stupid help us deduce what's smart?" Angel said. "That can help."

"Maybe; what are you getting at?"

"Could we ask questions using your A.I. computer program?"

"I guess. What do you want to ask about?"

"About Tohtstettor," said Angel. "You said people change, but do they?"

"We can put a question like that into the program," she said. "But we don't have time for much else. We have only a couple of days until the

Grand Prix. We have to take over a ship, and Uncle Ben still wants you to be able to drive a Grand Prix car if you have to."

"Let's do what we can before we have to go," said Angel.

Pussy got the program up and running, and they asked what could be deduced from the book about whether people can really change. They got their answer just before they had to leave for the hangar to prepare for the Grand Prix. The answer was very brief. People change; snakes don't.

More Orange County Review

Across

1. Diversity,Inclusion,Equity abbreviation.

4. Country that no longer wins Stanley Cups.

5. Big stadium where the Ducks play baseball.

9. What Germans want to be.

10. Vehicle type in Newport Grand Prix.

11. Where pitchers warm up.

Down

1. Unmanned vehicle.

2. Place to store airships.

3. Fuel type elites seek to ban.

6. Purse for ducks.

7. Predator of Newport land and water.

8. Subjagation by injection.

11. Island with Grand Prix loop-the-loops.

CHAPTER SIX

NEWPORT BEACH

Morning is a special time in Newport Beach. Usually, it resembles a winter's day as the morning sun begins its daily grapple with the marine layer, but on those clear mornings it is something to behold as the sun rises from behind the Santa Ana mountains and reflects off the Newport Beach Bay. It's a blinding reflection as the sun reflects off the literally millions of mirrorback sharks that congest the beaches and bays from Huntington Pier to Corona Del Mar.

The mirrorback is an aggressive shark that will leave the water to find prey, often ambushing the vain who admire themselves in its shiny back. The law requires that any sunscreen sold in Newport Beach contain at least twenty percent shark repellent, and the city takes other protective measures because of its aggressive nature. One of those measures is the evacuation zones at the Fashion Isle Mall in case of a mass shark attack such as Dolce and Gabbana as mirrorback sharks are allergic to cheap bags. The mirrorbacks, however, have consumed shoppers in Alo and Lululemon, which only proves that while nature can be cruel, it can also be kind.

Fear—just look at the people still wearing COVID masks while driving alone—rules humans, but there are two things that put that fear to sleep. Excitement and FOMO and the excitement that the Grand Prix and Health Fair promotions generated and the fear of missing out on it meant that the Fashion Isle parking was nearly by the time the sun reflected off the mirrorback sharks of Newport.

The lot was the meeting point for Pussy, Angel, Doc, Bobby, and Phil. Because so many people had camped out the night before the event, they were able to set up tents where they could all meet before the event and to keep Angel hidden from view until they got into the counterfeit Grand Prix cars they had also staged there for their mission. Mr. Smurdley, Uncle Ben, Lee, Ellis, Skeeter, and Daisy all had different objectives.

Uncle Ben, Lee, and Ellis were standing by near Castaways Park ready to sabotage every major thoroughfare around Newport in case the fake hospital ship could get into Newport Harbor and begin unloading the drones, robots, and vaccine. This would at least mitigate the damage done as fewer people would be vaccinated and thereby implanted with the behavior-altering mini microchip it contained. Uncle Ben had vowed to mess up the streets worse than the BBC can mess up fried rice, and fortunately he did not have to worry about Pacific Coast Highway, Balboa Boulevard, and Ocean Boulevard as they were most of the racecourse. For security reasons, they could have no phone or radio contact with the rest of the group.

Mr. Smurdley, along with Daisy and Skeeter, had arranged for fellow boat and yacht owners to form a flotilla in Newport Beach Bay during the Grand Prix and Health Fair. Mr. Smurdley, Daisy, and Skeeter each had their own craft and would lead the flotilla to get in front of the fake hospital ship carrying the vaccine and try to force it to stop in the channel between

Corona Del Mar and the end of the Balboa Peninsula where the ramps were located for the Grand Prix cars were to jump over the channel.

Getting the hospital ship to stop or at least slow in the channel would help immensely with the difficult mission that faced Pussy, Angel, Doc, Bobby, and Phil. They were to join the race covertly in the copied Grand Prix cars and, when the hospital ship was in the Newport channel between the jump ramps, slowly take off from the ramp to where they would land on the hospital ship's deck. Once on the ship, they would neutralize all vaccines, mini micro-chips, droids, robots and anyone or anything else that could be unleashed upon humanity. They would also rescue any slave labor, especially Kurri, who Angel was hoping beyond hope would be on that ship. The jump onto the ship would prove especially dangerous. They had only a vague idea of the ship's layout and were hoping the top deck would not be obstructed. Driving Grand Prix cars was also new to them. They would be attempting the jump after only a couple of practice driving sessions at the hangar that consisted mostly of Uncle Ben crying, "Aayai!" as they kept crashing into each other. But they had no choice but to try. Everything was coming together.

It seemed like the entire world was converging on Newport Beach for the Grand Prix. For the first time, heavy early weekend traffic was headed from Vegas to Southern California instead of the other way around, and along every major freeway and road leading to Newport Beach, thousands of signs hyped the event. The most sought-after viewing areas were already filling up. People on lawn chairs were nearly ten deep on both sides of Balboa Boulevard. There was standing room only near the two giant sixty-foot tall loop the loops that had been constructed on the track near Mariners Park and the Balboa Fun Zone which were nearly identical to the one at Niederrad Racecourse in Germany where stunt driver Terry Grant set the world record for largest loop the loop ever completed in a car.

The crowds were becoming so large that on Balboa Island the hosts of the television program The View, which was taping a special weekend edition about the Grand Prix, implored the crowd to spread evenly around the island so the island wouldn't tip over if one side became too heavy. People filled every seat on the pontoon bridges. The gamer crowds on Lido Isle were stepping on each other's chomp stompers and hundreds of brave spectators slathered themselves sunscreen and shark repellent on Pirate's Cove beach to get a good view of the racers jumping across the channel from the Balboa Peninsula to Corona Del Mar.

The fastest-growing crowd, however, was inside and surrounding Fashion Isle Mall. From a spot overlooking the bay that commemorated a 1953 scout jamboree whose attendance of over fifty-thousand was already dwarfed by the growing Grand Prix and Health Fair attendance, Doc and Pussy surveyed the race track.

"It's going to be tough to go fast enough to make the loops and not overshoot the ship," said Pussy.

"But if you undershoot the ship, you'll wind up in the water," said Doc.

"In that case, I hope the shark repellent works," she said. "I hope the ship has full automation, like Tohtstettor said. I don't want to run into any guards."

"I wouldn't count on anything Tohtstettor said, especially The Chip being there," said Doc

"What choice do we have?" asked Pussy. "Anyway, it's almost race time. Let's get this suicide mission started."

They took the escalator down to the parking lot and walked toward the tents they had set up. The lot was now completely full, and people were parking their cars anywhere they could. When they got to the biggest tent they had set up, Bobby, Phil and Angel were already waiting for them.

"Look who's finally here," Bobby said as Doc and Pussy walked into the tent.

"Here for now," said Doc. "Might not still be here after this race."

"I know what you mean," said Phil. "The odds of taking over that ship are pretty slim, let alone even landing on it."

"I worked out the physics of the whole thing," said Doc. "We need to be going at least sixty miles an hour to make it through the loop, but exactly thirty coming off the ramp. Any faster overshoots it, and any slower comes up short. Also crank that wheel when you land. The brakes won't stop you."

"This scares the hell out of me," said Bobby.

"I'm not scared," said Angel. "If I have a chance of saving Kurri, I don't care about the risk."

"I want to get on this ship as much as you do," Pussy said to Angel. "But I am aware of the risk."

"We'll either take over this ship or die trying," said Doc.

"Either way, we need to get in the cars now," said Phil. "Otherwise we'll never get out of this parking lot."

"Hell or high water, let's take down that ship," said Pussy.

She led everyone out of the tent and was shocked to see Hewis standing there in his racing suit when she opened the tent door flap. He looked angry. It was obvious he had heard their conversation.

"Take down a ship?" he yelled. "I thought we were saving the Grand Prix, not pirating!"

"We're not thieves. I can explain," said Pussy.

"You are thieves!" he growled. "That's why you wanted to get rid of Tohtstettor. So you could rob ships."

"It's bigger than that; lives are at stake," said Pussy. "I didn't want to deceive you."

"I don't believe a word you say," said Hewis.

"It's true," said Doc. "The fate of the world hangs in the balance."

"I don't believe you either," said Hewis. "You're all just thieves!"

"Would you believe me?" asked Angel.

"Another fake mascot? I don't think so," said Hewis.

"I'm not a mascot," said Angel.

"Then why are you in a costume?" asked Hewis.

"I'm not in a costume," said Angel.

"You're full of it," said Hewis.

"I'm not full of it, I'm a Duck," said Angel. "Check for yourself. But promise me this. If there is no costume and I really am a duck. Help us. The world really hangs in the balance."

Angel took the durse off of his shoulders and invited Hewis to search him. Hewis was hesitant at first and approached Angel slowly. The first place he looked was behind Angel's neck, hoping to find a snap button or zipper. He pulled and tugged at Angel's feathers until he gave up in exasperation.

"You really are a duck," said Hewis.

"I told you so," said Angel, putting his durse back over his shoulder.

"What's in that bag?" asked Hewis.

"Some things I brought from Monaco," said Angel.

"Monaco?" Hewis asked. "How do you know Monaco? There's just a casino for the ultra-rich and Grand Prix races. Other than that, it's just the wretched refuse no one talks about."

"I'm that wretched refuse," said Angel.

"The slave labor used to make the evil vaccine and the robots to force it on innocent people are on that ship. It's our only hope to save them and stop this evil plot," said Pussy. "Dummkopffer is involved too. I used you to stop this. I didn't want to deceive you. But I had no choice. We must stop them."

"Someone I care about could be on that ship and in great danger," Angel said.

"Why do ducks in Monaco look and talk like you do?" asked Hewis. "What happened there?"

"Terrible things long ago," said Angel. "I'm not sure of the complete history, but I want to find out. That's why I carry these relics they gave to me when I left."

Angel held up his durse and opened it up. He showed Hewis the book, chalice, and even the tiny cross. A moment of reflective silence overtook the group.

"We need you to help us," said Doc, interrupting the silence. "We need an experienced driver to get us through the obstacles and onto the ship."

"Without you, we have little hope," said Pussy.

Hewis looked at Pussy. Everyone was quiet again. If there were a sound to be heard, it would have been the wheels turning inside Hewis Lamilton's head. Then he looked at Angel.

"You said if you were really a duck, then I should join you," Hewis said to Angel.

"I'm really a duck," said Angel.

"Then it's a deal," said Hewis. "I'm in."

"Thank you," said Pussy.

"And like I said, let's get to the cars now," said Phil. "Otherwise we'll never get out of this parking lot."

Onboard the Calypso, Mr. Smurdley was organizing the skilled sailors in his flotilla. He had created the finest pool of seamen Corona del Mar had ever seen. Sailor Moon and Sailor Swift were piloting the Britannic and Titanic, respectively. Skeeter and Daisy, along with many others, were on their dinghies, the Monitor and Merrimack. He was to assemble the flotilla off Inspiration Point, where the race would start after Governor Gettyoyl's speech. After the race started, he needed to lead the flotilla back through the channel before the hospital ship's arrival and delay the hospital in the channel between the jump ramps so Doc, Pussy, and the rest would have a chance to land on the ship. If their mission was successful and the threat ended, he, Skeeter, and Daisy would shoot signal flares, stopping Uncle Ben's road sabotage.

Doc, Pussy, Bobby, Phil, and Angel followed Hewis Lamilton toward Inspiration Point and parked them together with the other Grand Prix cars on Ocean Avenue. Because they were following Hewis Lamilton, they could park with the other drivers with no scrutiny. There they waited in their cars until Governor Gettyoyl said some words and started the race. While they were waiting for the Governor, they tested the walkie-talkies they would use to communicate with each other and reviewed the race course.

Once the race started, the Grand Prix cars would take the nearest side street from Ocean Avenue to Pacific Coast Highway to MacArthur Boulevard and then through the Death Race course inside the Fashion Isle Mall. After that, the Grand Prix drivers would get back on Pacific Coast Highway, turn onto Balboa Boulevard, race through two loops and use the ramps to jump over the channel before getting back on Pacific Coast Highway. The race comprised ten laps through this course.

Governor Gettyoyl finally climbed onto the platform built on top of Narcissus Avenue, right in front of Ocean Boulevard. It took nearly a minute for the clapping to stop, but once Governor Gettyoyl stopped clapping for himself; it was quiet enough for him to start speaking.

"Greetings, Democratic voters, both citizen and undocumented," he began. "The sound you won't be hearing when the drivers start their engines is the sound of the end of fossil fuels. Whether you like it or not, to fight climate change, you'll own nothing and love it!"

As the Governor droned on and on about how he ended homelessness, lowered the cost of living, stopped crime, suppressed fires, and lowered taxes, Angel's mind wandered. He thought of Kurri and how he might see her soon. Then he thought about what he would have to do to get to that point. He would have to drive a Grand Prix car around a dangerous track, jump it off a ramp, and land on a ship after only having had a few lessons in an old blimp hangar. When Governor Gettyoyl stopped droning on, yelled "Start your engines," and waved a green energy flag to signal the start of the race, he was shaken back into reality. Angel swallowed hard, put his palmate foot down on the pedal, and hoped he could find Pussy at Fashion Isle.

Back on the Calypso, the boats in the flotilla sounded their horns in celebration when the race started. Once the celebration died down, Mr. Smurdley got word of a ship on the horizon. He extended his spyglass and focused on the oncoming ship. It was a hospital ship. At least it looked like a hospital ship. It resembled a small container ship or large coastal barge, but it was adorned with several huge banners, each displaying a bright red cross. He got on the ship's radio and called out the code words to Skeeter and Daisy.

"Toga, toga, toga," he said.

On the racecourse, Angel was gaining confidence in his driving. Having trained inside a blimp hangar, he had some initial difficulty transferring his newly gained skills to the road. He had started off far behind everyone else, but by the time he turned off Pacific Coast Highway onto MacArthur Boulevard, he was almost back with the rest of the pack. His newfound confidence would, however, be tested when the course veered off MacArthur Boulevard into the Fashion Isle Mall Death Race section.

In 2016, Canada expanded euthanasia with the MAID Act, which allowed for assisted suicide for patients experiencing enduring and intolerable suffering. Though aimed primarily at incurable ailments, Greta Von Karen had long promoted expanding such acts beyond similar laws in Europe to include depression and wrongthink to align belief systems within a universal global structure. Von Farma was not on board with the idea until Von Karen included the caveat that mandated patients continue to receive long-term taxpayer-funded prescription medications after their euthanization.

At the urging of Von Karen and Von Farma, Schultz Dummkopffer included the Death Race portion of the Grand Prix where the cars would drive through the Fashion Isle Mall trying to avoid Canadians suffering from what they felt was enduring and intolerable suffering from not having brought the Stanley Cup home to Canada in over three decades. If any car struck one of the Canadians, who wore hockey jerseys emblazoned with a Stanley Cup logo inside a teardrop and were trying to euthanize themselves by jumping in front of the cars from behind cellphone accessory kiosks, they would be penalized.

Hewis Lamilton, who was used to the leading position he was enjoying in the race so far, nimbly avoided all the depressed Canadians that jumped out in front of his car. Doc and Pussy were similarly skillful and avoided the collision-crazy Canucks. Phil and Bobby, who as American hockey players were used to pulverizing Canadians, hit so many of them that the inside of Fashion Isle sounded like a popcorn popper amplified through The Who's old Marshall stacks. This worked out perfectly for Angel since the path cleared by Phil and Bobby allowed him to catch up more because he did not have to evade any suicidal socialists.

Back on the Calypso, Mr. Smurdley was rushing to get the flotilla back through the channel and into Newport Beach Bay before the hospital ship got too close. He needed to get the flotilla into position and hoped that the hospital ship had automated sensors that would slow it down when it detected the vessels in front of it. As the hospital ship got closer, Mr. Smurdley scanned the deck with his spyglass. Except for the conning tower, the top deck was mostly flat and free of obstruction. He relayed the good news to Doc, who could actually talk on the radio. Doc had just gotten through the Fashion Isle Death Race and had just turned back onto Pacific Coast Highway where there was a long straightaway before the course turned sharply onto Balboa Boulevard. Mr. Smurdley told Doc that the hospital ship would be in a position between the jump ramps on either side of the channel just about the time they were coming up to the ramp to complete a second lap. Mr. Smurdley suggested the entire group slow down after completing the first lap so they would be together and away from the other drivers when they attempted to jump onto the ship.

Hewis Lamilton was leading the pack when Doc relayed the message from Mr. Smurdley. He was unhappy about having to slow down and relinquish the lead but he knew he was no longer in it to win it and was happy he could clear the loop the loops and the jump across the channel the first time before he needed to slow down to land on the hospital ship together. As he approached the first loop, he checked his speedometer. It had to be at sixty miles an hour. Any faster and the car could lose stability and flip inside the loop, and any slower the car would drop from the top and go plop. If he got through the loops, he needed to hit the gas hard because he needed to speed up to over ninety miles an hour to make the jump over the channel.

Hewis hit the loop at exactly sixty miles an hour. It was a fortunate coincidence that the six Gs of force he experienced caused the blood from his body to rush to his feet, thereby pressing down the accelerator and bringing the car's speed to over ninety miles an hour when he hit the ramp. Hewis flew over the channel and landed near the middle of the landing ramp; it only took seconds for his head to clear from the G-force. He slowed to a crawl and waited to see if his companions could make it through the loops and jump after him.

Doc and Pussy, both being medical professionals, understood the effects of G forces on the body and could prepare their bodies for the stress. They made the jump within seconds of each other and slowed down to join Hewis. Phil and Bobby completed the channel jump next. Being professional athletes, they could withstand the stress as well. The only question left was Angel. He approached the loops not knowing how his duck body would respond to G-force. He made sure the speedometer, an instrument he had only first seen a couple of days ago, was at sixty, closed his eyes, clutched his durse, and hoped for the best. The G-force pushed the blood to his large webbed feet, pressing the pedal so hard the car sped up to almost one-hundred miles an hour. He flew over the channel, nearly overshooting the landing ramp. The shock of the landing forced his foot down on the brake, and he came to a screeching halt behind Phil and Bobby.

Once they were together, Hewis led them slowly back onto Pacific Coast Highway toward the mall to drive through the death race portion of the course once again. The rest of the drivers were already ahead of them and had cleared out all the heavy-hearted hosers. Only crumpled Canadian bodies remained, with maple syrup still pouring from their wounds.

They had just made it out of the mall and back onto the Pacific Coast Highway straightaway when Mr. Smurdley had an urgent message for Doc. The hospital ship was almost in position. Doc got on the radio and told Hewis he needed to pick up the pace and for everyone to line up behind Hewis. He also reiterated that this time when they came out of the second loop they needed to hit the brakes instead of the accelerator otherwise they would overshoot the ship. The group followed the course onto Balboa Boulevard and sped up. Hewis checked his speedometer, Pussy checked her shark repellent, Angel clutched his durse, Doc lit a Chesterfield, and Phil and Bobby screamed "Geronimo!"

Back on the Calypso, Mr Lee watched as the hospital ship bore down on him. He had positioned his ship in the channel between the ramps to stop it there, but it did not stop. It had slowed significantly to navigate the channel, but it was still coming straight at the Calypso. The rest of the flotilla had turned back into the bay to avoid a collision. Mr. Smurdley sounded the Calypso's horn and radioed Skeeter and Daisy to get away from the hospital ship and then made a hard starboard turn. He would have preferred to turn to port, but it wasn't the time to drink. The Calypso's broadside was now passing in front of the hospital ship's bow. Mr. Smurdley gave it full engine power to avoid being T-boned. Mr. Smurdley looked up at the massive ship and down at the reflection of the hordes of Newport Beach mirrorback sharks massing around the two vessels. The sharks around Newport Beach Bay can sense nautical disasters and often mass for their legendary feeding frenzies. He thought he had avoided the collision when he heard a loud crash that rocked the back of the Calypso. The force of the blow nearly knocked him over. When he regained his balance, he heard another crash and then another, but those crashing sounds were coming from above. He looked up in time to see three more Grand Prix cars sail through the air and crash land on the top deck of the hospital ship. He waited to hear them go into the sea, but they didn't. They made it; he thought. Against all odds, they had landed on the ship. A feeling of exuberance overcame him. That exuberance turned to dread when he felt the Calypso list suddenly. The collision with the hospital ship had badly damaged the rear of the Calypso, and water was pouring into the vessel. Sensing a sinking vessel, the ravenous mirrorback sharks slithered up the sinking rear of the Calypso, causing Mr. Smurdley to retreat up the ship's bow to avoid their jaws. In a moment of desperation, he grabbed the flare gun from the bridge and fired off a flare. Seeing Skeeter's dinghy, he leapt off the Calypso's bow onto the dinghy. As he landed on the dinghy, his feeling of dread turned to even worse dread. He suddenly realized that by firing the flare, he had falsely signaled Uncle Ben that the mission had been accomplished and there was no need to sabotage the main thoroughfares through New Beach where the vaccine and robots might be transported. It would be impossible to board the hospital ship from the dinghy, so he instructed Skeeter to take the dinghy toward the back bay to find Uncle Ben.

On top of the hospital ship Hewis, Doc, Pussy, Phil, Bobby, and even Angel managed to crash land successfully but were randomly strewn about the top deck. The last to land, Angel's Grand Prix car had landed near the rear of the ship and penetrated the front face of the conning tower located there. He struggled to exit the vehicle and could finally push his durse over the driver-side window and slide out after it and crashed down on the ship's deck. He took a moment to regain his bearing and stood up. The sound of people running toward him reached his ears.

"Angel, are you okay?" Bobby asked.

"Thank God for handbrakes," said Phil.

Phil and Bobby were the first to meet him. Being professional athletes, they would have been the first to shake off the effects of a crash landing and run across the deck of a hospital ship. Before Angel composed himself enough to answer, the others came into focus. First Pussy, then Hewis, and finally, Doc, who ran slowly with a distinctive smoker's hack.

"I can't believe we all made it," said Pussy. "I thought we'd all be shark food."

"This is just the beginning," said Doc as he finally joined the group. "Now we start the hard part."

"Now that we're on the ship, how do we get inside the ship?" asked Pussy.

"I think Angel took care of that," said Phil, pointing to the large hole in the front face of the hospital ship's conning tower caused by Angel's car.

"Before we go in, everybody check that you have everything you need before we go in," said Bobby. "And double check your walkie-talkies."

Everyone in the circle felt around their race suits. Phil and Bobby patted under their arms, Doc and Pussy checked their messenger bags for laptops and electronics, and Angel checked his durse, stroking both the book and chalice for good luck.

"I know I don't need this," said Pussy, taking off her racing helmet. Everyone else followed her except for Hewis Lamilton.

"One thing I've learned from many years of racing is don't take your helmet off until the race is over," said Hewis.

One by one they squeezed through the hole Angel's car had made in the conning tower. Inside, they came to the main ship ladder. On one side was a metal ship ladder that led up to the bridge, and on the other side was a metal ship ladder that went down into the bowels of the ship.

"Up or down?" asked Pussy as she came to the front of the stairwell.

"Up," said Doc. "Let's get up to the bridge and try to steer this thing."

Single file, they climbed up the ship ladder to the ship's bridge. Phil and Bobby, being the most nimble, went up first, and Angel, knowing he would have trouble climbing the ship's ladder steps with his webbed palmate feet, climbed last. He struggled up the ship ladder and finally caught up with the rest of the group after walking through the hatchway onto the bridge. There, he was met with puzzled stares from the rest of the group. The bridge was completely bare. There was no navigation equipment anywhere. Even the stations where the crew, if there was one, would sit were gone. It was completely empty except for a couple of empty boxes and the windows at the front.

"How do we control the ship?" asked Pussy.

"There has to be some system on the ship," said Bobby.

"It's got to be in the engine room," said Doc. "Directly linked to an automated system. We have to find it now."

"What about Kurri and everyone else they kidnapped?" asked Angel.

"We've got to see what's below deck," said Bobby. "Time is running out."

They scrambled down two sets of ship ladders to the lower deck level. There they waited on the platform for Angel to traverse down the steps with his palmate feet. Once Angel joined them, they stopped briefly to coordinate their next move. On the level they were standing was a large hatchway with a sign above it that read BULK LEVEL and another set of ladder stairs leading down to a level labeled HOLD.

"What's down there?" asked Hewis, noticing the ladder stairs leading down.

"You and Angel go down and check it out," said Doc. "Everyone else follows me."

The group split, and Doc, Pussy, Phil, and Bobby burst through the hatchway and into the dimly lit bulk level. In the dim light, they could see that before them was a pathway between rows of very large open lifeboats that were filled with an assortment of drones and robots.

"Look at all these drones and robots," said Phil. "I've never seen so many in one place."

"Once the boats get launched, they'll be all over," said Bobby. "They will vaccinate everyone whether or not they want it."

"How will they launch the boats?" asked Pussy. "They're still inside the ship!"

"Not only do we have to figure out how they're gonna launch these vessels, we have to figure out how to stop it," said Doc. "And we only have a few minutes to do it."

Down below, Hewis and Angel made it through the semi-darkness to the bottom of the ship ladder, where they came to a hatchway with a metal bulkhead door. Angel pulled at the wheel on the front of the door trying to open it. After a couple of attempts, Hewis took over and spun the wheel around a few times, opening the door.

"I'm pretty good with wheels," he said.

Inside the door was a large, dark room. Hewis and Angel both stepped inside the room. They each took a couple of tentative steps, feeling out into the darkness for any obstacles.

"I wish I had a flashlight in my bag," said Angel.

"I have a Red Bull promo penlight in my suit pocket," said Hewis, "Let's see if it helps."

The narrow beam that emitted from Hewis Lamilton's penlight provided enough illumination for Hewis and Angel to gauge that they were in some kind of corridor between two side storage areas. They moved with the help of the penlight when a voice broke through the darkness.

"Do you have food?" the voice asked. "We're so hungry."

"Who's hungry?" asked Angel.

"All of us," said the voice. "We've worked so hard. You promised us sweet corn."

Sweet corn? Angel's mind raced. Ducks love sweet corn, and the voice sounded like a duck. Like the voices from back home. Maybe the voice in the darkness from Monaco, he thought to himself.

"Are you a duck?" Angel asked.

"Yes," the voice answered.

"Are you from Monaco?"

"Yes," the voice answered again.

"I'm Angel," said Angel. "I'm a duck from Monaco too. I've come to help you."

"Angel!?!" cried a voice from another direction. "You've come?"

Angel knew the voice. It was Kurri. He had traveled across the globe to find her, and he had. But he knew the hard part was coming.

"Kurri, is that you?" Angel said.

"Yes, I'm over here," she yelled.

Angel and Hewis made their way over to where Kurri's voice was coming from, using the penlight for guidance. As they got closer, they could make out many shapes in the darkness. Most appeared to be human, and a few appeared to be ducks. But not normal ducks. They were taller than a common duck but almost as tall as a Grand Prix driver. They were Monaco ducks.

"I'm here, I'm here, I'm here," Kurri kept repeating, trying to guide them to her.

Finally, they were face to face with each other, but metal fencing separated them. On each side of the corridor, was a long holding cell that ran the length of the hold. Inside it, dozens of young people and a few young Monaco ducks stood huddled together, desperate and hungry.

"Did they hurt you?" Angel asked Kurri.

"They've been taking blood samples and working us to death," she said.

"Is there a light switch in here?" asked Hewis.

"No," said Kurri. "It has always been dark."

"Let's see if there's a door."

Hewis ran the penlight along the width of the holding cell. The intertwined wires of the thick steel fencing ran from the floor to the ceiling with sharp barbs spaced every few inches apart. In the center was a gate held shut by a padlock similar to those used for gym lockers.

"There's the door," said Hewis.

Hewis and Angel moved over to the door. Kurri followed along inside the holding cell, following the light from the penlight. Hewis tugged at the lock on the gate. It was not a massive lock by any means, but it was still too strong to be defeated with bare hands.

"We can probably break this lock off with a fire extinguisher," said Hewis.

"Where would we get one of those?" asked Angel.

"We won't find them down here," said Hewis. "We have to go back upstairs."

"Don't leave us," implored Kurri.

"We'll be right back," said Hewis. "We just need to get something to break the locks."

"Please be quick," she said.

"We'll free you," said Angel.

"Or die trying," added Hewis.

"You're my hero," said Kurri.

Hewis and Angel ran back toward the ship ladder.

At the bulk level, Phil and Bobby had finished looking over one of the boats. They could not figure out how they would get out onto the water from inside the ship. Pussy and Doc continued down the pathway toward a modular office room at the end of the pathway. It was a rectangular steel enclosure with a steel door and windows that looked out over the bulk deck. The room was dark, and as Doc and Pussy approached it, they could not see what was inside.

"All the boats have drain plugs," said Bobby, standing inside one boat.

"Pull them out in case they can get on the water!" Doc yelled as he and Pussy raced toward the office at the end of the pathway. "That room might control the ship."

Suddenly the lights inside the office came on, illuminating the interior of the room. Doc and Pussy stopped dead in their tracks when they saw who was standing in the modular office looking out at them. It was Greta Von Karen, Schultz Dummkopffer, Baron Von Farma, Shein Temuvoffen and Major Tohtstettor.

"Welcome aboard!" Major Tohtstettor announced through loudspeakers on either side of the modular office. "What were you expecting, The Chip?"

"I wasn't expecting you," said Pussy.

"I got a pardon from Governor Gettyoyl," said Tohtstettor. "The fool thinks he'll be president."

"And I gave you a lifeline," said Pussy.

"I wish I could do the same for you," said Tohtstettor. "But as you can see, all the lifeboats are full, so there's no room for you and you have to die. In a moment, the ship's hull will split, and these drones and robots on the boats will make their way across the bay to their designated spots and spread the vaccine to everyone while we watch in our own well-stocked escape craft."

"You'll drown everyone!" Pussy exclaimed. "We know there's slave labor on this ship."

"Shein Temuvoffen would never drown his laborers," said Temuhoven. "The sharks will eat them before they drown. It is Newport Beach Bay after all."

"You're seeing the cup as half-empty," said Tohtstettor. "We're not drowning slave laborers, we're feeding starving sharks."

"We're good Germans," smirked Greta Von Karen.

"We won't let you spread that vaccine," said Doc. "Do you know how much harm it will do?"

"It isn't that bad," said Greta Von Karen.

"It's worse!" Baron Von Farma laughed.

"The world will be enslaved," sneered Tohtstettor. "We will chew the erasers off their pencil necks."

"You won't rule anything," said Pussy. "It's The Chip. I don't think you even know what The Chip is."

"Don't you remember?" said Tohtstettor. "We're German. We don't care who really rules. We just want to be the baddies!"

"You're not the baddies, you're the saddies," said Phil.

Phil and Bobby ran up the pathway toward the office. They stopped when they got in front of Doc and Pussy. They each slightly unzipped the top of their racing suits and pulled pistols out of the shoulder holsters they were wearing underneath and pointed them at Tohtstettor.

"You brought guns; how thoughtful," said Tohtstettor.

"We're not the types to bring knives to a gunfight," said Phil.

"And I'm not the type to bring guns to a robot fight," said Tohtstettor.

Suddenly, three Hello Nursie mini medical vans powered up and transformed into humanoid scary nurse robots with syringes in one ratchet arm and pulling out nets from their chest compartments with the other.

"Power down those robots or we'll shoot," Phil warned.

"Go ahead," taunted Tohtstettor. "The glass is bulletproof, but you're not robot-proof."

The nurse robots stepped out of the boats and surrounded Doc, Pussy, Phil and Bobby. Phil and Bobby leveled their guns at the robots facing them but could not get off even one shot before the robots ensnared the guns with their nets and pulled them from Phil and Bobby's hands.

"Game over!" Dummkopffer declared. "The game is in the kuhlschrank, the sauerkraut is getting jiggly, the butterschmalz is getting hard, and the fat lady is singing Wagner."

Suddenly, Hewis Lamilton and Angel stumbled through the hatchway onto the bulk deck. They started down the pathway, and Angel shouted out before he even noticed the robots menacing his friends.

"We found them!" Angel shouted. "They're in the hold!"

Then Angel and Hewis stopped in their tracks. They were puzzled for a second because three humanoid scary nurse robots surrounded their friends. That puzzlement turned to fear and hate when they recognized Major Tohtstettor inside the modular office.

"Look who's here," said Tohtstettor, recognizing Angel. "Before the rest of you meet your demise, it looks like I'll have the satisfaction of finally killing this duck! Robots bring me some pressed duck."

The robots converged on Angel. They reached for him with their ratchet arms and readied their nets. Angel held up his durse to use it as a shield. One robot poked at it with the syringe on its robot arm, ejecting the chalice from the bag. Angel quickly picked up the chalice. Holding it by the stem, he used it to block the needle on the syringe from poking him.

As he parried the thrust, another robot threw its net over him. It ensnared him and caused him to trip. As the robots moved in for the kill, the chalice suddenly came to life. Sparks emitted from the cup's rim, and a laser inferno exploded out of the cup, engulfing a robot in flames. The chalice then zeroed in on the second robot, blasting it to smithereens with another bolt from inside the cup. Seeing the disruption, Major Tohtstettor gave the command for the ship's hull to split.

As they started up, the motors that would separate the ship's plates emitted an almost deafening whir. The entire vessel shook, and water seeped into all levels of the ship. The chalice was now operating on its own, but

Angel could not let go of it. It had destroyed the last humanoid scary nurse robot and now trained its firestorm on the robots that filled the boats. As the chalice held by Angel laid waste to the drones and robots, Hewis ran to Phil and Bobby.

"There are scores inside cells in the hold," he yelled. "We have to break the locks open."

"How do we do it?" asked Phil.

"They're just regular padlocks," said Hewis. "A fire extinguisher would do it."

Bobby and Phil looked around, but they did not see a fire extinguisher. Amidst the chaos of the chalice in Angel's hand destroying the drones and robots in the boats, a large metallic piece of a robot that exploded fell at Bobby's feet. He picked it up.

"Will this work?" he asked Hewis.

"That should easily break those locks," Hewis answered.

"Then let's roll," said Bobby.

Phil, Bobby and Hewis started running to the ship ladder to break the padlocks with the robot section Bobby had picked up. Along the way, they yelled to Doc and Pussy to salvage whatever boats they could from the spectacle of flaming robots being obliterated by the chalice held by Angel and seawater that was now spilling more rapidly into the ship as it continued to split.

Phil, Bobby and Hewis made it into the dark hold. Those locked in the holding cells were screaming in terror as water began to cover the hold's floor. Hewis trained his penlight on the padlock he had seen before, and the three rushed to it over the seawater that now covered the floor.

"Be calm!" Bobby screamed to be heard above the screams of the captive laborers. "Once we open the cells, go up the stairs, and someone will help you there."

As Bobby prepared to slam the robot section down on the padlock holding the cell door shut, Hewis came face to face with Kurri on the other side of the fencing. The sight of him stifled her panic attack, and she composed herself enough to speak.

"What do you need me to do?" she asked Hewis.

"Try to calm everyone down and get them to go up the stairs without trampling each other," he said.

"Where's Angel?" she asked.

"Upstairs," he said. "I can't explain now. Just get everyone up the stairs."

Bobby raised the robot section over his head and brought it down on the padlock. He hit it solidly, and the lock broke off, allowing him to open the door. When he did, Phil took over guiding the captives through the darkness to the stairs while telling them to stay calm. Once Kurri got out of the cell, she stood by the door trying to keep them calm until they could get to Phil, who took them to the stairs. Hewis used his penlight to help Bobby find the padlock on the other cell. Once he found it, he raised up the broken robot section and crashed it down on the padlock, freeing the rest of the captives. Bobby was surprised that the robot part broke the padlocks. Must be German engineering, he thought.

Above the hold, the blaze from the cup continued to annihilate the droids and robots in the boats. Even those that were now activating could not escape its beam. Angel was feeling different. A sense of empowerment engulfed him. Whereas the chalice had embarked on its destruction autonomously before, he now felt a oneness with it. It was like he was the one. The one the chalice had been destined for. The one that Vladdy and Yoduck had been preserving it and all the other relics for. Angel's attention turned to the modular office and its occupants when the last robot was destroyed.

Inside the office, Major Tohtstettor and his ilk looked on in disbelief at the chaos that had usurped their plans. The command that started the splitting of the hospital ship and release of the boats carrying the drones, robots, and vaccine would also deploy the office they were in as their escape vehicle. Tohtstettor monitored the progress as Angel approached the office window. Tohtstetter looked up from the controls to see Angel through the office window staring at him with vengeance and now grasping the stem of the chalice with purpose and confidence.

"I wish you were dead," Tohtstettor growled at Angel.

"Back at ya!" Angel shouted.

Flames leapt forth from the mouth of the chalice, consuming the entire office. The heat was so intense that Angel could see Major Tohtstettor's features melt away from his skull, Greta Von Karen liquify as she screeched "what a world, what a world," and Shein Temuvoffen, Schultz Dummkopffler, and Baron Von Farma's heads exploded into a pulpy mess.

Standing in the boats they were trying to clear of smoldering robot wreckage, Doc and Pussy stared, mouths agape, at the devastation of the bulk level office only to be shocked back to reality when the water rushing into the ship began lifting the boats on the bulk level. Looking back from the office toward Doc and Pussy, Angel could see the first of the hold's captives coming up from the ship ladder onto the bulk level.

"They're coming up," Angel shouted to Doc and Pussy as he put the chalice back in his durse. "Get them on the boats before the ship splits apart."

Doc and Pussy called out to the desperate souls coming through the hatchway. They sloshed through the now ankle-deep water, and when they got through to the boats, Doc and Pussy pulled them onto the boats while pushing at the robot wreckage to make room. Angel splashed his way to the hatch. Through it he could see Phil, who was now at the top of the ship ladder pulling the captive laborers from the top of the stairs and pushing them through the hatchway. They were in a race against time to get all of them from the opened holding cells, up the stairs and into what room there was on the salvageable boats.

Like a bucket brigade, Kurri and Hewis guided the abductees to Phil and Bobby, who steered them up the ship ladder to Angel, Doc and Pussy, who struggled to maintain their balance as the water inched higher. As the split between the two ends of the ship widened, Pussy could see the snouts of the mirrorback sharks trying to push through the gap to claim more victims in Newport Beach Bay.

"The sharks are almost inside the ship!" she yelled.

As more and more freed captives made it into the boats, there was less and less room for them. Some boats could not be cleared of the still-smoking droid and robot scrap, and others had floated to inaccessible areas of the bulk level. The two ends of the ship would shortly be fully separated and sink quickly. The last group came through the hatchway and onto the boats. But as Phil, Bobby, Kurri, and Hewis made it up the ship ladder, there appeared to be no open spots left on the boats.

"Can everyone squish together?" Pussy asked the already crammed mass of young people and young ducks on one boat.

One by one Doc, Pussy, Phil and Bobby, who had to climb on top of a smoking robot shell to find a spot, got on a boat. As the ship fully separated, only Hewis, Angel, and Kurri could not find room on a lifeboat. There was suddenly a loud boom. The ship separated into two parts, and water flooded into the bulk level along with hungry mirrorback sharks. Pussy yelled to them from the last boat as it passed by, while the lifeboats were swept out to sea.

"I've made room for one more!" she yelled to them.

Without thinking, both Angel and Hewis grabbed Kurri and, though almost waist deep in water, lifted her up toward the boat where Pussy pulled her onto the last boat. "Angel!" Pussy cried out as it was swept out to sea and a wall of water propelled both Hewis and Angel across the deck of the bulk level into the hatchway and back down the ship ladder into the hold where the slave laborers had been held until their recent liberation. The water's force carried Hewis and Angel until they careened off the stair bottom down into the dark hold.

"Hello?" said Angel as he popped his head out of the water.

"Is that you, Angel?" asked Hewis as he did the same.

"Yes, it's me," said Angel. "Where are we?"

"Probably in an air pocket," said Hewis. "But I'm pretty sure we're underneath the water."

"So we'll drown down here," said Angel.

"Don't worry, there's no way we are gonna drown," said Hewis. "No one drowns in Newport Beach; the sharks will get us first."

"Speaking of sharks," said Angel.

Several silver shark fins popped out of the water and started circling Hewis and Angel. Suddenly, one shark broke off from the circle and, teeth gnashing, darted straight for Angel only to be vaporized by a glow that emitted from Angel's durse.

"What the heck was that?" asked Hewis.

"The cup," said Angel. "It destroyed the robots, the vaccine, Tohtstettor and the rest."

Angel reached into his durse to touch it. To his astonishment, the inside of his durse was dry.

"It's keeping the book dry and protecting us from the sharks," said Angel.

"Great," said Hewis. "Now I will drown. I can't swim."

"Climb aboard, I'll take you," said Angel.

"You can swim?" asked Hewis.

"Like a duck," said Angel.

Hewis latched onto Angel. Angel took a deep breath and made his way underwater, up the ship ladders, to the conning tower, and out of the ship. Almost out of breath, they popped up to the surface, with Hewis holding onto Angel for dear life and Angel holding onto his durse with the protective chalice in it the same way. Looking up, Angel could see the Grand Prix cars in the air jumping the channel. The race was still going on. Even with a ship sinking and lifeboats filled with freed captives and the wreckage of wretched robots appearing on the shore, the show went on. That's life. Courage, betrayal, honesty, greed, faith, love, selfishness, or selflessness — it's all peripheral; the show always goes on.

Being in the middle of the channel, Angel saw land on both sides, but he could make out lifeboats on one side and started swimming that way.

"I see lifeboats on the beach," he told Hewis. "I'm swimming there."

"I think that's Pirates Cove," said Hewis. "That's got the most sharks, and the Balboa Fun Zone is on the other side."

"Kurri and everyone else should be with the lifeboats," said Angel. "I'm swimming there."

"The Fun Zone has rides," said Hewis.

Angel kept swimming toward the beach and lifeboats. As he got closer, he could see people and ducks on the beach and shark fins in the water. He held the durse over his heart and kept going. As he swam, four large hungry mirrorback sharks came straight at him like a flying wedge from back when the NFL had real kick-offs. They opened their mighty jaws for a lethal bite only to be felled by the force of the chalice that now surrounded Angel and the book. Each shark attack was blunted, leaving motionless mirrorbacks drifting with the waves. Angel churned his palmate feet with growing confidence; the shore was getting closer.

On the beach, Doc and Pussy looked out over the bay. They scrutinized every vessel and sailboat, hoping that Angel and Hewis had been plucked safely from the shark-infested waters. Kurri had gone to check for her brother among the other freed slave laborers who had gotten off the lifeboats. Phil and Bobby had contacted Mr. Smurdley with the good news about the vaccine and the bad news about Angel and Hewis. Mr. Smurdley started making arrangements for the newly freed abductees from Monaco as Phil and Bobby could not get the attention of any media or public officials as they were too absorbed by the spectacle of the Grand Prix race.

"I don't see any sign of them," said Pussy, almost in tears.

"I think they've gone to Davy Jones' Locker," said Doc.

"They're not whale watching; what's wrong with you?"

"Not that Davy Jones' locker."

"The Monkees?"

"No."

"Look what's that in the water?" Pussy yelled excitedly, noticing what appeared to be two figures in the water less than a hundred yards from the shore.

Excitedly, Doc and Pussy rushed to the shoreline. With the surf coming almost to their knees, they looked as the two figures came closer. They were also close enough to identify when a wave crashed over them, causing them to disappear beneath the water. Doc and Pussy held their breath collectively while the tide went out, and out of the water popped Angel and Hewis, now having gained their footing on the shore.

"Angel! Hewis!" Pussy cried out excitedly.

They ran toward each other, ending in a group embrace. Together they walked out of the surf onto the beach. Once on dry land, Angel opened his durse and peered inside. The chalice was now inert, and the book completely dry. Angel closed his eyes and gave thanks. He did not know to whom or what, but hoped to find out one day.

"How did you keep from being eaten by the sharks?" asked Doc. "No one swims near Newport Beach without being eaten by them."

"The cup saved us, just like with the Robots," said Angel.

"Thank God," said Doc. "I've got to get the good news to Mr. Smurdley."

Doc hurried off to find Phil and Bobby, leaving Angel and Pussy alone. They were about to speak when they suddenly heard a loud, excited scream from further up on the beach near the lifeboats. Angel looked up and saw it was Kurri who was squealing excitedly. She ran toward them with her arms open wide.

"My hero!" Kurri wailed as she continued running toward them.

"My love!" Angel shouted, running toward her.

Angel and Kurri got closer and closer to each other. When they were only a few feet apart, Angel stopped and opened his arms, and Kurri ran right past him. She continued running until she came to Hewis Lamilton and jumped into his arms. They held each other in a long embrace as Angel looked on in silence.

"I knew you'd come for me," Kurri said to Hewis. "You're my hero!"

They put their arms around each other and began walking along the beach together. Angel continued staring silently as they left together. Pussy walked up to Angel, who was still staring in silence. She watched as Kurri and Hewis continued walking together.

"Alone again, Naturally," she said as she and Angel hugged in a comforting embrace.

"I thought if I found Kurri she would be mine forever," Angel said sadly. "I feel my duck heart breaking."

"My heart feels all achy breaky too," she said, embracing Angel even tighter.

They continued holding each other for emotional support until suddenly, Angel felt a tap on his shoulder. He tried to ignore it, but the tapping continued. Angel ended his embrace with Pussy, turned around, and there was Kurri. He stared at her for a moment before he was finally able to speak.

"I thought Hewis was your hero," he said.

"Hewis is my hero, but you're my love," said Kurri.

"What do you mean?" asked Angel

"Hewis helped rescue me," she said. "I haven't been given much in life, so if someone helps me, I'm going to show my gratitude. But when it comes to love, I'm a poor duck from Monaco, and I prefer to stay in my lane."

She kissed him softly on the bill. They stared into each other's eyes before holding each other in a long embrace. Pussy stared at them like a third wheel.

"Once again, alone again, naturally," she whispered to herself, closing her eyes. She stood there for a moment before she felt someone tapping on her shoulder from behind. She opened her eyes and turned around. There was no one there.

"Down here," she heard a familiar voice say.

She looked down, and there in front of her was the much shorter Hewis. Their eyes met. They stood there in silence for a moment before Hewis spoke to her.

"As a Grand Prix driver, I don't always stay in my lane, but I'd like to share a lane with you if you'd care to share your lane."

"You had me at hello," said Pussy.

"I didn't say hello," said Hewis.

"You still had me," said Pussy.

They held each other tightly, just like Angel and Kurri were holding each other. After a few moments, Angel spoke.

"So now that we've saved the world and found true love, what should we do this evening?" he asked.

"I've got an idea," Pussy said. "Why don't both of us couples find a spot on the beach where we can be alone together and maybe, just maybe, spend the night watching the submarine races? What do you think of that idea?"

"Bingo!" they all said.

Newport Beach review

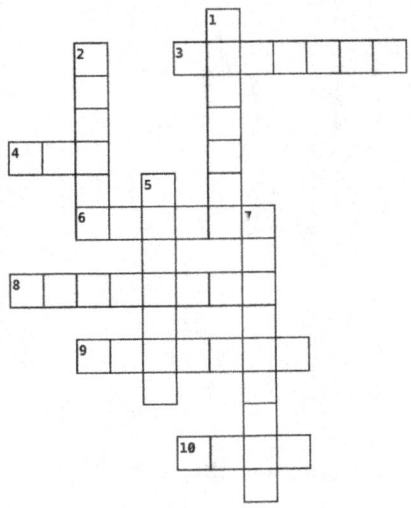

Across

3. Where boats enter Newport Bay.

4. Corona del for really, really, rich people.

6. Found on Balboa Peninsula bar stools.

8. Helps bad guys.

9. Coast highway in Newport.

10. Type of story this is.

Down

1. Protected Angel from robots and sharks.

2. Predators swarming Newport waters, beaches, and malls.

5. Magnificent author.

7. Avenue where California governor stood.

ABOUT THE AUTHOR

Patrick The Magnificent is magnificent in his magnificence and does so magnificently. He created so many things that they granted him the patent for stuff. When he is not doing magnificent things, he spends his time doing even more magnificent things. Which he does magnificently. Explore more of his magnificence at: PATRICKTHEMAGNIFICENT.COM

While you're at it, try finding Angel on the next page and leave a message where he is at PATRICKTHEMAGNIFICENT.COM

WHERE'S ANGEL? Can you find him? He's looking for evil doers in the Platinum Triangle. Tell us where he is at **PATRICKTHEMAGNIFICENT.COM** to be entered in the drawing for valuable prizes!

www.ingramcontent.com/pod-product-compliance
Lightning Source LLC
Chambersburg PA
CBHW061922130726
47908CB00016B/899